Bernard Ashley is one of the most highly regarded authors in the UK. Born in Woolwich, south London, he was evacuated during the war, and ended up attending fourteen different primary schools. After school, Bernard did National Service in the RAF where he 'flew' a typewriter. He then went on to become a teacher and later a head teacher – his two most recent posts being in east and south London, areas which have provided him with the settings for many of his books. Bernard now writes full time.

Bernard Ashley's other novels for Orchard Books include *Tiger Without Teeth,* a *Guardian* Book of the Week, *Little Soldier,* which was shortlisted for the *Guardian* Children's Book Award and the Carnegie Medal, *Revenge House,* also shortlisted for the *Guardian* Children's Book Award, *Freedom Flight,* and *Ten Days to Zero,* the first book about Ben Maddox.

Orchard Books
338 Euston Road
London NW1 3BH

*Orchard Books Australia*
Hachette Children's Books
Level 17/207 Kent Street
Sydney, NSW 2000

Orchard Books is a division of Hachette Children's Books

ISBN 1 84616 059 6
A Paperback Original
First published in Great Britain in 2006
Text © Bernard Ashley 2006
The right of Bernard Ashley to be identified as the author of
this work has been asserted by him in accordance with
the Copyrights, Designs and Patents Act, 1988.
A CIP catalogue record for this book is available
from the British Library
All rights reserved
1 3 5 7 9 10 8 6 4 2
Printed in Great Britain

IT'S A **RACE** AGAINST **TIME**
FOR **BEN MADDOX**

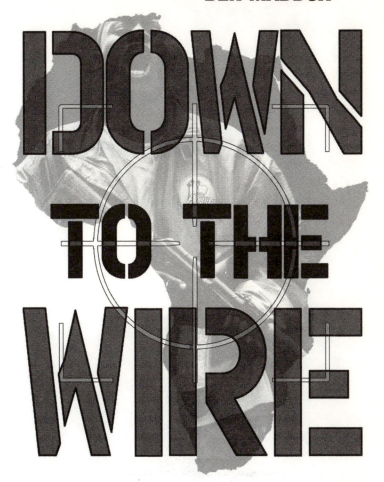

# DOWN TO THE WIRE

# BERNARD ASHLEY

ORCHARD BOOKS

*56. Ben Maddox – TV journalist*

There's no routine week for someone in my job. It all depends what's happening in the world, and what assignments I get given by Kath Lewis, my boss at Zephon TV.

Most days, when I'm not 'on the road', I'm in our South Bank office for the daily news conference at nine thirty. I'm among the youngest there (25) so I might get one of the more active assignments (I'm into sports big time, and often cycle to work from my flat in Hackney). I won't have read all the papers but I'll have listened to 'Today' and 'Zephon Radio News' on my Bluetooth radio.

Then it's out and about! But Kath Lewis likes initiative, so if I've spotted a potential story myself I might get a crack at it – till I'm pulled off when it's not getting anywhere.

Evenings – when I'm at home and not in the studio – are going to the gym twice a week, catching a  football match on TV or, better still, at one of the London clubs – or washing up after a great meal cooked by my partner Meera, who has the ability to use every pan and utensil in the kitchen, even for baked beans on toast. Then I catch up on newspapers and magazines, watch our own transmissions – if I'm not involved in them – or listen to some jazz.

No, all of that last bit was lies, the sort of stuff you'd expect to read – actually I sleep a lot or slouch around or read old Captain Marvel comics.

I still get letters about the Magayanan kidnapping of the last Home Secretary's daughter. But I was just lucky – in the right place at the right time – if I'm modest. If I'm being big-headed, I sniffed that story out myself, pursued it, and saved a couple of lives.

Brash? Doesn't that go with the job?

*(Ben Maddox was talking to Adèle Heath)*

## M4 HEADING WEST

*– The sub's on the ball again, going like a Red Fire down the left. Bill – this back four looks as scared as antelope of what he's going to do – and he's doing it!*

*Yes! It's a sweet ball, going over, head height – and perfect into the path of number eight – and...phew! Wow! He's hit it first crack! It's a goal! That bony forehead! Keeper no chance! A great goal! Who's the number eight?*

*– Charlie Akrofi!*

*– Charlie Akrofi's scored! But it's the young sub's goal, all the way! They're shouting for Akrofi in the stands, but some young genius made that goal. What's his name?*

*– Hang on, he's wearing twenty-three on his back...*

*– We'll find it! Number twenty-three, not been on the pitch long...*

Ben Maddox had thumbed the tuner of his world-band radio to the country he was heading for and hit on this crackly football commentary from the Lansanan Premiership – ideal listening for the mood he was in, because it didn't carry the vibes that music does. And with his radio cutting out the need for talk with the other passenger sitting in the back of the taxi, he could go on with the thinking that had to be done.

– *It's all over now, Bill, must be, sure! Two games into the new season and it's six points, top of the table, for Sikakoko Arsenal. Eh?*
– *True words! Hear that shoutin' an' jubilation!*
– *How long 'fore the whistle blows?*
– *Minutes. Minutes only. And we've seen something very special in this stadium here today…*
– *Praise God, we have!*
– *…a rare new talent coming up!*

The taxi took the DEPARTURES lane under the Terminal Four sign, and Ben Maddox pulled the phones from his ears, switched off the radio, and stowed it in his hold-all.

'Here y'are, gents,' the cabbie said, and Ben paid him, asking for a receipt – never forgotten these days; journalists' expenses are as crucial to the job as shorthand.

The doors to the terminal swung open, and now Ben and his cameraman were breathing international air in the departures lounge, and both of them suddenly relishing the excitement of heading off somewhere on a story.

# Joyce Avoka's story –
## written up by R. A. – part 1

Joyce Avoka's home was as poor as Lansana could offer. A few kilometres south of Sikakoko Township, up in the Yoori region, it was a roadside dwelling built partly of breeze, partly of mud, crouching under a rusting roof that flapped its tin wings whenever the wind blew. Fourteen years old, she had never been to school, but spent her days at the roadside selling whatever her family could gather together. In good times it would be food for the truck drivers who passed – bananas, plantains, a few melons, perhaps a young deer if her father's trap had worked – standing there under the palm fronds from sunrise to sunset. In bad times it would be fallen trunks of wood that she had herself dragged from the trees, for which others around might offer an egg or two to save them doing their own foraging. At night she slept as deep as death, exhausted – and growing old at twice the speed of most others in the world.

Tonight, it was raining. In the wet north east of Lansana the West African rains came and went in hard, frequent, spiteful bursts, and even if Joyce had been awake, she'd have heard nothing scary above the sounds of the downpour in her corner of the children's sleeping room.

So she didn't hear the men coming. Muffled not only by the rain, but by the creak and the strain and the dinning of the roof, the men lifted the scrappy mosquito screen aside and slithered through the high, small window like snakes, two of them – while other men were doing the same at other huts along this poverty-stricken part of the Sikakoko road.

They were child snatchers. Seeking children – to fight for the prophet Yusa and the Yoori tribal cause.

Joyce awoke suddenly in the rough arms of a different smell. These arms didn't belong to a family body; she was assaulted by the odour of a stranger, spiced by fear and action. A sweating hand was clamped over her mouth as she was grabbed from her place on the floor. She kicked, bit, and tried to scream as the little kids started to stir – but nothing could stop her from being carried like a log out through the doors and into the rain.

She heard screams and shouts as children from other huts were carried and pushed across the slippery mud in its funnelling to the road, where an open flatbed truck was revving in the roadside torrent.

'You talk – we come back and kill you!' And a high male scream was heard as a machete taught a father the lesson.

'Yusa! Yoori! Yusa fights for liberation!'

The raid was swift, cruel, and efficient. Within five minutes of the first waking, Joyce was being sat upon among a handful of other squirming children, all slithering in the truck like a boat-catch of fish as it bounced off north along the road. And Joyce knew as she lay there, her nose bleeding from the blow as she'd been thrown into the truck, that the Yoori Red Fires had at last hit their huts. Her family's fear that one day it would be their turn to be taken had come true. Like it or not, Joyce Avoka had been kidnapped for a 'soldier ant'.

# THIS IS AN E-TICKET
## KEEP IT SAFE.

..............................................................

**Travel Plans for Benjamin Maddox,
Johan Aaranovitch**

Trip Locator MQWNST7C

## Charter

Begin: **11 Apr**

Confirmation: **Confirmed**

Number of Persons in Party: **2**

Date: Friday 15 April

Flight: **BA00321**

Airline: **British Airways**

Depart: **14:10**

Airport: **London Heathrow**
..............................................................

## Terminal 4
### United Kingdom

Arrive: **19.55**

Airport: **Lansana Atlantic, Lansana**

Aircraft: **Boeing 767-3000/300ER**

Seat: **19-D/E**

Mileage: **3290**

Class: **Coach**

Travel time: **6.45**

Meal: **Yes**

Stopovers: **0**

With his e-ticket in his hand and doubt in his head – Ben still couldn't quite trust a sheet of paper from his own office printer to carry him all the way to Lansana and back – he pushed his hold-all along in the check-in queue for BA flight 321. But his companion Jonny Aaranovich seemed much more relaxed about whether or not they'd get onto the flight: his own sweat was for the camera equipment that he hadn't trusted to the hold.

'Stay in bed, I might as well – my camera landing at Kotoka International in Ghana and me in Lansana Atlantic,' he'd muttered to Ben, 'so it's coming with me.' Now he lugged and dumped the steel case as the queue moved forward, and Ben thought again how convenient pens and a palmtop were compared with camera equipment – even the 'lightweight' professional stuff issued by Zephon TV. It was like the difference between a piccolo player and a harpist on an orchestra tour.

But that was thinking 'awkward', not 'danger'; there was no difference between them otherwise. When TV reporters and their crews go abroad, they all share the same risks of being kidnapped or wounded or killed, the same chances of not getting to use their return tickets, self-printed or not. Newsmen and women in turbulent countries are like front-line troops when it comes to being where the action is. Not that where Ben and Jonny were going was a turbulent country, not yet, not unless they went out of their way looking for trouble.

There had been scents in the air, though; and one of them had been a small piece tucked into page four of a Sunday newspaper. It had alerted Ben's boss, Kath Lewis, to what might be coming up. Page four, a left-hand page, never has the reader impact of pages three or five. The eye always goes to the right-hand side first – and it certainly hasn't got the grab of the front page – so it was always a good place to go trawling for the news that other people might not be picking up. As Ben knew well, all news organisations – radio, TV and newspaper – have their own strings of local correspondents in various countries; and the international news agencies like Reuters and UIP fill the gaps in many news editors' schedules; therefore most good stories, once broken, get picked up quickly by everyone. So to be there first, to get the scoop, to transmit one news bulletin ahead of the rest, is to clock up viewing figures – and be at the top. But what might lie behind the urgent headlines could be weeks and months of investigating a story that isn't a story – until it breaks. And this was Ben Maddox territory. This was where Kath Lewis was trying to make him special.

# DEATH

## IN THE RAINS

The moderate Yoori negotiator in Lansana, Mbidi Renula has been reported killed in a road accident, heading north through a tropical storm. He was returning to the northern Yoori District from a visit to the capital of Lansana, Johnstown, on the Atlantic coast.

The Yoori people of Lansana have long sought independence for their traditional homeland, the mountainous region north east of the Ade river, allying themselves with the predominantly Yoori country Kutuliza which lies across the Lansana border. If they were to fly the flag of any country it would be Kutuliza's.

Details of the accident are scant. The road is notoriously potholed and poorly drained, but the carriageway is wide, and the chances of a four-wheel drive vehicle leaving it and crashing into a tree, as has been reported, are remote, even in a flash flood.

Lansanan government sources have not released details of the meeting that Mbidi Renula had with Dr Obed Abu, the president of Lansana.

*UIP local sources*

## ZEPHON TELEVISION – South Bank Studios

Kath Lewis had called Ben into her office on the Monday morning.

'See this?' she asked.

As if he had! He and his partner Meera had celebrated their second year together with an April weekend in Paris, Eurostar style, and he still hadn't sneezed the chestnut pollen out of his system.

He took the cutting from his boss and read it while she talked at him, fast. 'He was moderate, that man. The Yoori have got lots worse than him – hardline extremists who want independence, like the Tamil Tigers do in Sri Lanka. If he was trying to do some deal with the president, then this accident puts the kibosh on that.' She looked at Ben for a reaction. He sneezed. But he wasn't a messy sneezer. With some people you had to look away while they tidied up a nose job. Ben was as smooth as his television appearance; a quick apology, a no-nonsense blow and polish, and it was back to full attention from those hazel eyes. At the same time, a sneeze and its follow-up buys seconds; a longish cough a few more. Ben coughed. *What did he know about the Yoori of Lansana?* They were an old African tribe with a fierce reputation, not much more than that. *What did he know about Lansana?* It was a Christian country, with a predominant Lansan tribe, and a Yoori population in the north, and that was all.

'Okay, you know nothing!' Kath Lewis cut off his apology for the cough. People sometimes forgot that she'd grown up through television journalism the practical way; she knew all the tricks. 'Well, they want independence, the Yoori, their own state, form an alliance with Kutuliza.

Their tribal lands are where the rains fall heavy on the mountains, where the Ade Dam is, and the turbines that give Lansana its electricity. So, if you're Lansana, no nuclear power, depending on hydro-electricity, are you going to grant them independence, give it away?'

'Not unless they make me an offer I can't refuse.'

'Do you know the name for the Yoori extremist army?'

Ben shook his head.

'"Red Fire" – a vicious breed of soldier ants.'

He hadn't been asked to sit, and the weekend had been strenuous; travel and a big disappointment often are. 'Is this all off the internet?' he asked, leaning on a nearby table.

Kath Lewis ignored his rudeness. 'Some of it,' she said. 'Read this. It's off our own website.' She scooped up a printed sheet of A4 from the top of her in-tray.

Ben took the sheet and read it quickly.

# ZEPHON NEWS

## Fact File

Yoori Red Fires: A fearsome force from the late 1980s the Yoori Red Fires of North East District Lansana have been developed into a formidable fighting force involved in guerrilla attacks against the Lansanan armed forces, as well as on political targets. Deaths are thought to be in their thousands, although statistics aren't available

The Red Fires are terrorists drawn from the high, wet, mountainous north east, close to the border with Kutuliza, the predominantly Yoori country lying to the north. Some say that they operate out of Kutuliza, but this is denied by the Kutulizan government, which publicly distances itself from the terrorist force.

With weapons thought to be supplied from a foreign source, and with captured quantities of arms from the Lansana security forces, the Red Fires receive rigorous military training and a Yoori idealogical makeover ('brainwashing').

Boys (and some girls) as young as 14 are trained in special mountain camps – and with their fathers, brothers and cousins form a fighting force known as 'Red Fire soldier ants' who use artillery, surface-to-air missiles, and rocket launchers. Whole villages and townships in the north of Lansana are attacked in the cause of Yoori independence. Red Fire units have been accused of hacking to death women and children in predominantly Lansan tribal villages.

Kath Lewis talked on as Ben read. 'A young Yoori once watched one colony of ants fighting and defeating another colony of ants. He asked an elder how they had won, and the reply was, "By organising in bands and showing no mercy." And that was what the young man did with his enemies, his name was Yoor, and he became the first Yoori king and ruler of the region...'

Ben sneezed again.

'Are you allergic to something?' Kath asked.

'April in Paris,' he smiled. 'But I brought you a bottle of claret.'

'Well, you're getting out there. Lansana, not Paris. This story– ' she took the cutting back from Ben, left him with the internet fact sheet '–is going to kick off in a few weeks, because the hardline Yoori don't want a truce, they want a bloody independence, so they can link up with Kutuliza in the north. That's tribal. It's also economic – Kutuliza wants some of that water.'

'Are our viewers going to be much interested in that?' Ben asked, genuinely doubting Kath's focus this morning. 'We've got hose-pipe bans of our own...'

She blinked at him, three long, slow blinks that said, *shut up, you know nothing, and trust me, upstart!* 'If push goes to shove, goes to open and bloody civil war, Africa will have another Angola, Zaire, Sudan on its hands. And we'll have refugees and asylum seekers in our sympathetic cities the way we had them from Somalia, and British troops sent out as part of the UN being blown up on their streets – that'll interest our viewers!'

Ben blinked himself. He understood. Like a good chess player, Kath Lewis could see several moves ahead.

Lansana might well be the next big international story.

'And there's the human interest. Kids are human interest, the "Aaaah!" factor. On their recruiting raids for these young soldier ants, the Red Fire steal kids out of their beds and take them off to training camps in the mountains. Their parents never see them again.' She looked at Ben with an eyebrow raised, saying, *Story, or what?* 'And now someone's made cold meat of this Yoori pacifier so it's all going to boil up to fever pitch...'

'To mix a few metaphors,' Ben said.

'Get lost!' Kath told him. 'And bring that claret in before you book your air tickets.'

But Ben didn't go. He smiled his smile at her, the camera-easy smile – only spoiled by another hefty sneeze, which he got out of the way quickly. 'Why don't I know much about this?' he asked. 'Why isn't this conflict for independence as well known as the Tamil Tigers?'

'The boy's bright after all.' Kath got up. She went to her world map on the wall, pointed to Lansana in West Africa, the north east corner of it coloured dark with high mountains. 'Here's the only water in the country – but plenty of it – and they can't afford to pay for oil for all their energy needs. Capitalising on it, Lansana use their hydro-electric plant for their own energy, and – significantly – they sell it to countries around. So they can't let the Yoori have those mountains. But they don't want push to come to shove, they prefer to sit on it, or else their water customers will go looking for supplies elsewhere.'

Ben nodded. Now he really understood. 'And hence they've got to keep Yoori independence off the agenda – why their government's soft pedalling on trouble brewing in the north, and sitting on some of the atrocities.'

'Is my mixed metaphor guess.' Kath swung round at him, caught him by surprise, he was standing too close.

'Sorry!' They both backed off.

'So why does a moderate Yoori negotiator get killed?' Ben asked. 'The government doesn't want him out of the way. Is it his own hardliners…?'

'That, Benjamin Maddox, is why Zephon TV employs investigative reporters. Who did it? Which side?' She looked knowingly at him. 'Or, how many sides are there?'

Ben nodded. 'I'll book the tickets,' he said. 'Can Jonny Aaranovitch come?' Jonny was the best cameraman at the station and he and Ben had hit it off over the Magayanan political kidnap affair; another trip with him would be great.

Kath Lewis looked at her schedule on the wall. 'Sure, Jonny's okay; he's back from his kibbutz on Monday.'

'His Israeli bolthole. I know, that's why I asked.'

'In fact,' she made it sound as if she genuinely had just thought of this, 'I want this low key, no big production number, so just the two of you, sound on the camera – and Jonny can do the editing, be your producer. He knows what's what.'

'How long?' Ben asked. Television was a short fuse business; it was the magazines and newspapers that let a long cord of cordite smoulder for a story.

'Get an open return. I'm backing my hunch on this one. Things could move fast now this matey's dead, but you might have to be patient. I'll give it a fortnight, could be three weeks…'

Ben's eyebrows of surprise were being overworked this morning. With a pro's nod he went, all his sneezing done; the scent of adventure in his nostrils seeming to have seen to that. Paris was in the past.

## SIKAKOKO TOWNSHIP, LANSANA

Sixteen year old Mujiba Kalala sat on the edge of his bed with a ballpoint and a notebook. An active boy, a promising footballer on the books of an Lansanan premiership club, he could also be studious and reflective. And right now his mind was in turmoil as to where his life should take him. But there was no one with whom he could share his dilemma; he was no longer at school with a best friend, and the other apprentices at the club only ever wanted to talk about girls and football. His father was part of the problem – if problem it was – so he couldn't talk to his parents. Therefore he did what a bright teenager did with a mental tussle. He wrote it out – a sort of brainstorm – in the hope that seeing things on paper would help...

## *THE DILIGENT STUDENT NOTEBOOK*

*THESE PAGES BELONG TO MUJIBA KALALA, DEVOTED SON OF HIS FATHER, NOKONGOLO KALALA, OBEDIENT SERVANT OF THE LORD GOD AND OF YUSA, HIS PRIESTS AND ANGELS, WORDS OFFERED NOT FOR PRIDE BUT FOR HELP TO HAVE ABUNDANT WISDOM FOR UNDERSTANDING MYSELF*

*I try to know what is happening inside me. It is a strong body I have, with thanks to sweet Jesus and to Yusa and my ancestors, but it is split into two parts, through the heart, through the head. My arms and my legs pull me in these two directions, and* how can both ways be right? How can I best serve my father, my mother, eternal Jesus, the revered prophet Yusa, and myself? I have been given a special gift. I am different from many other boys, thanks to the genes of my ancestors. I play my football at a high level. I can say this not as pride but as fact. I am not clever to have this gift, I am lucky, so my head is not big about it. People say this gift can take me in a direction which will change everything for my family, but how do I know if these people are saying the truth? But I do know the truth of my father's strong priest-like love for the prophet Yusa and our Yoori people. This he would like me to have, and I love him. But I love my football, too. Can I serve both, and do justice to both? What is the right thing to do? I ask these pages. In writing them I seek God's mercy and Yusa's wisdom in sending an answer.

## BRITISH AIRWAYS FLIGHT: BA00321

The flight was full, and because the airtime would be nearly seven hours, people weren't just settling into their seats, they were occupying. Passengers sat in their places, then stood again to search for forgotten comforts from their cabin baggage in the overhead lockers. The aisle and the seats were cramped, the atmosphere claustrophobic, and the worst sorts of selfishness came out in everyone as they put themselves and their needs first. The BA packs of socks, eye masks, tooth brushes and blankets were not enough. And for the hundredth time on busy flights, Ben could see only hand-to-hand combat if the plane crashed or ditched. Which was why he and Jonny had reserved two aisle seats, near the emergency exit in the middle of the plane. Well, why not? Journalism was all about not being a loser. Plus, the aisle between them meant that on the long flight they could be private from each other, when they wanted to be.

But Ben had hardly settled, just let someone else into her seat and tested the girth of his seat belt, when Jonny was leaning across and poking him: a touch on his thigh.

'What?' He'd got his Stanley's guidebook on Lansana to skim before he tried to close his eyes.

'There. In front. The other side of the curtain.'

Ben looked to where the left-hand aisle curtain separated economy class from business, with him and Jonny on the cheaper side. The dividing curtain was looped back until after take-off, and cats could look at the backs of kings' heads for a while.

'Where?'

'Third row in, left–hand side, aisle seat.'

Ben stretched himself to see. In the third row from the curtain, port-side aisle seat, he saw the back of a white man's balding, grey head – as unremarkable as white men's balding grey heads always are. It was the sort of sight he'd fully expect to see up there in first class; it was only back here in economy that the heads were predominantly black. 'Who's that?'

They had to give way for a steward, shutting the overhead lockers with prim precision: 'Thank you, sirs,' as he shimmied between them.

Jonny came back. 'It's Eamonn Reilly!'

'Eamonn Reilly?' The name meant nothing to Ben. He stared into Jonny's sharp, bearded face, the dark brown eyes. He needed a clue – was he famous? Or someone in the job? Or a guy who owned a shop near the studios?

'Footballer. Spurs and Ireland. Legend!' Jonny was so excited: it was like Meera spotting Madonna in Kensington High Street.

'When?' Ben knew about football, played it and watched it; he knew a bit about most sports, but the name Eamonn Reilly meant nothing.

'Didn't play so long ago that I shouldn't know about him.' Jonny Aaranovitch, like many north London Jews, was a follower of the boys from White Hart Lane. 'Attacking midfielder, brought great distinction to the lily-white shirt...' He raked his fingers through his full head of dark hair.

'Good for him.' Pointedly, Ben opened his guide book.

'So what's he doing, going to Lansana?' Jonny was trying to keep the conversation low-key, which meant he was leaning right across the aisle, hampering the steward, coming back.

'Are sirs travelling together?' the steward queried, saying more than he was asking, the implication being that the friends should have taken adjoining seats if they were going to be an obstacle to his trolley service all afternoon.

'Sorry.' Jonny went away and came back when he'd gone. 'He's not signing players, Director of Football is Roy Jones, he does that...'

'At Manchester United? Newcastle?'

Jonny slapped Ben down with a disappointed stare. 'It would only ever be Tottenham Hotspur for Eamonn Reilly...'

'Oh, yes!'

'And there's no tourism in Lansana. For a holiday, he won't be going to Lansana. Sitting alone, see – so what's his business?'

Ben sighed. Jonny was great, but when he got hooked on something he wouldn't let it go. Besides, the answer seemed obvious. 'He's well retired from football. Now he's doing the job he was qualifying for while he played, using the money he invested from his inflated wages. They all do, football's a short life for a player. They don't all get their FA badges and go into coaching or management or become pundits. He'll be into timber, or gold, or oil, or own a chain of sports shops, opening one up in Lansana. Wouldn't be the Yoori problem, would it? Anyhow, he's not press, so no danger there.' The pair of them had scanned the passengers in the check-in queue but there hadn't seemed to be any competition from other stations or newspapers.

'You're right.' Jonny was nodding, but with his eyes still on the legend up in business class. 'To meet him would be very nice.' His sharp face melted with a schoolboy smile.

'Got your autograph book?' Ben asked.

Jonny turned his head to stare at him, more than a little offended. 'Memories, I've got.' He tapped his forehead. 'My father and me. You should be so lucky as to see a player like that, in action...'

Ben smiled, apologetically. 'Yeah. Sure,' he said. 'I guess I know how you feel.' And, a little uncomfortably, he stuck his head into his guide book again; but within moments he was reaching up to the locker for his wire-less laptop.

### Ben Maddox

**From:** benmaddox@talktalk.net
**Sent:** 23 April    14:01
**To:** bramsaran@zephontv.co.uk
**Subject:** Subject: Re: Eamonn Reilly

Bloom – could you look up Eamonn Reilly
in our biog files?
Ex Tottenham and Ireland footballer, few years ago.
What's he doing these days? Aaranovitch is excited to
see one of his heroes on the plane – but this is a
direct flight to Lansana, so what's he up to? Any
directorships with nuclear power companies?

Skulduggery is what we're into.

Cheers  Ben  x

'Excuse me, sir. Naughty! No mobiles, laptops, notebooks or electronic organisers until we're airborne. And then only if Captain Williams allows.' The steward, a tidy young man with orange hair, offered to take the laptop and stow it for Ben; which Ben let him do, because he'd already sent the e-mail.

'There's no taking him anywhere!' Jonny told the steward, but the boy was much less interested in Jonny than he was in Ben.

'I'm sure he's a delightful companion, wherever,' and the steward shut the overhead locker with a tender click. He went, and Jonny gave Ben a wink. Which made Ben feel less lumpy about having pulled the autograph thing on him just now. He could settle into his guidebook with an easier conscience.

## THE RED FIRES OF YOORI

The high and inhospitable mountains of Yoori District, remote from the coast and the capital, seem uninteresting at first encounter except to climbers; but as the traveller goes further north, Sikakoko – a town of two thousand people, mainly strict Yoori – sits below the huge hydro-electric dam at the foot of the long Ade Valley where the two main mountain ranges converge. The traveller will have come by road –

the Lansana railway system stops two hundred kilometres short of this remote area – yet it is here where the nation's wealth lies. The heavy rainfall and huge falls generate enough electricity not only for Lansana's needs but for export to Kutuliza to the north, Mashariki to the east and to Cote d'Ivoire to the west. But, as visitors to the country, our interest lies not in the economy, nor in the hydro-electricity, but in the wildlife. And, yes, there are lions, the animal everybody hopes to see on safari, but they laze for twenty-three hours of every day so the tourist would be better at a zoo. And as a resident, unless one's luck really runs out, they pose little threat to Man.

There is a strain of bold Red Fire in the region, though – solitary, secretive, stealthy and powerful – that has been known to take children from their beds, but the visitor's focus is much more likely to be on the striped hyena, the

green monkey, the olive baboon and the
Defassa waterbuck (see separate
entries), and for these a decent tip to a
local guide will get him to steer your
driver to various vantage points for
seeing and photographing most of
these animals.

Ben had shut his eyes before he closed his guidebook. The
safety instructions had been shown on the TV screens
while he read, and now the Boeing 767 was lumbering
round in the queue for take-off on Runway One. He
thought about that entry in the guide book. These things
seemed to be written for that small group of people who go
to other places to throw money about and gawp into other
people's lives, not to work; they're not even holidaymakers,
but *travellers*. Kath Lewis ought to write some of these
entries, she'd soon steer the intrepid traveller to where he
could have his backside ripped out by a Red Fire as he lay
beneath his mosquito net: ideally filmed by Zephon, of
course.

He opened his eyes and looked across at Jonny, smiling
to himself. The man was still giraffing his neck to see down
into Business Class. He filmed all manner of famous people
– Hollywood stars, top models, prime ministers, royalty,
sports heroes, celebrity chefs – but the sight of
a retired and forgotten Spurs player on the plane had him
twitching in his seat like a boy with worms. And a sudden
wistfulness enveloped Ben. What must it have been like to
have Jonny's sort of family background, where your dad
took you to your local team from the age you could sit still?

Or to do anything that was shared and regular? Ben had known kids like that, and he'd always felt jealous of them, having no dad himself since Infants school days, and a mum who'd had to work herself skinny to keep on having their own front door. *Weekend* was a concept she'd never known, and *leisure* to her was like a word from a foreign language.

Which was what Paris had all been about, the weekend before. Him pledging loyalty to Meera, taking her there to ask her to marry him, to have children – and being turned down, till he could live a lifestyle where he wasn't somewhere else half the time. Which was a demand that he could understand, but which he couldn't promise; and which he honestly didn't want to. So they'd made the best of the break, got over the awkwardness by driving along the Champs Elysee, climbing the steps to Montmartre, gliding on the fly-boat along the Seine, laughing and loving, eating the food and drinking the drink. And the first Monday back he'd jumped at this assignment in Lansana.

Now he snoozed; or, at least, he shut his eyes and let his mind drift again. Take-off was powerful and smooth, and the long uphill climb to their cruising altitude of forty thousand feet took them south beyond Paris. Soon the drinks and the food would arrive along each of the aisles; until then, with his eyes closed, Ben could be private from Jonny and think for a while about things.

The past weekend with Meera was still raw skin for him, he was still getting over the shock of it. And perhaps his shock had been greater because – telling himself the stark truth – he hadn't been one hundred per cent on the marriage idea himself. It had just seemed the right thing to do, now that he was well in with Zephon on the back of the Fran Scott kidnapping, in as secure a job as any journalist can have. And after his own vulnerable childhood, he wanted to pass that security on, to Meera. But, smack in the face, she'd said no, and he'd realised how much he'd been taking her for granted.

Sitting here now, though, he knew beyond doubt that the sort of assignment he was on was what he wanted to do, and he could feel free to do it – yet still have the partnership of Meera, on the same terms as when they'd first got together. No permanent ties. This was the only way it could be if he was going to be a front line journalist.

The Dell notebook on his lap, down from the locker again and sleeping like a sleek black cat under a camouflaging newspaper, suddenly sneezed. It was a reply from Bloom Ramsaran.

### Ben Maddox

From: bramsaran@zephontv.co.uk
Sent: 23 April     17:24
To: benmaddox@talktalk.net
Subject: Re: Eamonn Reilly

Hi Darling!
(High darling!)  Sorry.  No useful info on E.R.  All his football stuff is on the record, great player in his day, apparently – but no directorships or back-handers listed. Current occupation – 'retired', interest in Irish football.
Love
Bloom xx

'What's that?'  Jonny Aaranovitch had seen the smile on Ben's face as he'd read the e-mail.

'The office. About matey up there.' Ben nodded towards Business Class. 'Bloom's turned up nothing on your...old player.'

'It's the red on your face she's turned up, boy!'

Ben gave Jonny one of those really puzzled, *you-must-be-nuts!* looks, but his stomach had flipped with the way Bloom had signed off. Stupid! How adolescent could you get?

'Whatever...' he said.

*I love my father. He is a strong man - but he is not big and strong like a tough guy guarding the supermarket where drink is sold, he is strong in his spirit and also in his arms. He is a thin man but if he grabs to hold me, I cannot shake him off, and no-one will shake him off from what he believes is right and true.*

*My father Nokongolo Kalala is strong and faithful in the Yoori sect. He believes in the Yoori prophet Yusa and I think he would kill a man who disgraced Yusa or who sacrileged him. So it is hard for me.*

*I believe in sweet Jesus and his miracles and works, and I believe that our Yusa is at His right hand. I believe and I wish hard that one day I will be with Yusa and the angels in Heaven, but I also have this earth and what I wish for here.*

*My mother and my sisters say nothing, they will follow my father, and I will follow my father, too, in our beliefs. But also I like my life of sport and friends, and I am like a person with weighing pans. Jesus and Yusa go in one pan, and my daily life goes in the other. But it is not God but my father Nokongolo*

Kalala who is holding the scales. I swear I will never disappoint him, but I do not want to disappoint myself. Will it be him who makes my decisions, or the balance of what should be for me? This is my problem.

## JOHNSTOWN, LANSANA –
## ATLANTIC INTERNATIONAL AIRPORT

The queue at Immigration seemed endless, and Eamonn Reilly was somewhere up at the head of it: first class passengers always were. Visas were scrutinized hard for authenticity and more people than Ben thought customary were taken aside for interviews in side rooms, but he and Jonny eventually came through – and there, through the door on the far side of Customs, out where the placards and sheets of paper were being held up, was what they were looking for.

# ZEPHON

It was beautifully calligraphed in Times New Roman, and held up by a young woman who stood out from the crowd. She was late twenties, white, with short, almost flame-orange hair and pale, lightly freckled skin: not for her, the African sun. And cornflower blue eyes.

Jonny got there first. 'Miss Arens?' he asked.

'Rebekah,' she smiled, and they shook hands.

'Jonny Aaranovitch.' He rapped on the heavy metal case crowning their trolley. 'Cameraman and editor. And this is—'

'Ben Maddox,' said Ben and Rebekah together.

'Reporter,' added Ben.

'Me, too – but newspaper, and I'm your "fixer",' said the girl. 'Johnstown *Daily Graphic*, and yours for the assignment.'

'Somewhere good to stay, you got us?' Jonny asked. 'Nice and clean?'

Rebekah Arens gave him a knowing look and flapped the Zephon name card like a fan. 'Not far. Air-conditioned rooms,' she said, 'en-suite, but not the most luxurious place in Johnstown.' She rubbed her fingers, meaning money. 'Your Kath Lewis was quite tough about that.'

'She would be,' said Ben. 'We're lucky it's not a tent and two mosquito nets…'

Rebekah laughed. 'Only, not that much more lucky,' she said. 'Come on, we'll get a taxi. Your car and driver's paid by the day, so it wasn't worth employing him this time in the evening. He starts tomorrow.'

Ben and Jonny exchanged looks as Rebekah Arens led them to the taxi rank, out into the hot, heavy, air of a sea-level West African evening, Ben pushing the trolley.

'I'll deal with the taxi driver,' Rebekah said: which was as well, since Ben and Jonny had American dollars and no local currency yet.

'Where are you from?' Jonny caught up with Rebekah to ask, 'South Africa? Greece? The Middle East somewhere? Only, your accent…' It had a clip to it.

Rebekah threw it over her shoulder. 'Israel,' she said.

'Of the faith?' Jonny Aaronavitch asked, to which she nodded, as all their attentions were taken by a sleek black jeep with tinted windows sweeping past them on its way into the city, with the bald grey head of Eamonn Reilly leaning against the nearside glass.

'Where do the business people stay, and the 'A' list celebs?' Ben asked.

'Atlantic View Hotel,' she said. 'It's the only place like it. Behind golden gates, a palm fringed paradise in an international world of its own. And that's quoting from their brochure.' She turned to Ben. 'You'd hate it.'

'Would I?'

'I've read your stuff, you're not into that sort of privilege...'

'I am at nine o'clock on a hot night.'

'Come on, then,' she said, 'to the Volta!' waving her hand for the next taxi in the line. 'African river. The name of your hotel. Known locally as the Re-volta!' And she ducked into the car as Jonny and Ben made sure that their luggage got stowed.

# Joyce Avoka's story –
## written up by R. A. – part 2

The slithering bodies in the truck had dried out. The rains had stopped and the water drained off by the time the old Toyota laboured up the winding valley above Sikakoko. Dawn was breaking over the mountains, and now Joyce and the others could see the faces of the men who had captured them: younger than the monsters she'd imagined in the terror of the night. The captives weren't being sat upon any more, but were huddled at the front end of the flatback, sitting against the cab, some crying, some still calling their father's and their mother's names. The Red Fire soldiers, all in camouflage uniform but without hats or berets, were at the tailboard end, eight of them, sleeping, lounging, but one wide-awake man with a rifle sat staring at them, his weapon cocked and pointing towards the children.

Joyce knew all the others, they lived within shouting distance in their roadside cluster of huts. There were five of them beside herself – all boys – and most were younger, one older. And this older boy was Lame Daniel, who had always limped, but who could outrun them all in a chase for rabbits. She said nothing, looked with darting glances at the roadside, thinking of her chances if she threw herself off this truck as it wound its way slowly up the mountain road. She was as scared as the rest, and a great hole of loss ached inside her body. She had lost her family, she had been taken as children from other villages had been taken, and none of them ever came back. She wanted to scream out her hopelessness – because she knew that unless a miracle happened she would never ever see her people again: her mother, who could give a harder hug than she ever smacked, her father, who owned nothing in the world but was a proud man, and the brothers, who she missed desperately already, arguing over sleeping space, and annoying her. It was the end of her life as she had known it – a good girl who always said her prayers to Jesus.

Fearfully, she looked at the man with the rifle – had he seen her looking about? He had. He was staring right through her, and she pulled her old nightdress down as far as it would go. And he was shaking his head, jerking the rifle at her – don't dream of trying to escape!

The lorry picked up some speed as they came to the wide, level expanse of the Ade Dam – a huge reservoir of sparkling water that squinted the eyes, lipping over into a fall that filled the ears with its roar. Recent rains had been generous, the run-off heavy. And it filled the eyes, this huge man-made lake that none of the children had ever seen, bigger than their world. Their necks twisted to keep it in view as the lorry drove on to where the incline began again, putting the dam just below them, a few metres down a scrubby slope of volcanic rock and stunted trees. Suddenly, the lorry stopped, as if something had run out in front of it. The captive children and the Red Fire soldiers were thrown about, waking those who had dozed – but the man with the rifle kept it pointed where it had always been.

At Joyce.

With a slam of his door, the man in command, someone of higher rank, came around from the cab. 'Get down there!' he shouted – 'and wash.'

The young mud-spattered kids in sleeping shorts and underpants, Joyce in her nightdress, were forced off the back of the truck and down onto the road. Lame Daniel came last, limping across from the truck to the side. At the sight of him, the man in command said something to one of the men.

'You!' the soldier shouted at Daniel – 'Run to that rock! ' He pointed to an outcrop twenty metres back down the road. Daniel ran, and Joyce watched his limping, skipping run, as fast as he always did, until she was pushed roughly in the back and made to go down towards the reservoir. The soldiers lined their way on either side of the scree, and Joyce and the rest slithered and fell towards the water.

It was cold. It numbed Joyce's feet as she made first contact, but with shouts and threats and curses, and a machete being waved at them, she and the others were made to go out to waist deep, and duck themselves under in the clear water. It froze into her soul and wanted to stop her heart as she was made to scrub off the last of her old life. Embarrassed in her clinging nightdress, the men pointing at her and making lewd comments, she followed the boys out of the water and climbed the scree back to the truck.

Now Lame Daniel was being taken down to the reservoir, his body panting with the fast running that he had done to show that he was as good as the rest. But he must have known what was going to happen, his eyes had the terrified see-all look of the condemned.

Two soldiers went down the scree with him, and as the truck's engine restarted and began to move slowly forward up the valley, two soldiers returned, and climbed onto the back. Without Lame Daniel.

There had been no sound, no cry, no shot. But by the soldier's wet trousers and sleeves, Joyce knew that he must have been held under the water, and drowned.

Which was her first lesson. You had to suit to be a Yoori liberation soldier

# Atlantic View Hotel

### ROOM SERVICE

A discreet and friendly room service is available
at all hours of the day and night. Your floor waiter or
your floor housekeeper will attend to all your needs
at whatever time. Simply press button 1 on
your telephone handset.

Room service meals are available from the full restaurant menu, with a
5% added charge. A signature will be required at the time of delivery.

### MINI BAR

The mini bar in your room is replenished daily,
but your floor waiter will attend to any deficits
within five/ten minutes. Simply press button
1 on your telephone handset.

### AIR CONDITIONING

Air conditioning is controlled by the
bedside remote control. Please adjust the
temperature to your liking. To preserve the
climate control of your room, you are invited
to leave the air conditioning unit running
whether you are in residence or not.

### GENERAL

Our aim is to make your stay a memorable and
comfortable experience. Please remember that we are here
to attend to all your accommodation and personal needs
whilst you are our guest(s). Nothing is too much trouble.


THE MANAGEMENT

Eamonn Reilly fizzed his generous glass of Black Bush Irish whiskey with the smallest squirt of soda and sat himself down on the huge double bed. He looked around the room, pursed his lips and said, 'So here's a dandy place!' The floor was tiled and the walls were of marble, and the walk-in wardrobe, its door open with his travelling shirt hanging in it, would have accommodated a small office. The other open door, into the bathroom, let into a space almost as big as the old Spurs home team showers and tub.

He unzipped the black leather document case lying beside him and took from it his small book of contact numbers and addresses. He thumbed nimbly through to a name at the end and picked up his pay-as-you-go mobile phone. It took a short while to be registered on the local network, but before he'd one-handed unscrewed the top of his whiskey bottle for a refill, his call was answered – and he reported to the person at the other end that he was here, fit as Finbar's fiddle, about to make contact with the client, and after a good night's sleep and some fry, would be ready for business the next day.

# *Volta Hotel*

*We hope your stay will be comfortable.*
*Breakfast is served from 7 to 9 in the bar.*
*Please order boiled, scrambled, fried eggs*
*night before in the bar. All attention will*
*be paid to your order. Tea or coffee served,*
*no juices (can be bought from bar).*

*If you wish meals in the evening, next door*
*(Frankie's) has a good clean menu.*

*Switch off aircon machine on leaving*
*room.*

*Management is not responsible for valuables,*
*but safe can be hired from desk.*

*Bible in bedside locker. Sleep well and*
*rest in the Lord Jesus.*

## *Manager*

Ben Maddox hadn't brought a lot with him. From his local Milletts camping shop in Leyton High Street he had bought three long-sleeved khaki shirts with double pockets, the sort that wash out and hang to dry overnight, and two pairs of washable cotton trousers. From the start he'd been determined to travel light, especially after the

weight of the case he'd lugged to Paris and ba[ck]
two nights. Long cotton socks, three pairs of cotton [p...]
size nine suede boots and a beany sun hat made up h[is]
wardrobe; compact and efficient, leaving room for his
laptop, his chargers, several notebooks and a clutch of
pens.

He sat on the creaky bed and decided not to unpack
more than he had to: if they got the go-ahead to travel up
country to the Yoori region tomorrow, he was only going to
have to put the stuff back again. The ancient air
conditioning rattled above his head, and he sat in its
draught with a shiver and a sneeze while he sent a text to
Meera.

**R-ived OK  Volta hotel
Johnstown Lansana.
B good.  C U soon.
Luv u   Ben  XX**

The food on the plane had neither satisfied nor left room
for much desire to eat, so he took himself down to the bar
for a drink before bed, knocking on Jonny's door on the
way. But Jonny was sorting his camera equipment,
sounding as if he was going over his stock with Rebekah on
the phone, so Ben went on down and drank alone. A big
bottle of Star lager imported from Ghana seemed to be the
likeliest drink to hit the button, so he sat at a table, the only
one in the bar, and tried to make conversation with the
barman. s usual, he tried football as a useful way in. The
TV set high up in the corner was showing an Italian
*Serie A* match transmitted via South Africa.

'You follow football?'

...rman nodded, hardly turning his

...chester United.'

And before giving up, Ben idly asked,
...th seeing in Johnstown?' He knew that
...flourishing Premiership that was leading to
...uccess in the Africa Cup: he'd picked up that
radio com... ...ntary in London.

'Sunday,' the barman told him. 'Johnstown Lions versus Sikakoko Arsenal. That's the big one,' he added, showing an eyeball of interest.

Ben put down his glass. 'Sikakoko' had fingered his pulse. Wasn't Sikakoko in the Yoori region that was campaigning for independence? The place they'd come to investigate? 'That'll be big for tribe as well as for club, won't it?' he asked.

The barman shrugged.

'If I'm here in Johnstown on Sunday, can I get tickets?'

'No problem.' And the barman went back to leaning, and clicking his fingers at the television football.

So Ben drank up and went to bed. He was missing Meera already. Sitting in on some barman's life had to be a second-hand sort of existence. Could it be that the life of the lonely, roving investigative reporter wasn't one hundred per cent for him...?

# SIKAKOKO TOWNSHIP – LANSANA

Mujiba Kalala crept under the mosquito net that tented his bed and stretched the cramp from his legs. His light was low, sitting on the floor flickering beside him, sunlight had long since disappeared, the whole country went dark at around six o'clock. So there would be no reading, or writing in his notebook, bed was for sleep and nothing else.

But sleep wasn't his for the having, just yet. Outside, on the walking boards around the breeze-block house, were the Yoori religious men with his father, talking in loud and overlapping voices. Over the top of the dividing wall between his room and the kitchen – that stopped ten centimetres short of the tin roof for the circulation of the air – were the sounds of a South American serial being beamed out from the TV station in Mfinimfini, central Lansana. His mother, Eni, followed it night after night, and she knew the characters like her own family. And on the other side, his sisters' room, there was a fight going on for a comb that hadn't got broken teeth.

He turned flat onto his front, neither sheet nor blanket, it was too hot for covering, and tried to stuff his ears with the ends of his thin pillow. And because he was exhausted from his day's work, patience eventually paid, and before he had run through to the end of a long and fervent prayer for guidance, sleep overcame him – and he went to that place that changes every night, into the fantasy of his unconscious head.

*He came running out into the green and the light of the stadium.*

47

*The upper and lower tiers were alive with chanting and with arms waving in the sun, with white shirts and golden robes flashing from the VIP seats on the shadowed side. The noise rang around and around the football bowl like a throbbing cymbal, so loud and constant that shouting to team members on the pitch sounded in his head like the voice of someone else.*

*But he was ready for today, the dear Lord Jesus would see him play a noble game, his first chance not to have to wait for the substitute's call from his manager but with a place in the team, to start the game with his famous captain, who would feed off the balls that he passed through with skill and bravery. Shuffling his feet with the others, he lined up to face the benches and the main stand, the other team somewhere along to the right. Separating the sides stood the referee and his assistants and the fourth official, dressed in yellow and black. He looked down at the badge on his own blue shirt, the red eagle head aggressive and fierce, and he lifted it to his lips for a benediction. This was what he had waited for ever since he had first kicked those punctured balls around the family compound.*

*But suddenly the sky darkened. The chanting in the stadium stopped and there was a deep black hole of silence. He squinted towards the VIP seats, and out from the shadows, across the running track, came a man, walking fast and thin and ominous, his strong head shining bald in the sun – holding something in his hand, up before him at head level.*

*It was his father. His face was straight, not angry but not friendly, and he marched to where the line was waiting, directly to him, and in the glaring light of the afternoon, what was being held up could clearly be seen. It was a small Bible, held up like a red card, thrust at his face as his father stopped. And, 'Off!' his father commanded. 'Off!'*

*And with his heart beating and the crowd picking up its*

*cheering, Mujiba walked from the line of players and headed for*
*the shadow of the tunnel. Into the sudden darkness of night.*

He woke suddenly, knowing instantly where he was, no confusion between dream and reality. The house was dark now, and still, and only in this deepest night could the fast-running Ade river be heard, relieving pressure on the dam from the mountain waters. It was like the never-ending running of his conscience, always there as background to his life.

Did the sweet Lord Jesus send his will through such dreams as he had just had? Should he turn against his sport? Mujiba turned over and over on his bed and came back to lying facing up, eyes wide and seeing the first glimmer of light on the corrugations of the roof. Or was it only his father's will that the dream had shown? Was his father more clear-cut in a dream than he was in real life? His hints and looks and mutterings turning into an order to be obeyed?

A dog barked somewhere through the township, and the waking voice of one of his sisters called out a dream word that he couldn't understand. An early lorry rumbled along the rutted road, and for Mujiba Kalala there was no more sleep.

## JOHNSTOWN, LANSANA

'Right,' Rebekah Arens said, 'you've got to get a taste of this country.' They were sitting on the veranda of the Volta Hotel, wicker chairs creaking under Ben and Jonny's impatience to get going.

Ben looked out towards the street where, since they'd first come down to breakfast, people had been walking to Johnstown's main market, Gua, carrying everything on their heads. With deportment even better than Bloom Ramsaran's in the Zephon office, they carried fruit, nuts, bags of iced water, table cloths, cooked poultry, kitchen utensils, toilet rolls, sun glasses, and all sorts of other commodities in balanced tin bowls. On the road itself, mini-buses crammed with passengers hooted their way into the city, slogans displayed on their rear doors: *As At Now; Mighty Victory; No Weapons; Town Running; Obedient; King of Kings.*

'When are we going up country to Yoori territory?' Ben creaked, shifting his weight.

'Soon,' Rebekah told him. 'After the weekend. But today is orientation...'

'Done it. I did that in the scouts, on my five mile hike.'

Rebekah smiled at Ben. 'Background stuff,' she said, 'into the centre of Johnstown, see how the people live, get a feel of the place, sense the religious, tribal attitudes. You'll appreciate the difference when you go up to Sikakoko.' She nodded towards an old Vauxhall parked in front of the hotel. 'We'll go in the car.'

Which was their introduction to Richard – never admitting to a surname – who would be their driver and fourth member of the team; everyone travelling so light that all their stuff was crammed, incredibly, into the Corsa's boot. But that was for later. Today, it was Johnstown.

Ben had travelled about, but he had never seen anything like Gua Market. As far as the eye could see, along streets and streets of the east of the city, people were selling. On each side of narrow walkways everything for daily living was sold. There were no curios, jewellery, antiques or hand-made artefacts, just stalls and stalls of day-to-day stuff; and behind the street stalls were more stalls under colonnades; and above the colonnades, up steep stairs, were more and more of the same. There was cutlery, tableware, fruit, vegetables, toilet products, cleaning materials, buckets, bowls, locks and bolts – nothing particularly interesting to Ben, but the people compensated for that. Through the narrow walkway filed a continuous line, some buying, others delivering, everything carried on their heads, marvels of balance. As a circus performer for a few months between school and university, Ben had to admire the ease of the balance.

On every side, Rebekah, Jonny and Ben were beset by vendors. 'Boss–', 'Missus–', 'Uncle–', 'White boy–', 'Friend–' '–you buy?' Which was impossible without the currency that Ben and Jonny were going to exchange when they came to Kath's favourite *Forex*. Not that there was anything they really wanted here.

Until Jonny's eyes gleamed. He turned to Ben suddenly in the narrow passage-way, making Ben stop, and causing two following bowls on heads to collide and nearly spill to the ground.

*'Ani ka ase!'*

'Sorry!' But Ben had seen whom Jonny had seen: Eamonn Reilly, doing the same as them, strolling through the Johnstown market, twenty or so people further ahead.

'Come on!' Jonny said. 'We talk! Eamonn Reilly!'

Ben groaned; but if Jonny had a hero from his teens, who was he to spoil his worship? Jonny led the polite push through the crowds, but it was as if Eamonn Reilly had spotted them,because all at once he wasn't strolling the market any more. He was doing his own pushing, making a get-away.

'Eamonn!' Jonny called; every bit the Spurs' Paxton Road-end kid now. But if Eamonn Reilly had heard him, it looked as if he hadn't wanted to. At a crossroads, narrowed into four single files, he took a turning that Jonny didn't spot; and after twenty minutes of trying this way, and trying that, the chase had to be given up. Eamonn Reilly had eluded them. He had definitely and deliberately eluded them.

In a market café, eating rice and roasted chicken, Jonny wondered why. 'He's not besieged by fans these days, he's respected, not harassed – those years are past.'

Except for you, Ben thought, charging through the market like a kid.

'So, why?'

'Perhaps he's got something to hide,' Rebekah Arens put in, over a forkful of rice.

'Perhaps he has. But just to tell him what he meant to me – it would have been nice...'

Heroes! Ben thought. All the world wanted heroes!

Hello, Eamonn Reilly here. Switch off your answer-phone if you're there, you useless article. *(Pause)* Are you there? No? Well, just to tell you I've made contact with the man now, and I'm seeing him tonight, at the only decent eatin' house in the place. He's coming down south to me, which is a decent thing, given the hot of this place, and I'll ring again when I've anything to tell you. Over, an' bloody out!

The Irishman snapped shut his mobile and went into his marble bathroom for a hot shower – his room was too cold, if truth be known. Which might have contributed to the exasperated expression on his face; which might also have been down to the sight that day of two tourists off the London flight who seemed to have clocked him, and wanted to be UK friends abroad. Or something.

# JOHNSTOWN LIONS

## versus

# SIKAKOKO ARSENAL

(AWAY)

## SUNDAY 17th APRIL

Squad to travel – team coach noon
Sat. 16th April, no. 1 car park Sikakoko Stadium

| | |
|---|---|
| **Bodjona** | **Peprab** |
| **Olympio** | **Koomson** |
| **Eyadema** | **Wilmot** |
| **Kpotsra** | **Abankwa** |
| **Latevi** | **Kalala** |
| **Agama** | |
| **Atcho** | |
| **Gbeho** | |
| **Lawson** | |
| **Akrofi** | |

Manager: Chognon
Trainer: Adjei-Mensah
Physio: N'Gatta
Kit assistant

FINE FOR LATENESS – ONE MONTH WAGES

Mujiba Kalala ran into the canteen at the Sikakoko Arsenal training ground, a kilometre from the stadium. The squad to travel to Sunday away games went up on the noticeboard on Friday afternoons, after the morning training sessions. The stars of the team, three of whom played for the Lansana international side, would stroll past the list with their glasses of water, or coke, or cups of coffee, and casually check that they weren't being dropped – or left out to give them a rest if the opposition was weak. But the Johnstown game was always a big one, Premiership, at home or away, and some supporters would travel the length of the country in old cars and mini-buses to see the Arsenal play. Muj Kal – as the supporters called him – wasn't one of the élite, though. Some weeks he was in the squad, some weeks he was out. For home games, he was expected to turn up, on the bench, or not. But for away games when an overnight hotel was involved, to be picked to travel was an honour in itself.

Always there was the hurdle, though, and this had nothing to do with Sikakoko Arsenal, or its manager, George Chognon. This hurdle was Mujiba's father, Nokongolo Kalala. He seemed to reluctantly accept that his son played football in Sikakoko, that he was professional enough to be being paid an apprentice footballer's wage with a Premiership club, and he seemed also to be prepared to accept that sometimes Mujiba had to travel to games out of the north-east Yoori region – so long as he was back home at night. But when fixtures were a long way off, and the boy had to sleep in a hotel room with another player, there was always the same difficult conversation.

'If I let you go, and I will think and pray on this, you will at all times remember your religion and your roots. On the bus you will read your Bible, and you will think of the prophet Yusa at the right hand of the Lord Jesus, and at night you will pray to him on your knees. And the last thoughts in your head, the last words in your mouth before you go to sleep, will be of Yusa.'

'Sure, of course.'

'And when you go to alien towns, to towns that do not respect Yusa, then you will speak to no one besides the team and its officials. You will not be tarnished with any other air.'

'I know.' And Mujiba always obeyed his hard, loving father. It was difficult sometimes to pray when another player sharing his room was lying on his bed with poker cards, or watching the television; and when the officials from other clubs pointed the way, or a reporter asked a question, it was difficult not to say 'thank you' or to give some other answer. But he stuck to these rules because he wanted to go on playing football, as he also wanted to please his father.

He read his name at the foot of the squad for the following Sunday, and smiled modestly before he turned and anyone else could see his face. He would be in the squad, and if he was lucky he would be on the bench as a substitute. If he was luckier still, he would be given the chance to run out on the pitch, and take his place in the midfield, and win balls – and pass them accurately to Sikakoko's and Lansana's international striker, Roland Badjona, or to Charlie Akrofi.

He walked to the door of the canteen and waved goodbye to one or two younger players, and then he cycled home, thinking of football, and of his father and their

Yoori people. And of what would happen to Sikakoko Arsenal if the north east region ever did get its way and become independent. Even if it allied with Kutuliza to the north, Kutuliza had a poor international team, and no league like the Premiership. With Sikakoko in some other country, most of the Sikakoko squad would leave and play their football elsewhere.

But at least Mujiba's troubled mind would be made up for him, he could tear up his writing at home. He would not become a great footballer, but a disciple of Yusa, like his father.

# AFRICA INTERNET

## Background to conflict

*Conflict in the north east of Lansana is not a fact yet, but the signs of conflict are not hard to see. The north east region of the country, historically known as the Yoori lands, have long wanted independence, which would lead to an affinity with Yoori Kutuliza.*

*Historically, this part of Lansana and Kutuliza formed the Yusa kingdom, a territory that was a protectorate of Germany, and divided by the allied powers at the end of the 1914-18 war: Kutiliza to the French, and Lansana to the British. Both countries achieved independence in the 1950s, but the Yoori within them now seek to be reunited.*

*Water is the resource preventing a peaceful resolution of the Yoori tribal demands. The hydroelectric system in this mountainous region, with its plentiful rainfall, provides water – and energy – not only for Lansana, but for Mashariki to the east, Cote d'Ivoire to the west, and even Kutuliza to the north, contributing hugely to the Lansanan economy. It is inconceivable that the government in*

*Johnstown would allow this profitable region to become independent, free to align with Kutuliza.*

*Meanwhile, pressure is building in the region for action. The notorious Red Fires are training soldiers as young as fourteen to fight for Yoori independence; arms are being stored, some say over the border in Kutuliza, and guerrilla raids are made on non-Yoori villages. The Kutuliza government, officially neutral, could raise a formidable army to fight for its tribal cousins; the prize being Yoori unity again – and valuable water; but it stops short of violating international law.*

*The death of Mbidi Renula, a moderate Yoori, albeit through a road accident, is seen as an escalation of the call for action in the north east.*

Ben came off the internet and picked up Rebekah Arens's back copy of the Johnstown *Daily Graphic*. The report of Mbidi Renula's road accident was written up in more colourful style than Kath Lewis's Sunday paper news roundup, back in London.

# PLEADER FOR PEACEFUL SOLUTION DIES IN ROAD CARNAGE

**Story:** *Kwame Mensah*

The road was empty on Sunday night when Mbidi Renula drove into a torrential downpour on the Johnstown-Sikakoko road, north of Ntamu.

This road is ill-famed for its potholes and lack of run-off drains, but Renula's four-wheel-drive Land Rover, showing no tyre bursts or steering problem, crashed into a roadside tree, with whiplash that took off the driver's head.

He was returning from talks with president Dr Obed Abu in Johnstown, where sources say he had expressed ideas of peaceful coexistence in the North East District where the revenue from water could be fairly shared.

It is the higher mountains of Kutuliza that cause the rain to fall in the North East District, mostly on the Lansana side. Renula wanted recognition of this geographical fact, with some reduction of charges for energy to Kutuliza – but the government fears that other hardliners in the District want nothing

**short of a split from Lansana.**
**President Abu said, 'I am distressed by the sad death of Mr Renula, and send condolences to his family.'**
**Did the road and the rain kill Renula? It would be ironic if it was the rain!**

Ben read it through again, the article reaffirming his intention to seek an interview with the president, perhaps after he and Jonny had been north. A tough confrontation on camera with Dr Abu, as well as with the Yoori hardliners, would make a good report, and perhaps even play a part in the history that was being written here in Lansana.

Well, perhaps not that, he thought. Journalists shouldn't aim to be making the news; but quite urgently he and Jonny needed to sit down and decide on their plan of action: remembering, and he'd have to tactfully stress this to his senior colleague, that Rebekah Arens worked out here and would have her own agenda, as well as being a fixer. She might fix, but Ben and Jonny ought to be deciding *what* they wanted fixed. And tonight would have been a good chance, he and Jonny eating alone in the hotel: unfortunately, though, Rebekah had made other plans for them, which Jonny had gone along with.

## 'DYNASTY' CHINESE RESTAURANT, JOHNSTOWN

It seemed all wrong to Ben to be eating Chinese in Lansana – but, as Jonny had said – they *had* eaten local food so far. And if they were going up country soon, where they would have to eat what was served, it would be good to have a more international meal first, where he and Rebekah as good Jews could steer their way around the pork.

Going into the Dynasty was like walking into another world. From the stifling streets of Johnstown they came into an air-conditioned palace, a large Chinese restaurant with an international clientele; well dressed people talking many languages, immaculately dressed Lansanan waiters in white shirts and ruby waistcoats, and customers for whom this was clearly a social meeting-place: businessmen and women, diplomats, and the generally well-off. Walking up to the door while still being cajoled outside to buy toilet rolls from a box on a boy's head, stressed the differences in the two worlds that can exist in a capital city.

But what should have been a good meal was spoiled for Ben; because who had to be there also, sitting at a table for two over against the far wall, but Eamonn Reilly? Ben saw him first – he was facing the room – and decided to say nothing. But the Dynasty was all mirrors, and Jonny suddenly spilt plum sauce onto the table cloth.

'Don't look now!' he said. *'Mazldik!'*

'I'm not! And who's Mazldik?'

'Rebekah knows. Good luck, it means! It's Eamonn Reilly!'

'I know.' Ben watched Jonny fighting with his need to look around directly at the man.

'So who's that he's with?'

Ben shrugged. This Eamonn Reilly thing was getting out of hand. They were here on an assignment, and so far all they'd turned up was a pensioned-off footballer on some business trip. And all they'd done was have a chase through the market, and eat! Nevertheless, Ben was intrigued, because the man to whom Reilly was talking was a very large Lansanan dressed in golden robes, with plentiful gold on his fingers and wrists, and a large pair of golden spectacles – clearly somebody with money. 'You are *not* going across for a word!' Ben said.

When, 'I know him!' Rebekah Arens put in. 'I've seen him, the robed one, I know him...'

'Who?' Jonny asked, swinging round now.

She shook her head. 'It's gone. But I can look him up on Monday; he'll be on our photo files, I'm pretty sure of that. He's a known face.'

'Which is what we've got to talk about,' Ben found the chance to say. 'Where *we'll* be on Monday, and what *we'll* be doing.'

'Sure – where do you want to start? Which end of the country, whose version of the story?' Rebekah asked. 'Then I can start earning my Zephon fee.'

'What story?' Jonny said to his plate, suddenly serious. 'This is the problem I've got, what little there is to go on. Even if the car-death was murder, political assassination?' He shrugged, 'So what?'

'Not "So what?" – "Exactly!"' Ben said. 'Who did it? Are the Yoori's leading up to a big attack, getting rid of their moderates, building up their Red Fires, training their "soldier ants"? Or is the Lansana government manipulating a showdown, looking for a reason to start a civil war against their own people, before the ordinary Yoori people are really ready to fight? And isn't the lack of an obvious story exactly why we're here, sniffing one out? Do you see the press hordes yet?' He waved an arm around the restaurant.

Jonny Aaranovitch was nodding. 'This, I accept,' he said. 'I accept all this, a nice summary, and an accurate statement of fact. My trouble is, that could be Kath Lewis talking to me, across this table…' He looked up at Ben.

Ben blushed. He wasn't used to being criticised by Jonny, not even mildly.

'I'll tell you what you do see in places like this,' Rebekah put in like a peacemaker, 'without seeing them…'

Both Zephon men turned from each other to look at her.

'…You remember the ex-British Prime Minister's son who was allegedly trying to organise a coup in Equatorial Guinea? He was accused of putting up some money and a gunship, leaving some mercenaries rotting in prison right now?'

Ben and Jonny both remembered.

'Well, there'll be one or two of that sort in here, European money men wanting revolution, and the oil, gold, or water that comes up after it. People like Charlie Henderson – no, he's not in here, he won't show his face in Johnstown – but he's running with Red Fire, in and out of Kutuliza, but his real cause is Charlie Henderson, and he runs a tab in most of the best restaurants in Africa…'

'So there's a lot we don't know,' Jonny jumped on Rebekah's lines. And a few days using this– ' he tapped his nose '–and these, and these–' his eyes and ears '–will save a lot of overuse of these!' And he put a foot up on the fourth chair. 'And also my shooting stock isn't wasted.'

Ben nodded. 'Sure. Okay, that makes sense.' He ignored the earlier Kath Lewis remark, that was for thinking about later. Did the Zephon office think he was Kath Lewis's boy? Did fingers point, behind his back? 'Except you can't pull the "wasting shooting stock" wool over my eyes, Jonny, you're shooting digital.' He looked across the restaurant – 'Just so long as we're clear as to the reason we're here…' – to see that the table across the room was empty, was being re-laid quickly by two waiters. Eamonn Reilly and his companion had left while the newsmen argued. There would definitely be no autographs tonight!

Tomorrow we drive to Johnstown, and I am proud to be on that bus. The team bus is splendid, with air conditioning and comfortable seats, but as a junior player I will have to sit at the back of the bus, where I am put. This has a problem for me. I will be with the young players, not the senior stars whose boots I have cleaned, who read newspapers and listen to music in their earphones on long journeys. They are wise, thinking men, but the young players around me play cards all the way, and have magazines with pictures of girls in them that I try not to see. I think of my father, as if he were sitting near to me and seeing such things, and I know how disgusted he would be. So I turn my eyes away, and the others laugh at me, and say words in my ears, to make me think of the pictures they are looking at. It is hard to be good, but thinking of Yusa in my head — Jozea the prophet at the right hand of Jesus — I will try to have his help on that bus. Perhaps it would be wise, I am beginning to think, to follow my father in his wishes, and turn my life into being a priest for Yusa. Then my existence will not have the terrible conflicts that I suffer.

# Joyce Avoka's story –
## written up by R. A. – part 3

Joyce and the other girls sat cross-legged and with straight backs on the hardened mud floor under the canopy. The crossed legs had to form a perfect diagonal – too flat or too raised and the sergeant's cane swished across a back – and the arms had to be tightly crossed across their chests. They were soldiers, not individuals any more, this was shouted at them day and night. They served in the Yoori Liberation Army, the Red Fire. Under General Lakle, they had no personal family – there would never be any return to their former home, not even in a body bag – and their lives would be dedicated to the liberation of the Yoori lands, in the fight to join up with Kutuliza, their rightful state.

'In the name of Yusa!' the sergeant shouted from the front.

'Praise Yusa!' they had to shout back.

The canopy above Joyce was large, a khaki canvas top over-reached by camouflage netting, like the rest of Camp Vodi. Outside were lines of winter tents all of a similar size, with 'UN' stencilled on them, 'vanished' from United Nations stores somewhere. The mess tent was bigger, and so was the insulated assembly tent; while General Lakle and his officers had tents of varying sizes, according to rank, most of them patched and sewn. The height above sea-level froze out the stink from the rubbish tips and the latrines, but nothing could disguise the bleakness of the empty, rocky landscape – it was like living on the moon.

Joyce Avoka tried to keep her folded arms rock still as she breathed in and out. The Camp Vodi plateau was so high in the mountains that for a few days her breathing had been laboured, her head light. But now she was in what Sergeant Six called Stage Three. 'Stage One, you get recruited; Stage Two, you get used to this place; Stage Three, you get education; Stage Four, you get basic training; Stage Five, you get active service; Stage Six, we get liberation! And very possible, Stage Seven, you get heaven.'

He had told them that even if he shouted as loudly as a hundred lions roaring, if blank ammunition echoed around like a thousand thunderstorms coming all together, and whatever lights were shone, this camp was impossible for anyone to find. On the Lansana side was a narrow pass that led here from the road, where your knees were skinned either side as you rode, easy to hold kilometres down by a small band of fighters. From any army! And the camp was placed so high in the world that the mountain down-draught crashed helicopters if they flew too low. Even a bombing raid by a Stealth B-2 Spirit was impossible. It would need to over-fly Kutuliza air space coming in or going out – with all the international trouble that would stir up – beside the fact that finding the camp in the first place would be like finding a solitary stone in an avalanche.

Joyce had never ridden a mule before, but when the Toyota truck had reached where the road ran off into a track, a pack of ribby mules had brought them all on a two day climb up the winding pass. Like her, her parents had never been up beyond Sikakoko as high as the dam, and they would certainly never get to her here. On the way, there had been more shouting, some beatings, and on the first morning up here the new recruits had been kitted in one-size khaki, heavy cloth against the cold, and black trainers from boxes marked 'Korea'. They were people no more but soldier ants with 'last twos' instead of names. Which meant that Joyce, who was arm-tattooed the number 145, was 'Forty-five': her new name. The boys, and there were many more boys than girls, were known by 'last threes.: This was the only difference between the sexes: otherwise, with all hair cut short and wearing thick, baggy shirts and long trousers, no one could tell boy from girl, not by just looking at them.

And looking at Joyce, no one could know what was happening inside her head. Everything had been made so clear to her: she could never escape, and there was no chance of earth of being rescued. She held her head high and her face receptive, but her thoughts were not here, they were of home. That hole in her soul was even bigger now than it had been on that first night, because now she realised more clearly how her past life was over. Like a slave taken to another part of the world, this was a place of no return. Her mother, her father and her little brothers no longer existed. They had been part of her childhood. Now she was a soldier ant, and she had to try to think like one. But it was hard, and when she saw another's face she might see a pair of eyes, or a nose, or an expression that reminded her of one of her family. But, strangely, in all that she didn't cry, because those who cried were given whip-lashes to cry for, and fear of such pain kept her eyes as dry as death.

'Yusa was a fightin' prophet, praise him!' Sergeant Six shouted under the canopy. 'Yusa showed the way that dedicated Yooris must go. Never flinchin' from the battle, never runnin' from the war. Hear what the Bible says…' He flipped open the small, thin-leaved book he was holding, his voice parade-ground hoarse as he read from it. "And Jozea" – that's Yusa – "proclaims, 'There shall be a mighty scourge across the laxful land, and, question not, the just lashes of the scourge shall dwell with God, the king everlasting."' He shut the book. 'Thus said the prophet Yusa, you hear? We are the just an' righteous lashes that shall scourge Lansana!' He suddenly reached out an arm and smacked a girl across the face with the Bible. 'Say it!' he commanded. 'Say them words from the book!'

The girl couldn't: she mumbled. Sergeant Six smacked her with the Bible again, the other way, back-handed. 'You all listen!' He pointed the Bible along the lines of soldier-ants-in-training. 'I read this again, and you get it in here.' He thwacked his own head with the book. 'You kick out from your brains your family names, and their images and your memories. I am your father and your mother and your brother and your sister, your what-was, your here-and-now, and your what-will-be! Kick everything else out and make room for the words of the holy prophet, and make space for all the training you're going to get. You master that!' And this time he spoke Yusa's words from the Old Testament without using the Bible, except to give a rhythmic beat; saying them slowly, and the recruits repeating them, chanting them with him. Which went over and over in Joyce's mind as she drilled that day, and as she ate the thin food, and as she tried to sleep in the mountain cold, squeezing her eyes to shut out those memories of family faces that were so destructive. She had had no schooling, so she had had no practice in reading and memorizing words; but she had to keep these Bible words in her head, and everything else, out.

Because those who limped, whose memory was lame, or who did not obey orders in every detail, would not live long, she knew that. And while she thought she didn't care whether she lived or died, something in her spirit wanted to survive.

## PRESIDENT ABU SPORTS STADIUM, JOHNSTOWN

Sunday afternoon, three o'clock, not so different from many premiership matches in the UK – the big match was on, and Ben and Jonny had got tickets. For next to nothing in pounds sterling, they were with Richard their driver in the VIP seats on the shaded side of the President Abu Stadium. In London they would have had to pay almost a month's salary to be sitting where they were, but the rates of exchange made every visiting European a rich person in Lansana. The VIP seats were strictly segregated by high railings from the Directors' Box on their left, and from the home supporters on their right and, unlike the cramped plastic seats of the English premiership, these were armchairs, casually arranged in rows. It made Ben feel like an emperor at a Roman games.

Across the well-watered green pitch, the stadium swept round in the sun – white, low, modern but with old-fashioned floodlights; not a huge crowd in the Sikakoko Arsenal 'away' section, but a big, vocal contingent of Johnstown Lions' faithful fans chanting and dancing in anticipation of a good win over their northern rivals.

With some local money in his wallet now, reckoned in 'shillings', a thousand to the pound, Ben bought three bottles of cold water and held his bottle to his forehead. It was very hot in the sun, and close and sweaty even in the shade. But rubbing the bottle around his head gave him the chance to turn and get a good look into the directors' box. Traditionally, if it were the same here as it was in England, the Sikakoko directors would be in there with the Johnstown directors, which made for an interesting political situation: as he'd said to the barman at the Volta, this match had to be about tribe as well as about sport. How would they behave, all sitting together? He hoped very well, because Jonny had reckoned that he wouldn't be allowed to bring his television camera in here, so he'd come without it – and if the worst happened, he'd be mad at himself for missing a scoop. But this early the seats were hardly occupied, a local youth game keeping the crowd partially entertained, and Ben guessed that hospitality – and the hostility – was happening back in the directors' lounge.

In the 'away' dressing room down at ground level, Mujiba Kalala was getting changed into the Sikakoko Arsenal kit. The two teams' colours didn't clash, so he was pulling over his head the famous first team blue shirt with number 23 on the back. He was excited, his eardrums near to bursting with the proud pressure of being on the bench, the chosen substitute for attacking mid-field. The manager, Mr George Chognon, had told him the news on the bus that morning, driving from the Atlantic View Hotel to the stadium. Being an away game, he had notified the squad of the men that were to play by walking down the bus and tapping people painfully on the head with a knuckle, saying, 'Start,' to eleven of them, and 'Sub,' to three. One substitute was always the reserve goalkeeper, the other two picked from the remaining three who travelled. And today Muj Kal was one of them – although whether or not he got on to play was a matter of luck regarding injuries, and the score. He had spent matches for the first, the second and the youth teams as substitute in his time and sometimes not got on the pitch at all, after the warm-up. Nothing in football was a safe bet, even for the gambling boys.

He jogged up and down the dressing room, studding the concrete floor, enjoying the shirt and its laundered smell for a few minutes before he pulled on his thin tracksuit top. He attended to every word that Mr George Chognon said at the whiteboard, but his name wasn't mentioned in the last minute tactical talk. He felt sick, anyway, and when coach Adjei-Mensah led them out of the dressing room for the warm-up, he nearly keeled over against a row of pegs. But he kept his feet, he kept his purpose, and as they ran out, kicking balls towards the 'away' goal, he repeated, 'Yusa, Yusa, Yusa,' over and over in his head.

Why shouldn't his football, even if only the warm-up, be a tribute to the prophet? Every action in life should be such...

The names of the two sets of players were called out over the public address system – there were no programme sellers that Ben had seen. Some in the VIP lounge were scribbling names down, but as the seats filled and people greeted each other, there was a general air of everyone knowing everyone else – including a familiarity with the names of the players in both teams. Football was big in Lansana.

The youth teams had been clapped off, and the premiership players were out warming up. In the directors' box next door, men were emerging – all men – from the lounge and taking their seats. Friendly words were exchanged in Ben's section of seating, most of the VIP seats occupied by large men in cool clothing, all very relaxed and acting pleased with their positions in life, these 'haves' who were seated comfortably in the shade. Through the railings, the directors and their guests were seating themselves, a touch more anxiety on their faces: this match was more than a Sunday afternoon out for these men, it was business.

Including Eamonn Reilly's dinner companion from the night before. Ben spotted him, sitting four or five rows back from the front of the directors' box, in white robes today, wearing his large, gold, tinted glasses. Ben nudged Jonny.

'I know, already,' Jonny said. Ben had concentrated on the warm-up while Jonny had been eye-balling the directors. 'Eamonn Reilly's here.'

The old Spurs star was leaning over to talk to someone in the front row of directors. But, which directors, which team? And Ben realised, from the chat through the railings, that the Johnstown Lions' directors were on this near side of the box; the opposition, the Sikakoko Arsenal, were on the further side, where Reilly was.

'He's here for a Sikakoko player,' Jonny muttered, on the same wavelength as Ben. Because Golden Man was also talking to – and hugging – someone else in the 'away' directors' seats.

'You reckon?'

'Who are the Sikakoko stars?' Jonny asked Richard, their driver, who was relishing his armchair view, king for a day.

'Three internationals – Badjona, Olympio, and Eyadema; and a good forward, from Ghana, Charlie Akrofi.' He pointed them out, with their numbers. 'Badjona, captain, big at the back, number five; Olympio, striker, in the hole, number eight; Eyadema, in goal, number one.'

'And Charlie Akfrofi?'

'Number nine, twin striker with Olympio.'

'So who would you buy, if you were a big London club?' Jonny wanted to know.

Richard shrugged, thought for a moment. 'None of them.' He waited for the surprise to come off the others' faces. 'We want to keep our football first class in Africa. You mustn't buy any!'

Muj Kal walked out of the tunnel in his tracksuit top as the selected team ran out onto the pitch to a police escort, their white numbers against the blue shirts almost fluorescent in the sun. The Lions were in white, and while the Arsenal had been received with wild cheers from the travelling supporters, their small numbers made the cheers sound thin compared with the chanting, dancing, and roaring that greeted the Lions. The stadium went mad, and a hand seemed to clamp around Muj's throat as he walked to his place on the bench. These big games were always known for the ferocity of the support, but there was tribal enmity in this reception, as well as football rivalry. The noise was deafening, and dire. All around the stadium, a horseshoe of Johnstown supporters were raising clenched fists in a rhythmic shout – *'Lansan! Lansan! Lansan!'*; merging with, and swelling into, a hateful, *'Yoori dead! Yoori dead! Yoori dead!'* And Muj Kal's heart seemed to give the eagle badge on his chest a push, push, push as he sat; this was dangerous; and he wondered if he really wanted to be called upon to run out there.

And when the kick-off whistle went, he threw his head back and prayed to Yusa for spiritual strength.

Up in the stand, Ben Maddox was recording the tribal hatred on his mobile phone. Jonny Aaranovitch was discreetly using the camera on his; and Richard was sitting there mouthing, 'Worse than before; this is worse than before...' Through in the directors' box, the Sikakoko people sat rigid, while a few faint smiles could be seen on Johnstown faces.

'Worse than Chelsea/Liverpool! We've got a story,' Jonny said to Ben. 'We have got a story to chase!'

Ben gave him a look. 'Yup,' he said, 'that's what Kath Lewis thought.'

# CAULDRON BUBBLES AT JOHNSTOWN ABU STADIUM

**Graphic report:  Michael Kasea**

## Johnstown Lions 0
## Sikakoko Arsenal 1

The crowd won this dull match at the President Abu Stadium yesterday.  Although there were seven internationals on the pitch, four in the home team and three in the opposition, none of them could light any fires. That was left to a near-violent crowd, thankfully only verbally.

Remembering the crowd tragedy of four years ago, when twenty spectators died in a surge towards the pitch, there was a high police turn-out for this needle match, where, to re-use a hackneyed phrase, sport was the only loser.

Bad blood between the north of the country and the south, with abuse and spitting and threatening behaviour – not, for a change from the players but from the crowd – put nerves rather than flair on display, and the game would hardly be worth reporting except for its few final moments.

Chances were missed at both ends, the main offenders being Arsenal's Olympio, who kicked over the bar in the first half, refusing the invitation of an open goal, and Lions' Lewis, the South African international, who missed a penalty opportunity and gifted the ball into the welcoming arms of Sikakoko goalkeeper Eyadema – hardly an international level save.

But in the last ten minutes, Muj Kal, a Sikakoko home-trained midfielder, was brought off the bench to replace Latevi, whose day it wasn't. With some youthful wiggles and a promising series of passes, Kal, in the last seconds, persisted to chase a lost cause down by the corner flag, and against all the odds, floated a ball across that Charlie Akrofi scuffed at – and scored, more by luck than judgment.

The important fact to report is that the away crowd was safely escorted from the ground without real violence, but the crowd behaviour seems to have reflected the on-going political and economic situation in the country. It was as if the continual chanting of abuse was underlining the stadium's name – that of the president – and the mainstream Lansanan attitude to the North East Region. 'We run this place – and you should know yours.'

## JOHNSTOWN, LANSANA

Michael Kasea, the *Graphic*'s chief football writer, was a colleague of Rebekah's, and she wasn't too happy fixing Ben Maddox's interview with president Obed Abu. Already, the paper's editor-in-chief had roasted Kasea over the tone of his report, telling him to stick to the football in future, and Rebekah pleaded with Ben not to make his interview sound too much as if it had been prompted by the *Graphic* piece.

'Why should it?' he asked. 'We were there, we heard it. We don't need to refer to your paper.'

'How shall I sell it to the president's aides?'

'You're the fixer,' Ben told her. But Jonny shot him a look, and took over. As producer.

'Tell them we're doing an Africa special – a week of programmes for the British viewers to see how the global aid programme is working. Good things we've heard, about what Lansana is doing for itself; so where does it see its economy moving in the future?' He didn't look at Ben.

Ben nodded all the same. 'Get us in through the front door any way you can,' he said. 'We can lull him with a public relations piece, and when he's all smiles with the soft questions, I'll hit him with a hard one.'

Rebekah looked from one to the other. 'Okay, that's the line? Global aid?'

'That's the line. Self help.'

Ben changed the subject, as Rebekah headed off to the Volta veranda with her mobile phone. 'And I've had a text message from Bloom, about Eamonn Reilly,' he told Jonny.

'Oh, yes?' Jonny was more prickly on this trip than he'd ever been before; now it was as if Eamonn Reilly was *his* hero, why did Ben get the text message?

Ben flipped his mobile, and found the text, handed the phone to Jonny.

**E. Reilly. Spends a lot of time in Dublin. Liffey Ath FC. director, unpaid. Luv Bloom xx**

'So that's it!' Jonny said. 'The Irish league. Most of their best players play abroad – *their* abroad – have done from George Best onwards. But they're like the African nations, they want to keep the best Irish players for domestic use...'

'Washing up and that?' Rebekah asked, which Jonny laughed at as if it was the joke of the century.

'*Washing up!*' Another laugh. 'The domestic game, is what I'm saying.'

'So he's here poaching a player from this other country that's also trying to hang on to its own home-grown players. Ironic,' Ben said.

'Ironic!' Jonny repeated. 'Well, it's good to know. We could get a little sports exclusive on the side, if we knew which one he was after.'

'Right!' said Ben. 'But let's fry our big fish first...'

'I've got the numbers, I'll hit the phones,' said Rebekah.

'"Washing up",' grinned Jonny as she went.

*I am in the biggest fix. I am so nervous of
what my esteemed father is going to say. I
have played a good game, for ten minutes
only, but I have made a goal for my team,
Mr George Chognon the manager is pleased
with me and hugs me as I come off the
pitch. It is comforting, amid the boos and
hatred shouted from the Johnstown crowd,
and all I can do is shut my eyes and think
of Yusa. I am proud, though, of helping to
win the game. Now Sikakoko Arsenal goes
third in the premiership, a place above
Johnstown Lions.*

*My real trouble is, on the bus home to
Sikakoko — we travel straight after, all the
evening and part of the night — there is
another man on the bus, who was not there,
going. He is a big man in white robes,
dressed more like a president than the
president, and he has golden glasses with
diamonds in the corners. He is a rich man.
He comes down the bus and tells Glebo next
to me to move, and he sits in his place.
Before, he has been sitting with Mr George*

Chognon. He smells of perfume, and his voice is low and dark, like a prowling panther. 'I have been watching you at the game,' is what he says. 'Yusa watches me always,' I tell him. He waves his hand, and up his sleeve a big gold watch goes round and round like a king's bracelet. 'I have been talking to your manager, and I have permission to talk to your father.' Words like that, I cannot remember exactly. 'Please tell him that Mr Gerald Abowa is coming to see him.'

And now I am very worried. I write this in my bed by the light of my torch, I cannot sleep. What is this important football man going to say to my father? How can I explain that this has happened to me, I have not caused it, only by helping my team to win.

Yusa, I ask forgiveness for being a conceited sinner. May my father not be very angry at me.

## THE PRESIDENT'S SUITE,
## GOVERNMENT HOUSE, JOHNSTOWN

Ben, Jonny and Rebekah were waiting in the ante-room for permission to go in and set up before President Dr Obed Abu appeared. Guards dressed in white, with pistols in shining leather holsters, stood at both doors, the one going into the president's office, and the door through which the Zephon team had come. There wouldn't be a lot of setting up to do, Jonny Aaranovitch had said that he needed five minutes only, his camera would be on a lightweight tripod, with a lamp above the lens. Ben would ask his questions off-camera, and Rebekah would take them down in shorthand. He would then repeat his questions on camera when the president had left the room, as if it were happening simultaneously: this way, one camera served for two. It was standard practice 'on the road' and the session would be completed with Ben doing his 'noddies', appearing to listen to the president's answers, nodding, frowning, smiling, for Jonny to edit-in later, as appropriate.

Ben felt nervous – he always felt nervous before an interview, and before a news broadcast when he was reading off an autocue. If you wanted to be the best, you had to have the best butterflies, but you also had to know how to keep them in their place. And this came down to breathing, and to concentration. Today he felt nervous because the president's aides had approved the line of his questioning – on Lansana's self help programme – but before the end of the interview he was deliberately going to go 'off message', and throw some awkward questions at the man. How would that go down? Would the Zephon team be thrown out on their ears, Jonny's equipment – or, at least, the digital card – be confiscated? It was hard to tell; but news people always had to take that risk.

Ben consoled himself that Dr Obed Abu – a doctor of theology from Redcliffe College – was not a tyrant dictator like Idi Amin or Sadham Hussein; he wouldn't have the three of them thrown into a verminous jail. But he could have them expelled from the country, their visas cancelled, and how would Kath Lewis feel about that?

Yes, if the truth be known, Ben was more nervous of Kath Lewis than of this president.

While Jonny fiddled with his equipment, checking in his steel box, Ben looked around the ante-room. Every room you ever went in as a journalist held clues to personalities, and there was no doubt at all what sort of ego Dr Obed Abu had. It was huge. Already, nowhere near dead, and nowhere near out of office, he was creating his own legend here in Government House. His photograph – the same one – was in every corridor and room they had come through, even in the lift; and here, just outside his office, his memorabilia was already on show. In glass cases around the room there were labelled exhibits: 'the pen used to sign the United Nations treaty on human rights'; 'the walking stick used on the long walk to freedom from Aids'; and 'the "stars and stripes" lapel pin given to Dr Abu by the president of the United States'. There was even a pristine copy of Dr Obed Abu's book, *My Africa*, open at the autographed title page. This man, like many leaders, was as concerned with his place in history as with current affairs. So flatter him, Ben decided: start by asking him how long it took him to write his book.

Suddenly, while Jonny was still groping in his camera case, a man and a woman came out of the door to the presidential office. The man was white-skinned, the woman more olive, and as Jonny looked up his eyes widened, and *'Sholem-aleykhem,'* he said.

The woman nodded, briefly. *'Aleykhem-sholem.'* And the pair of them hurried out, clutching their document cases.

'Jewish?' Ben asked.

'Of course, Jewish. He looks like my uncle. For a moment I think I'm in the kibbutz.'

'What are they doing here?'

'Selling something?'

At that moment an aide appeared and they were ushered into the presidential office, with its polished ebony desk as big as a full-size snooker table; and on it, nothing more than an ivory telephone and an inkstand with a golden Mont Blanc fountain pen. Whoever had just been in there, the office was empty, awaiting a fresh entrance by the president.

Jonny worked fast. Straight off, he identified his problems as the 'shine' coming off the desk and the bright light from the window, because he'd been told that the president wanted to be filmed in an executive position, with the tops of the Government House garden palms in the background.

'Tight, I'm getting in tight, after the establishing shot,' he told Ben. 'To cut that glare.' Ben checked with an aide that he could sit almost opposite the president, on a humbler chair, and he wired himself for sound with a lapel mike, running back to Jonny's camera. In his hand he held the mike that he would have to use if the president didn't want to be miked-up, too, although it would be a long reach.

'You ready?' Jonny asked, who'd been as swift as a cameraman at a crash site.

Ben nodded. Jonny looked round at Rebekah, notebook and pen ready for the transcript, who nodded.

'Okay, we're ready,' Jonny told the aide.

Ben's stomach turned over, as the president of Lansana, Dr Obed Abu, without any visible or audible signal, appeared from the door to his private sitting room. He was a small, slight man, receding dark hair, lightish skin, steel glasses, and intense eyes. Power, Ben had noticed, always lay in the eyes.

'You got butterflies?' he asked Ben, coming over and shaking his hand. 'I've got butterflies. I ask you as a professional, why is this? I do this stuff all the time...'

He was all smiles, which was never reflected in the pictures of him. It would be good to get him smiling, Ben thought: everyone in world politics knew the face, but not this disarming manner.

'So, what are you boys here for?' he asked. 'And don't bury me under that 'self-help' deceit. Why come from England all this way to one of the minor African countries to talk about self help? Eh?' He laughed. 'Wire me up,' he told Jonny, 'I hate those animals!' And he laughed again as he flicked his fingers at Ben's furry microphone.

Ben was sitting back in his chair. This guy was cool! It was this man who was springing the surprise!

Jonny's face was very close to the president's as he clipped the lapel mike to the man's smooth, light-grey linen suit. He didn't look around at Ben as he told the president in a low voice, 'Yoori District. Secession. The death of Mbidi Renula...'

The president nodded. 'Okay,' he said. 'This is what I thought.'

Rebekah cleared her throat, a whole apology in a guttural sound – for failing to be convincing enough when she'd set this up over the telephone.

'On condition.' The president was settling into an interview position facing Ben, suddenly showing the flat of a hand.

'What's that, Doctor President?' Ben asked.

'I see the edit – and if I take two stabs at an answer, you let me choose which one you use, an' which one goes on the cutting-room floor.'

'That's great,' said Jonny.

'Of course,' said Ben, simultaneously.

'Okay, studio–' said Dr Obed Abu, with a confident smile all around '–let's roll!'

# ZEPHON TELEVISION
## Transcript of interview with Dr. Obed Abu

PROGRAMME: ZT/JA/19/4  67
WORLD VIEW
TRANSMISSION: TO BE DECIDED

April 19.  Government House, Johnstown, Lansana

## BEN MADDOX REPORTING

### Ben Maddox (walking towards camera, exterior. Government House):

Here in Johnstown, capital of Lansana, life is typical of a
smallish, medium economy African state – so far as any
country in Africa can be called typical in as wide a diversity
of countries.  Here, minerals and coffee beans play their part,
as diamond and gold and oil play their parts elsewhere,
*(intercut shots of the Ade Dam.)* but Lansana's main export is
energy, from the hydro-electric plant in the mountains of the
north east.

### Ben Maddox  (close up, still exterior):

But the north east district, the home of the minority Yoori
people, is not a contented area.  For years they've been looking
to separate themselves from Lansana, and sometimes by
violent means.  Their most moderate leader was killed in a
road accident last month – and I asked Lansana's President
Obed Abu what Yoori independence would mean to Lansana,
if it happened.

**Dr Obed Abu (interior, the presidential office):**

Independence is not on the agenda, it won't happen. No matter what the extremists do, however many of us they kill, the north east region is not going to be separated from Lansana. We are determined about that. Most of the people in this Christian country are Lansan, but we embrace and celebrate our Yoori people, too. Diversity is the watchword for every civilized state. We want them in, not out, and 'in' is where they will remain.

**Ben Maddox (voice over library pictures of power cables running across savannah):**

Your hydro electric system in the north east provides electricity to Lansana and to several neighbouring countries. *(Close up on Ben Maddox.)* Is it really to celebrate diversity, or to hold on to this resource, that makes Lansana refuse to let the Yoori people form a coalition with the Yoori people north of your border? *(Sceptically.)* Are you really saying it's your sense of tribal inclusion?

**Dr Obed Abu:**

Believe it or not, I really am. And by 'people north of the border' I presume you're talking about Kutuliza. *(Abu's voice over library footage of the rapids north of Sikakoko.)* More water falls on our side of the mountain than it does on theirs, this is geography, whatever they say, and the Ade Dam is on our side of the mountain. *(Abu's voice over spinning turbines)* We invested in all this. We used world aid to help ourselves to create one of the most modern plants anywhere, millions of dollars of investment. What did Kutuliza do with their aid? I ask because I don't know. *(Close up on Obed Abu.)* Would the United Kingdom give something like this away? Did your government allow Northern Ireland to become part of the Irish Republic? *(Laughs)* What is this? Why are we the villains?

### Ben Maddox:

Do you see yourselves as villains?

### Dr Obed Abu:

Certainly not! Why should we?

### Ben Maddox:

So, if a moderate negotiator like Mbidi Renula dies, and you want a moderate solution – like better tribal recognition of the needs of the Yooris – his death couldn't be laid at Lansana's door...

### Dr Obed Abu (big close up):

The police have yet to release the vehicle, but my understanding is that Mr Renula died in a road accident. His death is not laid at any door, except the final exit of fate.

### Ben Maddox:

The Yoori hardliners wouldn't dream of having him killed themselves?

### Dr Obed Abu (big close up):

You're talking dreams. Fantasy. It's not for me to speculate on what Yoori hardliners might do.

### Ben Maddox:

What about meddlers in Africa's affairs, people like Charles Henderson, Europeans who could make money out of coups

and uprisings?  I've heard that name since I've come out
here…

**Dr Obed Abu:**

Or British news teams, looking under rocks for stories that
don't exist? *(Doctor Abu's face lights up as he laughs into the
camera, a shot cut out at his demand). (Abu leans forward
earnestly.)* As I said, extremist, hardline terrorists – or even
meddlers, as you call them – can do what they want. They
can do it to their people or to our people, but take my word,
Lansana is not going to give ground.  Literally. *(A long pause.)*
We are not…giving…ground.  *(Abu turns away slowly and
looks out of his presidential window, terminating the interview.)*

**Ben Maddox:**

One last question, Doctor President?

*(Dr Abu swings back, frowning.)*

**Ben Maddox:**

Have you any trade connections with *(a couple of beats)* Israel?

**Dr Obed Abu (looks at the door through which his visitors
always exit):**

I receive diplomats from every country in the world.
It is protocol.

**Ben Maddox:**

No one selling nuclear energy potential, then?

**Dr Obed Abu (Laughing, waving his hand airily):**
   With our economic, environmental water power? Who...
   would...want?  Uh?


**Ben Maddox:**
   Thank you, Doctor President.


The president took off his own microphone and placed it
precisely onto the desk, equidistant between the
telephone and the inkstand.  His face held its questioning
smile until Jonny's camera light went out – when he
suddenly whooped.
   '"One-take Abu!"' he said. 'Lose the laugh – and use
it, boys!'

## CAMP VODI

The 'Yoori' mountains change like scenes in a film – sunny, hard, and hot one day, or dressed in cloud, invisible, and cold another, or possibly beaten by storm, drenching, and loud yet another. Here, in the confusing ridges and valleys high in the northern mountains of Lansana, there was no need for the Red Fire secret camp to move about, it was as if the changing conditions did the moving of the mountains for them. Camp Vodi, north of Sikakoko, north of Nsraban township, was high inside Kutulizan country, accessible to the Yoori capital only by a remote pass and a poorly maintained road.

As Joyce Avoka had learned in her brainwashing, neither spy planes nor satellite systems could exactly pinpoint the camp, hard as the Lansanan military tried. Under camouflage tents and netting, set on an enclosed plateau three quarters the size of a football pitch, the camp was served with meagre food by Kutuliza, with water from the sky, and with recruits abducted from the poor townships and villages of the North East District. With a well trained look-out system and weaponry commanding the approaching passes and tracks, it was safer from attack than the Pentagon, since taking it on the ground would cost too many lives, and an attack by air – even with smart bombs aimed at the exact map reference – would mean over-flying Kutulizan air space and defying international law. And Kutuliza insisted on the sanctity of its air space.

General Lakle was a fighting man, more used to a blanket in a cave than a bed in a house. Dressed in camouflage khaki, he was lean and fit, grizzled, and with a black eyepatch covering a sniper-blinded eye, coming up to fifty, and a Kutulizan Yoori, not a Lansanan. To the Red Fire soldiers he had become a god, as well as an unpredictable, spiteful leader. A joke could be greeted by a laugh, or by a fist in the face: the same joke, on different days. His was a mood that could never be taken for granted. At the end of a successful operation, he was as likely to be in foul humour as in fine.

The recruited children of the liberation army lived in tents of eleven, but were counted in tens – General Lakle always allowed for losses – and were quickly trained in weaponry, military tactics, and obeying orders. These soldier ants became familiar with M24 bolt-action sniper rifles, AK-74 automatic assault rifles, M26 fragmentation grenades, and the operation of BM-21 multiple rocket launchers. Anything bigger, like the heavier artillery, was left to the older men, although they were woefully short of everything. The military tactics were the basics of survival, ambush, sabotage and booby traps. And the following of orders: unquestioningly, blindly, instantly – and suicidally. The regime was harsh, with brutal punishments.

To the recruits it was a simple, order-following life. They were fed daily, although the food was poverty-poor, but they were fighting for the glory of Yoori unification, and for the recognition of Josea, known to the Yoori by the name of Yusa, as the prophet nearest to the right hand of Jesus Christ. And, above all, their goal was the Yoori right to profit from the heaven-sent water.

The typical townships that General Lakle selected for attack were of two sorts. In the Central Region, south of the Yoori lands, the townships would have economic reasons for wanting to be left in peace; good crops, or grazing lands, or mineral mines. Attacks on these areas could lead for calls to the Lansanan government to give the Yoori lands to the Yoori people, live and let live. But in the poorer townships of the north east region, the attacks would be for recruits, where they would claim boys and girls of fighting age – which was anything from ten upwards – to come to be trained in Camp Vodi. This was a sort of national service; except that it was never declared over.

Now an attack was being planned, a small scale affair at Botae, east of Sikakoko but a loyal Lansanan township. General Lakle was briefing his troops, a guerrilla group of twenty seasoned fighters, who would go with a 'tent' of newly recruited soldier ants, to blood them. It had to be small scale because, in truth, until a new supply from a fresh source arrived, the Red Fires were short of arms, artillery and ammunition.

'We take the Sikakoko-Botae road by truck,' the general said, his mahogany stick scratching across a map on a blackboard. 'We trail down the mountains by mule to Nsraban, we rendezvous with the truck, we journey to the Botae outskirts, arrive 03.00 hours.' The men in the tent nodded, this was a familiar routine. 'You will know, Botae is manganese mining for the Lansana steel industry.' The men nodded again; most of them didn't know. 'Main mine, one kilometre north of the town.' He looked around the tent of men sitting straight-backed upon the floor, everyone focused on him. 'The cadets, the soldier ants, throw grenades through main street doors and windows in the town, create a diversion, and regroup at the truck.'

The men again signified understanding; although they all really understood that while there might be some grenades, the rest of the missiles would be rocks.

'The main force, the men, kills the mine guards.' General

Lakle draped a cloth over the blackboard, painted with a diagram of the mine grounds – perimeter fence, admin. building, mineshafts one, two and three. 'And a twenty kilo bomb is dropped down mineshaft three, the deepest.'

Again, the nodding. For twenty kilos, read ten.

'All regroup at the truck rendezvous, drive north on the north-west road, the wrong direction for us coming from Nsraban, but unexpected for the police and military, we hide out at Dedie for thirty-six hours, and return to Nsraban by night, rendezvous with mules and return to camp.'

'Mission successful!' a soldier called out.

'Stupid talk!' General Lakle shouted at him. 'Make questions, not predictions!'

And the rest looked at their knees, and quickly found strategic questions to ask.

**Ben Maddox**

From: Kath Lewis klewis@zephontv.co.uk
Sent: 20 April     11:06
To: Ben Maddox
Subject: Progress Report

Thanks for your info. report.  Presidential interview
sounds good, send it ASAP for filing. No action
re transmission here yet, we'll hold it for the 'special'
when the story really breaks. Don't want to alert the
opposition – you two still look like the only players
in the game re British press.

Keep digging. Go secretly to the accident scene,
footage would be good, Ben talk through the
accident with <u>slightly</u> sceptical voice.

Go north to Yoori lands, noses to the scent-trail
of terrorists. Can you get hold of this Charles
Henderson that Rebekah spoke of? The president
didn't deny his existence, and he seems to be a
player in the game. What's in it for him?

But always remember, time is money!

K. Lewis

## SIKAKOKO TOWNSHIP

Mujiba Kalala came home from the training ground, straining to glimpse the look on his father's face. From the rutted street he could see the veranda where his father sat, and talked with elders, and read his Bible. Right now, the man was alone, his head bowed over a paper in his hand, his wire glasses down his nose; but from where Muj was, his expression couldn't be seen.

What paper was his father holding? Had the man with the golden glasses already visited? Was the paper something left for Nokongolo Kalala to read? There was no knowing; so Muj Kal, the loyal son and the football prodigy, approached the veranda like Joseph coming before the Pharoah. Would his father look up, and fix him with his stern eyes, and beckon him to stand before him? Or would he ignore a sport-loving boy who seemed to put Yusa in second place, and his own trivial ambitions first. Whichever it was, Muj Kal thought it would be good if the man *had* visited, and the shock of his message had already been taken by his father.

It was the worst. As Muj Kal approached the veranda, his father looked up from his paper, waved a hand at his son, and said, 'Praise to Yusa', the way he greeted everyone. Routine. Normal. There was no doubt that man had not called yet.

Muj Kal went into the house. It was hot in Sikakoko, even in the higher ground of the foothills. Working days began early in the cool hours. Arsenal training – both sessions – was over by eleven-thirty, and a light meal was eaten at midday before the heat of the afternoon led to resting wherever cool could be found. Then evening activity began: which in Nokongolo Kalala's house was all to do with Yusa and the Yoori cause. These hours of meetings, and readings, and prayer sessions were when Muj read, or wrote his anguish out, or dreamed of being a premiership footballer – and, sometimes, a priest.

Strangely, Muj's mother Eni talked to him more of football than of religion. She was interested in what he had done that day, and in his place in the order of things at Sikakoko Arsenal. She kept him well-fed and fit, and while she always nodded devoutly in the family prayers, she seemed impatient for the end of them when she would give Muj a bowl of goats' milk, and measure his height in the doorway.

Today, as he came in past his father, she welcomed him and made him wash his hands outside before giving him a piece of maize bread, and a ruffle for his shining black head. But he ducked away under it, spurned the bread, and headed for his room.

Today, he was at a crossroads in his life.

# LANSANA NATIONAL POLICE DEPARTMENT

## CENTRAL DISTRICT
### Accident Report

**Date:** 29th March, current year

**Time:** Reported 01:30

**Location:** Approx. 3 kilometres north of Ntamu, on main road.

**Vehicle(s):** 1996 Land Rover LSN61

**Reg. Owner:** Mr Mbidi Renula (61), PO Box 23, Sikakoko Township.

**Details:** The vehicle must have left road in bad weather (storm), run into ebony tree at roadside. Driver (alone) killed, apparently on impact (head off). Body taken to mortuary, Mfinimfimi, Central District.

**Further enquiries:** Autopsy reports no physical (human) reason for accident, victim had not suffered by heart or stroke, no drug or alcohol in blood. Also vehicle's brakes and steering OK.

**Action:** Next of kin (sister, victim address) informed. Body released for burial.
Vehicle write-off. Scrapped 4 April.

## MFINIMFINI, LANSANA

Ben and Jonny thanked the police sergeant for letting them see the accident report. A tall, slim, young man, the sergeant handed back their press passes, which had impressed him.

'You want I should show you the place?' he asked, turning round and reaching for his beret from the top of the rusted filing cabinet.

'Without bothering you, could we find it ourselves?' Jonny asked.

The sergeant sucked his teeth, shook his head, standing and putting on his beret. 'Follow my vehicle,' he said, 'but no camera on, that needs permission from the boss.'

'No camera,' Jonny assured.

Back in their own car with Richard and Rebekah, they were free to speak. 'They're not hiding anything, then,' Ben said.

Jonny agreed. *'They've* got nothing to hide, and there may be nothing to hide at all. On the other hand, what's hidden may be hidden at a higher level than the Mfinimfini police.'

They followed the blue police car, an oldish, unremarkable vehicle except for the police light-baton across the top. This part of the road was good, and it was no trouble for Richard to keep twenty metres behind on the smooth tarmac. But on the way north from Johnstown, they had travelled stretches of red, rutted clay, and swerved from side to side to avoid potholes where road works were seeking to make improvements. It was a laudable project except for the labour involved at the roadside – whole families, where the men were breaking large rocks into medium sized rocks, the women were hammering medium sized rocks into small rocks, and the children were sitting on heaps hammering small rocks into stony aggregate to mix with the tar.

Jonny was appalled. 'In school, they should be!'

'We pay for school here,' Richard muttered at the wheel.

Now the police car in front slowed, one of its red tail lights coming on; the road was running into a poor stretch again. Here, where the ruts and potholes slowed the traffic, stalls under shading palm fronds were set up on either side, selling bananas, plantains, and even a small dead antelope that was swung towards them. Further along were tin-roofed shacks, with walls of red clay. One shack, end on to the road, carried a bright painted advertisement for Omo washing powder; and, indeed, poor as the Lansanan population looked around here, everyone seemed to be in bright, clean, shirts and dresses.

As Ntamu village was passed, the police car pulled over to the concrete rain run-off, in better condition than the road itself. Car doors slammed, and everyone but Richard got out of the two vehicles. The police sergeant took off his beret and threw it behind him onto the car seat, a signal of not being strictly on duty.

'Here,' he said. He pointed to the stretch of broken road ahead of them and to the clusters of trees, fifteen or so metres off to the right. He walked fast to the first, most prominent mahogany tree. 'And here is the wound where the vehicle hit.' He paced ten metre steps back, looked at Rebekah apologetically, and pointed to the hard ground. 'And here is where his head rolled.'

Rebekah stared at the policeman, unblinking. She was

a journalist; she had seen and heard everything.

'Thanks,' said Jonny. 'We're grateful to you.'

'You want I stay?' the policeman asked. 'But I mustn't be in the film.'

Ben shook his head. 'No thanks. But we can walk anywhere here?'

'Of course,' the policeman said. 'It's not a crime scene.'

'Sure.' Ben put his hand into his shirt pocket. 'Here, some shillings for your police charity.'

The policeman took it without any sign of surprise. 'I got no receipt book,' he said, stuffing it into his back pocket. Ben waved that necessity away. 'I'll leave you, then.'

The three of them watched as the police car screeched a tight turn in the road, and headed back to Mfinimfini.

'Okay,' said Ben – 'What did they miss?'

# ZEPHON TELEVISION

## Transcript of Accident Location Report

**PROGRAMME:** ZT/JA/19/4  67
**WORLD VIEW**
**TRANSMISSION:** TO BE DECIDED

### BEN MADDOX PRESENTING

### View of Road, Ben Maddox aproaching camera:

This is an ordinary stretch of road in Lansana, about a third of the way north from the Atlantic coast and the capital Johnstown. And here an ordinary and unremarkable thing happened. There was a road accident.

*Intercut library shot of a dun-coloured Land Rover*

### Ben Maddox (to camera):

A car like this ran into a tree like this *(turns head to the roadside trees)*. Mahogany. Hard.

*Intercut shot of a scarred mahogany tree*

### Ben Maddox (to camera):

A man died here, someone a bit special. Mbidi Renula was a moderate negotiator for the Yoori people of the north east, living on tribal lands that President Obed Abu wants to hold on to. Renula's death was an accident – apparently – in heavy rains on a bad road, his Land Rover hitting the tree with such force, although mahogany scars don't admit to force, that the whiplash took the head off his body.

**Ben Maddox (walking among the trees, long and medium shots):**

The police are open about it, Zephon television has seen the accident report, and we were brought here by the authorities with no restrictions on filming wherever we wanted.

**Ben Maddox (close up):**

But are things as they seem? If we put accident aside for one moment – and let me stress that we have no evidence for putting accident aside – who might want the moderate Mbidi Renula dead? Possibly? *(Turns, facing north.)* Well, there are the hardline Yoori, the Red Fire fighters striking terror into the northern lands in the cause of their independence.

*Library shots of guerrilla soldiers in a file, carrying modern weapons*

**Ben Maddox (voice over):**

*They* might want a moderate negotiator out of the way. Or, there's the government of Kutuliza –

*Map shot of West Africa, highlighting Kutuliza:*

**Ben Maddox (voice over):**

– they profess not to want the Yoori lands; even though their links with the North East Region are tribally strong. But would a foreign government stoop to murder?

**Ben Maddox (in a stooping position, picking up a handful of soil, standing and throwing it back to the ground):**

Dust to dust. What price Yoori soil? *(Turns to face south)* Or would the Lansanan government itself want a moderate negotiator out of the way – because with a moderate settlement the problem would remain, rankle, boil up again – and might the Lansanans prefer to have the excuse for an all-out war with their own Yoori people, to finally tame them before foreign meddlers provide them with the serious arms and ammunition for an uprising?

### Ben Maddox (close up):

Unthinkable! Probably one of the best bets – if accident is discounted – would be those Yoori Red Fires, a fierce and terrorist organisation determined to get Yoori independence and alignment with Kutuliza. Would they get more Yoori support for direct action if the moderates are off the scene? *(Turns away, looks into the trees.)*

### Ben Maddox (in the thick of the trees):

Snooping around, I found this. *(Camera down to Ben's feet.)* Preserved in the mud after the accident-causing rains had dried – footprints.

### Close up of footprints – Ben's voice over:

Two sets of prints, clear markings. And not studded army boots, nor ribbed and silent rubber sniper soles, but trainers. Ordinary trainers perhaps, one pair size nine and one pair size nine and a half, at a guess. And a quite distinctive pattern on the soles, that zigzag. *(Ben's finger traces the zigzag.)* Evidence of two people standing back in the trees but with a view through to the road.

### Ben's POV of the view through to the road:

From here I could flash a bright, blinding light; or I could catapult a rock to shatter a windscreen.

**<u>Ben Maddox (close up to camera):</u>**

Just possibilities. Just improbabilities – because the cause
of the accident and the cause of death are known. *(Pause.)*
Atrocious driving conditions.

# Joyce Avoka's story –
## written up by R. A. – part 4

The raid was to be the first test of Joyce's loyalty. Her tent of girls was told they'd been chosen by Sergeant Six, as was a tent of longer-trained boys – the mission an attack on an enemy Lansan township, where all their faithfulness to the Yoori fight would be under close observation.

'You try to run off, you think you go back home – you make the biggest mistake of your life!' the sergeant rasped at them from the doorway of the tent. He pointed his finger at each of the girl soldier ants as he spoke. 'You, an' you, an' you, an' all of you – we know where you come from.' He came further in and stood over the girl next to Joyce. 'What's your last two?'

'Twenty-three,' the girl told him, her back like a board.

He thought for a moment. 'Nsraban village!' he snapped. She nodded. 'We know all your home places.' He went back to the tent doorway, and suddenly turned in again, his face fierce. 'And if you run we come again in the night, and we bring you back for hanging in front of the camp.' He put his hand to his throat in a gruesome gesture, making a choking sound. 'You master?'

'Yes sir!' the girls said smartly back. Joyce was sitting up as straight as she could, the required way. She knew that she wouldn't run away; she was too scared. She tried to tell herself that she believed in the Yoori cause that she was being taught, that she would willingly strike against Lansanans for Yoori justice, that fighting – as Yusa preached in the Bible – was the just way to righteousness. But in truth she knew that she was scared to the depth of her being, for her deeply-missed family, who would be punished if she tried to run, and for herself. A single noose was always dangling from a cross beam outside the assembly tent, empty up to now, swinging in the air currents like a kids' playing rope from a teak tree, but it gave its own message – and she didn't want to be hanged.

Meanwhile, she knew all the answers to the questions Sergeant Six asked; she could recite back the bits he taught them; and she was starting to learn to read, from a small children's book about Yusa. So, yes, for her own reasons she believed in Yusa – and she would not run away. She told herself that she would do her soldier's duty to the full, and Sergeant Six, and General Lakle, and Yusa himself, would be proud of her. She told it to herself, and she tried to believe it. And as Sergeant Six left the tent she recited to herself, 'And Jozea proclaims, "There shall be a mighty scourge across the laxful land, and, question not, the just lashes of the scourge shall dwell with God, the king everlasting."'

Now Forty-five was going to be a just lash against the Lansans. Or so she hoped.

## SIKAKOKO TOWNSHIP

The man came at around six o'clock, and he was cool. His silver Mercedes Benz was so air-conditioned that as he emerged from it the lenses of his golden glasses frosted over. He wore city-black shiny shoes, and a white collarless shirt under a white suit whose lack of crease gave him the appearance of an international operator.

Muj saw him first, he'd been on nervous look-out since he'd got in from training, and as the car pulled up in the road outside the Kalala house, he ran around from the side shadows to the back, climbed in through his window, and curled up tight on his bed.

He heard his mother say, 'Who's this?' and his father scrape the chair in his cupboard of a study, before walking through to the front veranda, muttering. A running knot of kids from along the road had strung themselves behind the expensive car, and were being eyed by its driver, who had got out and was trying to stand on all sides at once, in protection.

The Kalala bungalow house stood thirty metres back from the road, sparse patches of grass surviving beneath the tall trees that stood on either side of a wide dirt-way walk up to the veranda: Muj Kal's early training pitch. The stranger's car had not presumed to drive up to the house, but kept a polite distance. All the way from the road to the house the stranger smiled as he strode, swinging a small crocodile skin briefcase.

'Have I the honour of addressing Mr Nokongola Kalala?' he asked from below the veranda, in English with an American accent.

'I'm Nokongola Kalala.' Muj heard his father reply. 'Come into the shade.'

Already, Muj's mother, Eni, was arranging a tray with lemonade to take to her husband, a traditional hospitality. Muj heard the two glasses clinking together as she carried it, and then the scrape of chairs as he knew that the man with the golden glasses was being invited with a wave of his father's bony arm to sit at the bamboo table. He pictured his father's face, asking the question *what do you want?* as the lemonade plopped into the glasses.

His mother's head was suddenly around Muj's bedroom door, asking the same question as her husband, but with theatrical strength. Muj sat up and put his finger to his lips, and together they listened.

'I presume your son has mentioned that I may call upon you?' the man asked. His voice had a deep authority to it, the sort one listens to.

'I've got a son, Mujiba, but don't presume, Mr...?'

'Ah. I apologise, sir.' Muj could hear the flap of leather as a business card was being brought out. 'Gerald Abowa. I am an agent.'

'For good? Or evil?' Perhaps the card was not being read. 'Or an agent for change?' It was Nokongolo Kalala's contentious voice, the one he used for arguing and sermonizing for Yusa, sort of jokey, but very much meaning what he said: because Muj hadn't had the courage to tell him that this man might call.

Gerald Abowa laughed, a rumble like the gathering of heavy waves before they hit the rocks, and yet eddying away quickly. 'An agent for the better, I hope. So my clients tell me...'

There was a silence, and Nokongolo Kalala didn't fill it.

'I'll start from the beginning. My clients are footballers. I represent football players in their dealings – welfare, wages, transfers. I like to think I represent their best interests, obtain for them the best deals, find for them the best clubs, make the best matches between management and players…'

There was still nothing from Muj's father, except a slight shift of his chair legs, the little shunt that prepared for a push away from the table.

'…And it will be no surprise to you to know, sir, that your son Mujiba is a talent that everyone has been watching – on the threshold of a remarkable career in football. Sikakoko Arsenal is understandably cautious about him, they are not over-exposing him yet, but–' the man lowered his voice, '–he has been spotted by a European club, and by invitation from the representatives of this club, and of Sikakoko Arsenal, I have been given permission to speak to you, his father, his legal guardian. I have the honour to make you a proposal…' The expensive click of a briefcase catch could be heard. 'As a man of intellect you will see that by acting now, we are ahead of the game, no one else is on his trail, but he has been watched at junior matches, reserve games, and his few senior appearances. The offer I am prepared to make for the exclusive right to negotiate for you is very good indeed.'

There was a long pause. Muj and his mother, two people breathing lightly for one, listened for what Muj's father would say. Depending on what he said, one sentence could take Muj down one road, or down another.

And Muj was about to be impressed by the man – not by the man with the golden glasses, but by his own father.

When Nokongola Kalala finally spoke it was not like a devout Yusa follower, throwing out worldly opportunity, not like a father protecting a young lad, and not like a Yoori who was strong for the tribal cause. He spoke like someone who was used to the market place.

'You sound like a salesman, Mr…Gerald…Abowa.' Now the card was being read – and silence from Golden Glasses. 'You sound like someone who offers *this* if we jump at it quickly, a second-best *that* or a lost opportunity if we don't leap at your offer, whatever it may be. Like telephone sales. But you're talking about my son, and I've never made a rushed decision concerning him since the day he was born…'

*Except when the rushed decision was to smack his legs!* Muj could have put in, but he was listening hard for what might come next.

'…He's sixteen years of age. He has my permission to earn his living as an apprentice sportsman, but it is conditional.'

'Conditional upon what?' Some of Mr Gerald Abowa's golden edge had rubbed off.

'On family conditions, of no concern to anybody outside it.'

'Well…' There was a very long pause, but no closing click came from the briefcase yet. 'These are your affairs, naturally. I will say this, though.' The man with the golden glasses coughed deeply, a thinking cough. 'If your son wishes to continue as a footballer, and if you give this permission – a permission required only until he is eighteen, after which he can decide for himself, whether to go this way, or that— '

'This way, or what way?'

114

'He plays Lansanan football, and is much admired, perhaps the way of transfers around the Lansanan clubs, perhaps even of playing internationally for his country.'

'For Lansana?'

There was another pause, as if Golden Glasses were frowning as to which other country there could be. 'If he wishes to continue as a footballer he will earn himself a wage as good as any civil servant in the country. Or, the other way, sir, is that he plays upon the world stage. Which he is good enough to do. He moves to Europe, he plays for a top club, he lives a fine life, and he sends you back sufficient money to live in grandeur here...'

'Who wants grandeur?' An instant response. 'We live in luxury already...'

The agent was too polite to look about him and question that statement.

'Clean drinking water. What percentage of the world's population has that on tap?'

Now came the closing click of the briefcase, the scrape back of a heavier chair. 'I think we have probably concluded our conversation, Mr Kalala.'

Nokongolo Kalala pushed back also.

'My telephone and e-mail details are on the card,' the agent said. 'I may not tell you which club is interested at this stage, but it is a big one! And sadly, despite your impression of it, my offer will not last for long, sir.'

Muj's father must have shrugged. Muj could picture that typical answer to a statement that meant little to him.

The man went, and the air-conditioned, tinted-windowed Mercedes Benz vacated the road, and the district. Long before which, Nokongolo Kalala had walked back to his little study, saying nothing, until

Eni appeared in its doorway.

'Your son could be a world class footballer,' he told his wife, over his shoulder, 'if that's what he wants.'

Muj's ears were so fine-tuned through the plaster walls that he would have heard a mosquito at a thousand metres.

'If that's what he wants to do,' his father repeated, his voice up half an octave – as if he knew that Muj was listening. 'If that's what he wants to do,' he said once more, but very quietly, to himself.

# Joyce Avoka's story –
## written up by R. A. – part 5

It was mule and truck in the dead of night, glimmers of light
from shaded torches showing the way down the steep,
winding pass to where the Toyota truck stood waiting. It
was the first time that Forty-five – as Joyce had to
remember to think of herself – had ridden with the real men
of the Red Fire, she and the other young soldier ants having
to give way to men's outstretched legs, the discomfort
overcome by knowing that General Lakle himself was riding
with them, in the cab of the truck.

There was a melon-slice of moon that picked out both
mountain top and slides of shale as they went down, and
then they were at the wide, flat, dark of the reservoir, where
Forty-five found herself looking away in case she caught
sight of the floating corpse of Lame Daniel circling in the
water. All around her everyone was hiking themselves up for
the raid: the men kept checking their ammunition box of
explosives, and Sergeant Six nursed the canvas bag of
grenades that the young soldier ants would use.

At a junction in the road somewhere outside Botae, the
truck stopped. The men jumped smartly off as General
Lakle alighted from the cab and checked his map with a
torch. Up on the back of the truck, Sergeant Six pointed to
a huge redwood tree that dominated the crossroads.

'We rendezvous with the men of Red Fire here!' he told his
recruits, cut down now to eleven altogether, six boys and
five girls – a matter of supplies, he'd told them. As his men
became part of the roadside foliage, General Lakle waved
the vehicle away for the recruits to be driven a further

kilometre nearer to Botae where, on the manganese mining town outskirts, they were jumped off. 'For Yusa! For Yoori!' Sergeant Six exclaimed, hoarse but quiet.

'For Yusa! For Yoori!' the Red Fire soldier ants whispered back, finding their legs and feet after the cramped and bumpy ride.

'Where we've come along just now is one road, single – you run it back to the giant tree, you hide, an' you wait for the truck.'

Forty-five and the other recruits nodded.

'If you get wounded or get captured, you say only one word…Yoori! Nothing else, you master?'

They nodded again. Forty-five shivered; well, she told herself, it was cold here in the night.

'You hold the plan, in your heads?'

They held the plan. Forty-five had it pictured in her mind as it had been drawn out on the large piece of cardboard back under the canopy at Camp Vodi. They were to creep into these outskirts of the town, along the main street, off which six side alleys ran, where there were long, joined-up abodes for the miners and their families. Two Red Fire recruits were to go into each alley, just one into the furthest alley. The boy who went into this last alley would have an M26 grenade. When he threw this grenade in through an opening to a building and it exploded, this was the signal for the others to throw theirs. If they had grenades, they pulled out the pins and threw them in through openings, one to each side of the alley, shouting 'Yoori!' and running away fast. If they had grenade-size rocks, they threw them, too, just the same. This would cause panic, people running out of their dwellings into the narrow alleys, along which

Sergeant Six from the main street would be firing his AK-74, before he ran giving covering fire to follow his recruits. 'We soften enough places like this, and we get them wanting our Yoori liberation!'

Now Forty-five and the others were ready to do it. Sergeant Six gave out the missiles from his canvas bag, and stealthily, in twos now, the new soldier ants crept into the sleeping township, eyes sharpened, ears pricked. They were about to become real Yoori soldiers. A dog whined somewhere, and a drunk shouted obscenities in his sleep, while the moon and the silent stars above took no notice: so much happened under their blind gaze.

Forty-five, in her Red Fire uniform and her black trainers, held her hand tightly around the smooth rock that she had been given. She was with a boy, older, taller, than she was. He had a grenade, she knew by the way he carried it – two-handed, one hand cradling its body, the other on top with a finger in the ring of the pin. He led the way, creeping into the second alley on the right side of the main road. It was darker along here, but as they trod softly their eyes acclimatized, and the boy pointed out an archway.

Forty-five stopped as the boy went creeping on. She looked into the opening, an empty room with a table and a chair, and, beyond it, a closed door. She listened. She thought she heard a cough, a child's cough, someone in the far room, perhaps. But it was hard to listen, to overcome the dinning of the pulse in her ears, the waiting for the signal of the first grenade. It was as if the world was standing still, the moon above stopping its movement in the sky.

Was that the scrape of a chair? Was someone going to the child who had coughed? For a second she thought of her small brother, Idi, when he had croup and her mother boiled water up for him; but she straight off wiped the disturbing image. Instead, she pictured how, after the first loud bang, and with her rock rolling across the floor of the living room, this Lansan enemy family would be running out, screaming into the alley – by which time she would be back in the main street and running herself – for the redwood tree at the crossroads, her job done.

This was right, wasn't it? This was for the greater good of the Yoori people and the glory of Yusa, scourging these enemies of righteousness. People had to die, it was for the Yoori and Yusa good – wasn't it? What had her family ever gained from being Lansan? *Small deaths, big victories!* Sergeant Six said. She had to believe that, to throw this rock, didn't she?

She was gripping the rock so hard now that it seemed almost to give, to mould a little to her hand.  And never mind grenades, her head was ready to explode with the pounding of her blood in the fervour and the excitement of what was going to happen.

General Lakle and Sergeant Six said there had to be deaths!  Always!  It was for the greater good.

A flash in the sky suddenly started the attack, followed by a resounding bang as the first explosion ripped the sleeping air.  It echoed in the confines of its alley as it scourged and seconds later, nearer explosions joined the terror of the night. In her own alley, the boy yelled, 'Yoori!' and Forty-five heard the clatter of the grenade as it went in through a window opening and rolled across a concrete floor. In the main street there was screaming, and wailing, urgent shouting under a thick smoke that blackened out the sky.

The boy ran past her, shouted, 'Yoori!' at her as she drew back her arm to throw, and shouted, 'Yoori!' herself. And was transfixed in that position as she dropped the rock to the alley floor, couldn't throw it – in her head she'd suddenly seen her mother watching. But she ran after the boy as if she had done her Red Fire duty, into the mayhem of the Botae street and the sound of the AK-74 spraying its shells – and on a further kilometre to the redwood tree.

General Lakle and his own bombers from the manganese mine assault were there already, soon joined by Sergeant Six and his recruits. All of them – not a Red Fire soldier killed or captured – clambered into the back of the Toyota and bumped off along the road to Dedie – in the opposite direction from which they had come, where the pursuit would surely go.

And with the greatest, most immovable lump in her throat, Forty-five sat in the back of the truck and quietly joined in the Red Fire jubilation at this successful mission.

# KIBBUTZ NEGEV

Welcome to Kibbutz Negev, a growing, thriving kibbutz located twenty-five kilometres north of Eilat in the Arava Rift valley, a uniquely tranquil region of Israel.

Our communal mode of living and the high value we place on Jewish tradition, gives us that feel of utopian community that other kibbutzim have lost.

Negev continues to expand in its public, communal sector...and we are building, building, building. Our present building projects include new neighbourhoods, artist studios, a modernized library and a new film and photographic enterprise that will empower our young people in the modern world.

Come on in and explore our way of life, from our myriad of expanding businesses to our cultural values and goals.

Rebekah Arens read the information printed off the internet and looked at the pictures of the kibbutz that Jonny Aaranovitch had been speaking about. In her room at the King's Hotel, Mfinimfini, she had just served two scalding hot cups of an apple-juice drink, flavoured with clove. Now she read as the two of them gingerly sipped, sitting in tight armchairs on each side of her dressing table.

'This is where you were this year?' she asked.

'Go every year. Just back.'

'It made such an impression?'

'It always does. We all need a spiritual home.'

She looked at him sharply. 'Time out, communal living, putting self last…is that you?'

'Plus religious tolerance,' he put in. 'Kashrut and Shabbat are observed in the dining room and at cultural events, but everyone's free to do what they want in their own homes.'

'And this is what you want?' She waved the paper, partly for cooling her drink. 'A go-getting, top class cameraman wants the kibbutz life? An isolated community, looking in upon itself?'

'Not so.' Jonny shook his head earnestly. 'Kibbutzim have produced many national leaders, political, intellectual, military…' He sipped his drink and didn't flinch. 'I can help with the film and photography, everyone can help with their own expertise. Give it a try some time, you should.'

Rebekah laughed. '"Arabic Jewess in Israeli Utopia!"' She ran a newspaper headline across between them with her hands.

'And, "Once a journalist, always a journalist!"' Jonny countered. He fell silent, so did she. Until he added, 'I'm getting a bit tired of seeing the world through a camera lens.'

To which she stared down into the steam from her mug.

**Ben Maddox**

**From:** Meera Sharma meeras@vintage.co.uk
**Sent:** 22 April      14:30
**To:** benmaddox@talktalk.net
**Subject:** How are you?

Bumped into Bloom Ramsaran at Liverpool Street. She said you've sent back a couple of good clips and you sound well.

I'm OK, too. Getting on with life at Vintage Books, possibility of a promotion to assistant editor – be good, wouldn't it?

E-mails to this address are fine, not public, also texts and voicemails work on my mobile – you've got the number. Look forward to hearing from you.

You dog.

Meera

The e-mail arrived as the Zephon team checked out of the Mfinimfini hotel. It was handed to Ben as Jonny paid the bill for the four rooms.

'Who's that from?' Jonny asked.

'No one. Not from Zephon, it's for me.'

'Ah. Meera.' Then, facing away, towards the receptionist, 'Or Bloom, is it?'

Why should Ben bristle? 'Meera, of course. Personal, not work. No one's cutting you out of the loop.'

'So I would hope...'

Rebekah was already in the back of the car, talking into her mobile phone, while Richard polished the windscreen, going lightly over the cracks. Ben threw his rucksack into the boot and sat in the back, nothing to say. Disgruntled, he took little interest in Rebekah's end of the phone conversation.

'You'll let me know... Right... That'd be brilliant for us... Yes... Yes... Can you find out?... Okay... We're going north, but there's good cell-phone coverage... You can reach me...' She turned to Ben. 'That was my office...'

'Uh-huh.'

'They're trying to locate us a name to interview, someone to speak for the Yoori people.' But the slight soprano roll in her voice said she was quite excited about whose that name might be.

Ben's hand was still in his shirt pocket, where he'd folded away Meera's e-mail. He buttoned the pocket. 'A leader? Extremist? Or a moderate, like the dead man?'

'We're already seeing Mbidi Renula's sister, that's the moderates covered. No – they think they can set us up with someone who's close to the political situation – thinks some international publicity might be appropriate.'

'Right.'

'And guess who that is!'

'Bob Geldof? Jamie Oliver?'

'Are you Okay?' Rebekah suddenly asked, as Jonny came to the car and dropped his own rucksack into the boot, beside his camera equipment.

'Indigestion,' Ben said. 'It'll go. Who are they setting us up with?'

'Charlie Henderson!

'Henderson showing his hand in Lansana?' Ben queried. 'Why would he do that?' Suddenly, the reporter in him took over from the guilty-feeling partner. He clapped his hands. 'Right, things are stirring – so let's get north!'

But they were hardly five kilometres out of Mfinimfini, past the accident spot and on the Sikakoko road, when Rebekah's mobile rang again – a stupid, frog ring-tone that Jonny always laughed at. Rebekah listened, Ben tried not to, and Jonny fiddled with the map, refolding it for the day's journey until, with the frozen mouth of bad news, Rebekah turned to them and said, 'There's been an attack. Last night, early hours. They've bombed Botae, the manganese town.'

'Who has?'

'Yoori Red Fires are claiming responsibility.'

Jonny was already fighting the map again, to find Botae.

'It's on our way,' Richard said, 'more or less.'

'Right, let's get there!' Jonny found it. 'Any casualties?'

'No details yet,' said Rebekah. 'But the *Graphic* wants me to file on this.'

'Sure,' said Jonny, 'and I'll get you some pictures…'

'Since you're here!'

And while a quick look flashed between the two, and the car drove on towards the location of a hot news story, Ben found himself eagerly leaning forward in his seat.

My respected father has said nothing to me about the football agent's visit. Not to me directly. He has made me ask myself the question of what I want to do in my life, but he has put no pressure on me to decide this way or that. This is my problem, he is saying. It would help if he did say something. From a little boy I remember how he can be disappointed in me. When I played too long with my friends and not been at home for the start of the family prayers, he would not chastise me, but add a long prayer for Yusa's forgiveness. When I became very interested in playing football he sent to Johnstown for the best football boots in my size. But when he gave them to me, he also gave me a new Bible, in superior leather.

Premiership first team matches are played on Sundays, and when I have

to miss church meetings and prayers, he gives me a text to carry in
my pocket; and when I run to the pitch or the bench I always think of Yusa - although my father does not know this. To tell him would sound wrong, like showing off how holy I am.

When I read this, I see that I do not write enough of my feelings for God, and Jesus Christ, and the holy prophet Yusa; but I am a serious boy, I do not consort with girls or with the gamblers in the team, and if the call comes more strongly for me to be a priest for Yusa, I will think about it very deeply.

Also when I read this, I see that I have not been honest in my writing. The big, big question burning in my head is, which club? Who in Europe — IN EUROPE — wants to sign me?

## ATLANTIC VIEW HOTEL, JOHNSTOWN

Eamonn Reilly shivered again in the air conditioning. He had had no phone call the night before from Gerald Abowa, and the man had not been answering his mobile phone that morning.

He looked at his watch, and switched off the cold air. The new quietness descended around him like settling dust. He picked up his pay-as-you-go mobile and, from memory, he dialled a longish number.

'Johnstown, Lansana here,' he said. 'I'm still waiting for news regarding bucko boy. I'll give it a while. Jee-sus, a drink takes half a day to come out here, what price a spankin' contract? Be in touch soon.'

He went back into his room and turned on the television, with the bored flick of someone not caring what he saw. But when picture and sound emerged, it brought up a news bulletin from the Botae bombing, which he stood to watch, reaching for his phone again as he did so.

## BOTAE TOWNSHIP

With the professional skill of a good journalist Rebekah Arens filed her *Graphic* story by telephone from the back seat of Richard's car.

'Last night Botae (B...O...T...A...E) was hit by bombers (stop). They struck at the number three shaft of the Amalgamated Manganese Company's mining operation (stop). Three mine guards were killed as access was gained to the spoil shaft and a bomb of as yet unconfirmed size and composition was dropped into the void (stop). Deaths underground are not reported since the mining company does not operate a night shift (comma), but the pit head deaths are reported to be Robert Akona (26), Enoch Peprah (33) and Kwabena Avoka (45), who between them leave six grieving children (stop). Spelt A...K...O...N...A, P...E...P...R...A... H, A...V...O...K...A.
'New para. Responsibility for the atrocity has been claimed by the Red Fire Yoori Independence Movement in a telephone call to the Botae police (stop). Botae Chief of Police Edward Gbeho (G...B...E...H...O) said (comma, open quotes), "This was a cowardly attack on a peaceful and law (hyphen)- abiding town (comma), by people who are not Red Fires but lice (stop). No warnings were given so townspeople had no chances to protect themselves (stop, close quotes)."
'New para. As a diversion, grenades and

missiles were thrown through open windows in the hot and sultry town (stop). Details are still being collated of casualties (comma), which are likely to be high (stop). Certainly deaths and serious injuries can be expected (stop). The contact telephone number for the Jesus Lives Botae Hospital is 03982440131.

'New para. The Mayor of Botae (comma), Councillor John Salia S...A...L...I...A (comma), says (comma, open quotes) "We mourn the deaths and sympathise with the bereaved (comma), these mine guards were only doing their job (stop). We are a town of peace and industry (comma), going about our lawful business (stop). No one will intimidate us into calling for Yoori independence (comma), and indeed we do not think that most Christian (capital C) Yoori people support these murderers (stop, close quotes)."

'New para. Eunice Biri (B...I...R...I comma), a market trader in the main street of Botae, told me (comma, open quotes) "We are Lansan tribe (comma), but our Yoori friends in Sikakoko have sent us their sorrow (stop). Terrorists will not drive a wedge between the peoples of this country (stop, close quotes)."

'By-line Rebekah Arens, staff reporter.'

Ben and Jonny hovered outside the car, with Jonny sending a mobile phone picture of the pit-head to the Johnstown *Graphic*. He, Ben and Rebekah hadn't been able to get through the police cordon at the mine so the pictures were more to occupy a space in the paper's lay-out than to show anything very specific. This space would be filled with the paper's own photographs for the next edition. Now the Zephon pair were preparing to get their own television package together, both agreeing that the human angle was the one to pursue next: the grief in the houses where grenades had killed and maimed sleeping townspeople. The police couldn't cordon off every home that had been hit, and in a street of bungalows, their white walls spattered with red earth and blood, they found a knot of people wailing and grieving in a shady alley, beneath the jagged and enlarged window of a blown-out room. Ben walked quietly into the alley and approached them while Jonny set up his camera.

He saw that they were weeping over something blue, lying in the alley; something small and flat to the ground, like a starved body. But as Ben came nearer he saw that it wasn't a body but a dress, a school uniform, tattered and empty. The women were lifting it, kissing it, cuddling it, treating it as if life was still in it. He stood on the edge of the little group, and tapped an elderly man on the shoulder. The man turned, his eyes red with rubbed tears.

'Who was this?' Ben asked.

'Victoria,' the man told him. 'Seven years old. Asleep in her bed.'

'Killed by a grenade?'

The man snuffled, and nodded. 'Age seven! The dress

was new, for her next school.' He bowed his head, and wept again. 'She…was…so…proud…of…' He couldn't finish, too choked for breath to give body to his words.

Ben knew that behind him Jonny was shooting. It was always difficult, shooting tragedy. But the story needed to be told, Ben was convinced of that. He was not a voyeur, he got no kicks from being in places of tragedy like this; he did it because he was a journalist; and he was a journalist because he wanted to spread information and knowledge about the world he lived in. To do so, he normally asked permission for his cameraman to shoot, made it clear with his microphone that he was a journalist, and would record what people said to him. But there were times when formally setting up interviews was unhelpful, it seemed intrusive, and today was one of those. And he knew that Jonny would stay where he was, shoot his angle, and not become obtrusive into these people's grief.

Ben shuffled into the group and knelt beside the empty blue dress. 'Are you her mother?' he quietly asked the woman who had a fierce grip on the material. He nodded towards his small hand-held microphone; he wasn't trying to fool the tragic woman.

'Yes, sir,' she said.

'And where is…she? Have they…?'

'She's gone to the hospital, but she is dead. Her father is with her, they are busy, there is no room for everybody.'

Ben was surprised to see that the woman's eyes were wide and dry, she was beyond mere tears.

'Children!' she suddenly shouted into Ben's face. 'Children! We heard their voices!'

'Children did this?'

'Children! In the road, running, children's voices,

133

swearing at us, how we were dead. Throwing bricks and rocks into some houses, bombs into others, and into ours...'

'You didn't see them?'

The woman stared a blank face into Ben's.

'Children!' the other women muttered, as Ben quietly withdrew, ensured that his mike cable was still in tact and running into Jonny's camera, discreetly entering the alley and closing in on the pitiful scene.

And not for the first time, Ben noticed how, at the site of an explosion, the debris isn't made up only of bits of walls and windows and beams, but of strands and rips of soft furnishings, cushions, curtains, clothes. Tatters and duck-down floating up in the air.

Like the departing spirit.

# DEFIANT BOTAE GAME GOES ON DESPITE TRAGEDY

**Graphic report: Michael Kasea**

Wednesday evening's premiership clash between home club Real Botea and Sikakoko Arsenal will go ahead with strict security the order of the day. In travelling, the Yoori club is underlining for the world that the board, the players, the officials and the spectators of Sikakoko may live in a Yoori township, but they are not Yoori extremists.

The match – and the three points it carries – is important to both clubs, who are in the top half of the premier league, Sikakoko Arsenal third.

Teams have yet to be announced, but there's a rumour that Sikakoko's Latevi may have a groin injury. Manager George Chognon is confident, though, that his squad is strong enough to cover any absence. Meanwhile Real Botea will probably field an unchanged side from that which defeated Ntamu Wolves on Sunday.

Black armbands will be worn by both teams, and a one minute silence held before the game to show respect for those who died in the recent atrocity. The bill for the police presence, however, will be huge.

## APOLLO HOTEL, BOTAE

Jonny released Rebekah for a few hours to get on with her first responsibility, reporting the atrocity for the Johnstown *Graphic*. This was part of the Zephon deal with her newspaper, but he would have done it, anyway. Jonny stood for the responsible side of journalism which isn't all 'dog eat dog'. But he had been serious and sombre as he saw her off.

'I shoot wars,' he'd said, 'and I shoot tragedy in communities – my job, it's not all film stars and prime ministers. I shoot distressed children and their parents – but too much today this world brings war and mutilated kids together.' He'd sighed, breath long enough for a Sabbath prayer – and he'd tangled his fingers like a wreckage. 'I should train to use my other eye for shooting, this one has seen too much...' and he'd pulled down the skin beneath his right eye to show how bloodshot it was.

Then, snapping to business, he and Ben decided to seek official press permission to be at the Botae/Sikakoko premiership match, with camera and comment. Through the usual satellite channels – set up with local broadcasters – Jonny had sent their tragic Botae footage back to Zephon in London. The response was a text from Kath Lewis.

> **Stay with it. Trnsmtd yr Botae pckge lst nite's news. Small item, no reaction, but kp going on story.**
> **We R still only team on 2 this.**

'So what is our story?' Jonny suddenly asked. 'Let's remind me what the taste of the juice is out here.' He was lying on Ben's bed, shoes and all, while Ben sat at the dressing table in direct line of the inadequate fan. 'When they're writing fiction they ask, where's the jeopardy? So what are we chasing here?' Jonny took a swig from Ben's bedside glass of flat Coke. '*Whose* jeopardy?' 'Both sides'. Civil war. That's the story,' Ben said. 'It ravaged Zaire, Sudan, Somalia, Angola, Sierra Leone – is it going to ravage Lansana?'

'*Ravage* – that's a word! I like it. "Rav-age"!' As a photographer Jonny had a focused appreciation of words. Some of Ben's voice-overs he would criticise as 'a bit blurry', but others had him giving a thumbs-up, and saying, 'Sharp as a lancet!'

Ben went on. 'And would such a civil war be engineered from outside, by Kutuliza next door? Yoori helping Yoori, across national boundaries, aided and abetted by this Charles Henderson?'

'To get control of the water and the hydro-electricity…?'

'And to return to the pre-1914 boundaries, put the former country back together again.' Ben stared across at Jonny, tapping his ballpoint on his pad. 'Yes, *and* to get control of the water and the hydro-electricity.'

'And then? After?'

'After what?'

Jonny sat up. 'What does Kutuliza do after, with the north east region, when it's been annexed? Does it make its new Yoori brothers rich on water profits – or does it sell them down the river?' He laughed. 'The pun – forgive!'

'Not strictly a pun,' Ben said. He thought for a few

moments. 'But you're right. Kutuliza's the key to all this, probably not the Red Fires at all – the Yoori Red Fire extremists could be being used.'

'So.' Jonny got up, scuffing off half the covers. 'Since we're in Botae already, we cover this match – which can be background if it's peaceful, and hot news for Kath if it all kicks off between the Lansans and the Yooris.'

'*That's* a pun!' Ben pointed his ballpoint at him.

'We interview the moderate's sister, probably a waste of time – if it were sixteen mill film I wouldn't bother loading the camera – and we talk to Charles Henderson…'

'…then onto the real story. We head off to Kutuliza!' Ben pronounced.

'Having my sentences finished, I hate that! So, what are we waiting for? More metaphors, yet?'

'Cover tomorrow night's football match,' Ben told him. 'Then we move further north.'

Jonny put his hands on his hips. Stood, and thought. 'That Coke's flat,' he said, 'let's go down to the bar and call for a nice, cool beer.'

'Right. Let's.' And from the dressing table Ben picked up his draft letter to Meera and followed Jonny out of the room.

Down in the bar, their cool Star lagers in front of them, Jonny suddenly said what was on his mind; the matter of importance that he'd clearly been thinking about back in the room. 'Kutuliza – so what do you know about Kutuliza?'

Ben shrugged. 'Not a lot – yet. It's Yoori, used to own the Lansana North East Region before lands were redistributed after the First World War.'

Jonny stared at him. 'It's a hell of a scary country. I know,

I was there four years ago. Just about got out with my life…'

'Yes?'

'Guns they carry like we carry bags. Highest murder rate in Africa. Look at someone as if you're on a story and you need bodyguards to get you from the hotel to the car…and a bullet-proof car when you get there.'

Ben took a long swig, from the bottle. He knew what was coming already.

'Forget Kutuliza,' Jonny went on. 'Rebekah, I wouldn't let anywhere near the place. And I don't fancy it myself, not just on the strength of what we've got.'

Ben wiped his mouth. He'd wondered how long it would take for this Jonny-Rebekah thing to surface. At mealtimes these days Ben was finding himself talking more to Richard the driver than to Jonny, while Jonny and Rebekah were mostly talking of the Israeli kibbutz he saved his leave to visit for six weeks every year.

'For how long do we wait here? Months, it could be before any moves are made…'

'So, what do you think we should do?' Ben asked. 'You can't say things aren't buzzing right now…' It took only a glance out into the Botae street to see the mud and blood still being wiped from the walls of buildings.

'We cover what we're covering. We do our interviews, we get some shots of this European meddler Henderson, perhaps even a militant Yoori breathing fire into the camera…'

'And then?'

'We go home. Seven hours, we can be out here again if your civil war ever starts…'

Jonny clicked his finger to the barman for another

couple of bottles of Star. In an ungracious thought, Ben told himself that cowardice could be thirsty work.

'Definitely not go to Kutuliza?'

'Definitely not – not without the United Nations behind us.' Already, Jonny was into the second bottle.

'See how we go, eh?' Ben didn't want a row right now. But he had come here to do a job, and the Ben Maddox maxim was that he finished the jobs he went out to do, whether or not they ended up on the cutting room floor. But his own feelings of guilt about not taking time to be in touch with Meera froze his unkind thoughts about Jonny suddenly finding a kindred spirit. So he went to work on his own second bottle of Star.

# REAL BOTAE

## versus
# SIKAKOKO ARSENAL
(AWAY)
## WEDNESDAY 27th APRIL

Squad to travel – team coach 8 am Wed. 27th April,
no 1 car park Sikakoko Stadium

**Badjona**          **Sinton**
**Olympio**          **Peprab**
**Koomson**          **Kpotra**
**Eyadema**          **Akrofi**
**Wilmot**
**Kalala** (see manager)
**Abankwa**
**Agama**
**Atcho**
**Gbebo**
**Lawson**

Manager: Chognon
Trainer: Adjei-Mensab
Physio: N'Gatta
Kit assistants (2)

FINE FOR LATENESS – ONE MONTH WAGES

Brilliant! Was Yusa smiling? Or testing him? And what was that note by his name, 'see manager'? Mujiba Kalala stood and read the team sheet for Wednesday evening on the canteen noticeboard. He was hardly dry from his shower after training, and ten minutes earlier he'd been out on the pitch with Mr George Chognon shouting at him, and at all the others. Why did he have to see him especially? This sheet had been put up on the manager's behalf while they'd been out there, but right now the manager would be in his office, waiting for him.

Picking his way through the small knot of players around the noticeboard, Muj went out of the long hut and up to the smaller portacabin next door. There were too few metres between the buildings for much thinking to go on, and perhaps he should have had a slow drink of water before he came, but he'd made his move and couldn't go back now. Players were called to see the manager for club discipline, or a roasting for being lazy, or acting greedy with the ball – or for being told that they weren't wanted by the club any more. On the other hand, he *had* been picked for the squad, so it couldn't be that.

Or had his father changed his mind and objected after Golden Glasses' visit? Was Muj himself going to have to make some decision in front of the manager about his future – to go *with* his father, or *against* him?

He knocked on Mr George Chognon's door.

'*Oui!*' The man spoke good English, all the training was in English, he was *mister* not *monsieur*, but '*oui*' with a nod, or '*non*' with a waggle of the fingers were trademarks of the manager: the players impersonated them.

Muj Kal went in. The manager was a white Frenchman, quite old to Muj, a former international whose name most people wouldn't remember. He was bent over his desk, ruffling his hair and trying to find a paperclip for fixing some receipts together.

'Ah.' But Muj was not invited to sit – and he hadn't expected to be – only the internationals ever sat in Mr George Chognon's office. 'Real Botae,' the man said, still paperclip hunting.

'Yes, *patron.*' That was the only other French thing. Mr George Chognon hated 'Boss' and 'Gov'nor' and 'Sir'. French managers were always 'patron', anywhere in the world.

'You will start the game.'

'*Start?*'

'You will play where Latevi plays, right side, but when I signal you, you will switch with Agama and play left side.' He found a paperclip, couldn't pick it up with his short fingernails, so licked a thumb and stuck it there for long enough to grab it. He turned and smiled his small satisfaction at Muj.

Muj should have smiled back, but he was still recovering from what he had just been told. He had only ever started against bottom-of-the-table teams, and in some minor tournaments that hadn't mattered – never in a top-of-the-premiership clash.

'It will not be easy. Especially, Yoori players will be facing the abuse and the booing. But you must use your skill, and hold the ball, keep tight to it, slow the game – Botae like to rush at things, so you can twist and turn, and slide some clever balls through to Akrofi. You feed Akrofi, okay? He's up front, we play the four-five-one.'

'Yes, *patron.*'

'You do not let them bully you. A big tackle is coming in, you miss him, you dodge.' Mr George Chognon had finally fixed his receipts together; now he opened a drawer and threw them in. 'All the world must see you are good...'

Muj nodded. So, this was to be the game! Others in the team who had been transferred out for good money had been given their matches like this, where they had been put on show. Now Muj Kal was going to be watched especially. His stomach rolled. At such times, in Mr George Chognon's office, internationals would lean back in their chairs and talk about a better contract. As it was, Muj Kal bowed respectfully.

'But if you are not good, I will take you off. No problem. Sinton goes on.'

Muj bowed again.

'You will not miss this team coach?' The manager smiled. Muj had never missed a team coach in his short career, nor would he ever miss a big opportunity like this.

And the roll, the excitement still in his stomach, was telling him how he was really feeling about his dilemma. His pleasure *had* to be saying that he was coming down on the side of professional football: with Yusa's blessing, he hoped – which the prophet could give to him by allowing him to play a good game on Wednesday evening under the Real Botae lights.

There was nothing more to be said. Now Mr George Chognon was searching for something else on his desk, Muj Kal's meeting with him was over. Except for, 'Thank you, *patron*.'

'You do as I say, uh?'

'Yes, *patron*.'

Muj Kal went: but which way should he go? Back to the

canteen to tell his friends in the squad – or straight off home to tell his father and mother that he was a starter on Wednesday?

He went home. This was not a time for crowing, this was a time for asking his father to say some special prayers to Yusa for him – in which he would join. Worshipping Yusa, and being Yoori, were still vital parts of being Mujiba Kalala.

# ZEPHON TELEVISION
## Transcript of Football Coverage
## Real Botae/Sikakoko Arsenal

**APRIL 27 Botae Africa Olympic Stadium, Botae, Lansana**

PROGRAMME: ZT/JA/19/4  67
WORLD VIEW /PM NEWS
TRANSMISSION: TO BE DECIDED
PACKAGE 1

### BEN MADDOX REPORTING

*Exterior shots of Botae Africa Olympic Stadium, night, floodlights on, a smallish crowd heading for the entrances*

#### Ben Maddox (voice over):

This is Botae, a few short hours after bombs killed manganese workers in the town, and grenades and missiles thrown by child soldiers killed and maimed sleeping citizens. And the local team's match against Sikakoko Arsenal has not been cancelled.

#### Ben Maddox (facing camera among spectators passing him on their way into the stadium):

This is a defiant gesture – although my guess is that the gate receipts will show it to be a costly one. Who comes from a funeral to a football match. Furthermore to a match against a team from the area of the rival tribe, whose extremists have claimed responsibility for the bombings – the Yoori Red Fires?

**Ben Maddox (speaks to spectator walking past, man of about 30):**

Excuse me, sir – Zephon News, United Kingdom.
Is this a needle match tonight?

**Spectator:**

Needle?

**Ben Maddox:**

It's top of the table stuff, yes? Three valuable points?

**Spectator:**

Is right.

**Ben Maddox:**

But important in another way?

**Spectator:**

What other way, man?

**Ben Maddox:**

Tribal? Aren't Sikakoko Arsenal from the Yoori district? And wasn't it the Yoori extremists who bombed your town the other night?

**Spectator:**

This is football, yes? You know how many Botae players comes from Botae, or Lansana? You know how many Arsenal players comes from Yoori? *(He flicks three or four fingers on his right hand.)* This is football, okay? *(Makes to move off.)*

**Ben Maddox:**

And you've got the stomach to watch football so soon after the attacks?

**Spectator (moving away, over his shoulder):**

What else am I going to do? Hospital's shut to visitors six o'clock. Sit home an' look at my wife's bare chair?

**Ben Maddox (to camera):**

Which seems to sum up the feeling here. Life goes on. Not to let it, is to take a further hit from the terrorists.

**Jonny:**

Cut it there. Nice. We can file that.

Ben tucked his microphone into his shirt. 'Poor bugger,' he said. 'So let's get inside and see what's what. Twenty minutes to go, and it's quieter than Milton Keynes reserves.'

Jonny was nodding. 'Some football match!' he said.

In the away dressing room the hardest bit for Muj was getting the black armband to stay in place on his number twenty-three shiny shirt; it kept slipping down. Too tight and armbands constrict the blood, too loose and they come off – and Muj's arms weren't as thick as some of the muscly back four's. But fiddling with it somehow kept his mind off the importance of what was happening for him here tonight. His stomach kept rolling, and he'd been to the toilet three times. His head went light with the thought: he was in the spotlight, being showcased – because Raoul Letavi was no more injured than Muj Kal was. Sikakoko Arsenal was putting him on their market stall, for someone big and important to buy.

Mr George Chognon came over, put a fatherly arm around him. 'You remember what I tell you, in the office.

149

You feed Akrofi, run the right channel; and when the bench signal– ' he did the signal, the fingertips of both hands meeting on the top of his head '–you make the switch left with Agama for ten minutes.'

'Yes, patron.' Muj came out from under the fatherly arm; he had one father already, and one in heaven. He started jogging on the spot as an excuse.

'And you use size, your size. You are small, so you will jink and run, jump the heavy boot.'

Muj nodded, as Charlie Akrofi came over. Charlie was the captain of Sikakoko and the captain of Ghana, a brave player who had played in England but who was now back in Lansana to finish his strong career. 'I'm hungry, boy! What am I?'

'Hungry, Charlie!'

'I'm hungry for the ball. You feed me.' Playing four-five-one meant that there were four at the back, five in the middle of the pitch, and only one striker. It was an 'away game' unspectacular system. 'All the time you feed me.'

Mr George Chognon was smiling benevolently, letting his captain take over the pep talk, about to go elsewhere in the dressing room.

'I'll feed you, Charlie,' Muj said, but his stomach had suddenly risen to his throat, and he heard himself adding, 'when it's the right ball to play. If not, I'll do my thing. Okay?'

What had happened? Muj had suddenly gone effervescent inside, saying this to such a man, to this towering international player. Well, he knew what had happened. He was starting the match, one of the Sikakoko first eleven, and he was going to count equally in this game, up until he made some terrible error and Mr George

Chognon had to pull him off. If he really was any good, it was because he played his game within the team. In the second team he played balls as he saw them; he would assist his forwards, feed them when it was the right thing to do, but he was his own man. As a first team substitute it was different, you fitted the situation out there; but now, in the first starting eleven, Muj Kal wasn't going to be Charlie Akrofi's servant. When you started the match, you were up there with the others, to do your thing within the team. Playing four-five-one meant that the midfielders had to come through, to give weight to the attack.

All the same, Muj had still gone cold, saying what he had.

Mr George Chognon had hesitated in his going, but now he walked away, smiling quietly.

'Sure,' said Charlie Akrofi. 'But you remember, "Hungry" is still my real name! If you get greedy, forget the other team, I'll kick your ass over the stadium!'

'Yes, Charlie.'

But Muj Kal had made his point.

# ZEPHON TELEVISION

## Transcript of Football Coverage
## Real Botae/Sikakoko Arsenal

### APRIL 27 Botae Africa Olympic Stadium,
### Botae, Lansana

PROGRAMME: ZT/JA/19/4  67
WORLD VIEW /PM NEWS
TRANSMISSION: TO BE DECIDED
PACKAGE 2

## BEN MADDOX REPORTING

*Shots of the interior – Botae Stadium – floodlights on a lush green pitch giving a theatrical feel to the evening. Both teams – Real Botae in all red, Sikakoko Arsenal in blue shirts and white shorts – are warming up.*

*The camera pans around the ground. It is half empty, and the Sikakoko end has no more than a hundred youngish men dancing and chanting for their team: We are Sikakoko! Fear us! We are Sikakoko! Fear us! The camera closes in on this group, concentrating on some of the fervent faces.*

*The camera pulls back from the Sikakoko end and pans to the Real Botae end. Here, by contrast, the spectators are standing still, with their mouths closed.*

### Ben Maddox: (voice over):

I have never heard anything like this. Look at these still, silent faces, and wait for a gap in the Sikakoko chanting. Watch with me, and listen.

*Cut to a Sikakoko quiet moment.*

**Ben Maddox (voice over):**

Listen! It's uncanny! I hope our microphone can pick this up.

*Against a panning shot of Real Botae spectators' faces, all their mouths in a wide, fixed smile, a sinister hissing can be heard.*

**Ben Maddox (voice over):**

*(Whispering)* Can you hear that hissing? It's the sound of derision, of a dignified sort of disgust for the atrocity of two nights ago, when the Yoori extremists struck.

*Cut to close-ups of the Sikakoko Arsenal players, some kicking in, others turning to look at the hissing spectators – intercut standing still – most of whom are in black, looking like death themselves.*

*One young Sikakoko player, number 23, stares, and then runs to foot-juggle a ball.*

**Ben Maddox (voice over):**

*(Whispering)* I have never heard such a sinister and effective protest – although, as the Botae spectator said earlier, these players are not all Yoori. And there will be Yoori players in the Real side, too. But what effect will it have on the game? How do players' nerves deal with this sort of thing? They're used to booing, they have overcome racist chants in England, but how do they cope with this sibilant sound of hostility?

Muj Kal had never heard anything like that. The sound the Real Botae crowd made seemed to seep into the skin like a poisonous gas. The stadium here was smaller than at Sikakoko, the hating crowd tighter and closer. And being in the starting eleven at this level was a nervy experience, anyway; nothing had had the chance to happen in the game for him to go on and improve upon as a substitute – tonight someone on the bench would be wanting to replace *him*. Which is what fired-up Muj Kal, the reaction that could make the difference between a useful player and a potentially great one. Hostility, nerves, fear, they all call up the adrenalin that makes players like him take chances, be special, play their own game. No one's ever a genius in a training match: skilful, technically brilliant, yes – but sporting greatness comes with the nerves sucked out of you by the drawn breath of the occasion. Facing the 'home' end he defiantly kept up the ball for fifty, before turning on it and lashing it into his own net.

He looked around him, at his own Arsenal side of internationals and greats, to see that no one was especially looking at him. Before lining up he'd had no ruffles of his hair, no slaps on the back, no special words of encouragement, no more than the usual gee-ing up passed around between the team anyway. He was out there. He belonged. He had a full and equal place in tonight's team, and a fervent need to do well for himself. That was why he was wearing the shirt from the first whistle, wasn't it?

The sinister hissing went on. But thoughts of the bombing, the attack, the deaths and the terrible injures had to be pegged back with his clothes down in the 'away' changing room. Right now, under these floodlights, winning the game was his only concern.

# SIKAKOKO'S SAVIOUR

Graphic report:  Michael Kasea

## Real Botae 0
## Sikakoko Arsenal 1

This politically charged match could have been a flat affair. Local derbies often disappoint, where there's too much testosterone in the air for the game's good. The Botae crowd hissed at Sikakoko to spread a shroud of contempt over the visiting team, Lansans scorning Yooris, making it not only a local derby but a racial derby, too – although Arsenal's Yoori players number only five.

It was one of them, though, a Yoori boy brought on through the club's youth policy, who decided this match.

Okay, it *was* a turgid first half, where the modest floodlights were the brightest participants. Botae's leading scorer Nkruma wasted a heading opportunity in the twenty-eighth minute, meeting the ball as awkwardly as a man bumping into his ex-wife. Charlie Akrofi, for Sikakoko, was put through into the penalty area by an incisive pass from Muj Kal a minute from the end of the first forty-five, but he trod on it as if it were a supporter's balloon, and the chance was missed.

It was this same Muj Kal, though, who enlivened the second half. As the game wore on he took more and more responsibility for what the Sikakoko team did. Seen in previous games as a champagne cork substitute, last night as a starter he popped and bubbled enough for a whole vintage of Bollinger. For the last half hour he dominated the attacking midfield with steadfast tackling and astute passing. He saw possible angled balls like a snooker player, feeding Charlie Akrofi until the striker was taken off, and then feeding his substitute, Ken Koomson.

But Kal's greatest moment was for himself, in the seventy-seventh minute. He came back to the edge of his own area for a rolled-out ball on the left, took the diagonal that the referee runs, deep into the Botae half – beating Jessop with what seemed like five quick feet, remarkable in itself – then played a quick one-two with Atcho who was tight-roping along the touchline, and cut inside to thread through the Botae back four like silken embroidery. Wrong-footing international defender Lemaire – brick wall suddenly turned to gauze – he chipped the advancing keeper to secure the Sikakoko lead, which they weren't going to be giving away.

With five minutes to go, Muj Kal came off, for manager George Chognon to bring on solid defender Abankwa, and sit heavily on the lead.

This was a sad night at a tragic football ground, lifted by the emergence of a young player to watch. Muj Kal. I won't tell you to remember the name – there's no need: it's with us now.

Muj Kal clattered into the 'away' changing room on his studded boots, trying to look normal and modest. But whatever did or didn't get said now, he knew that he would never forget having the life hugged out of him by Lansan internationals and premiership greats. Making and scoring that winning goal had mixed their perspiration with his: real, professional, shared sweat. He was so high that he saw over the heads of players he'd looked up to before. He'd never forget it: it was a run of play that he knew would be with him for ever, marked in his life like one of the boxed passages in his father's Bible. The game at nil-nil, a draw and one point a satisfactory result in this difficult away fixture. All game, the ball had been slow coming from the back; the defenders had passed about among themselves too much. So, midway through the second half, he'd started going back for the ball himself, collecting it and using it as well as he could to feed his lone striker. But suddenly, about a quarter of an hour before the end, he'd seen a gap in the Botae pattern of defence. There was a diagonal channel – he could see it like a track through trees – while the game had been all straight up and back so far. He took the channel, and the Botae midfield didn't know whose responsibility he was, and whether to track him for a tackle or fall back and leave him to a defender: by which time he was well into their half on the opposite side of the pitch. Botae's number six decided to take him on, came in for a Block, but with a double step-over he passed him, leaving the man to his obscenities, and slid a quick ball to 'Birdy' Atcho on the wing. Birdy tapped it on beautifully, seven or eight metres ahead of him as he ran into the space. A quick look up, and Muj could see that Botae's back four was square, contorting into a diamond as he beat the left back and ran across and through them – the best route because it was the one they didn't anticipate.

Don't do the obvious thing!

Forget the training pitch instructions!

Beat them once, and go around and beat them again if that's what surprises!

The hissing from the crowd had stopped; now they were shouting scared at their defenders, and suddenly it was Johnny Lemaire the great international coming at him. He was as big as a redwood tree, and growling as he tried to time his tackle, those great legs ready for a left or a right-hand tap past, leaving his feet a bit too far apart – just room for Muj to slide the ball through them. Nutmeg! And the rest was easy. The keeper came off his line like a Baoulé bull, and the ball had bobbled on a scuff of pitch, sitting up nicely for Muj to get an instep under it, and lob it half a metre over the keeper's head and into the Botae net. Sweet. Memorable. As an old man, he knew, he'd sit and remember that run – if Yusa spared him that long.

When Mr George Chognan came into the changing room Muj shook the French coach's hand with the strongest of grasps. 'Good!' said the man. He put a palm on each of Muj's cheeks. 'Three good points, we go second, and for you– ' he pinched the cheeks, tweaking them painfully '–for you we can ask two million dollars more.' He moved away to talk to others in the changing room as they stripped to go padding towards the showers; with Muj Kal staring after him.

He knew he was called 'home-grown talent': but with a shiver in the humid room, Mujiba Kulala suddenly felt like something to be sold at the roadside. Merchandise.

# ZEPHON TELEVISION

## Transcript of Football Coverage
## Real Botae/Sikakoko Arsenal

**APRIL 27 Botae Africa Olympic Stadium,
Botae, Lansana**

PROGRAMME: **ZT/JA/19/4  67**
WORLD VIEW /PM NEWS?
TRANSMISSION: **TO BE DECIDED**
**PACKAGE 3**

### BEN MADDOX REPORTING

*Shots of the football pitch as the players of both teams walk off, escorted by
forty or fifty police, who form a protective corridor for the players to walk
to the tunnel and the changing rooms. Players from each side are talking
to one another, no aggression between them, only a professional respect.*

*The camera pans the emptying ground. There is no more hissing as the
tiers empty quickly into the night.*

<u>**Ben Maddox (voice over):**</u>
So the game ends and the Real Botae spectators go home
to their families. The sporting contest is over, and real life
resumes. But let's be clear – the roots of football are in the
poorer quarters of our cities, it has always been a game to
take the mind off the drear and grind of real life; and off its
tragedies, too.

## Close-up of Ben Maddox in the stand, microphone in view, sporting commentator mode:

And in the way these things happen, a young man has tur ned the focus of a difficult night away from tragedy and onto himself. His name?

*Intercut with individual shot of Muj Kal as he walked off the pitch moments before.*

## Ben Maddox (voice over):

Mujiba Kalala, known as Muj Kal.

*Replay of Muj Kal's run from his own penalty area to the scoring of his goal (insert 24 secs. of match coverage, 77th minute courtesy Lansana National Television), crowd effects added.*

## Ben Maddox (as before):

The goal that was the climax of his night. The player who silenced the Botae hissing. So, are the Botae directors pleased that they carried on and staged this game?

*Corridor behind the directors' box. Men in suits, colourful shirts and kaftans are coming towards the camera and into the hospitality lounge, camera left.*

## Ben Maddox (voice over):

We're high above the terraces, it could be a normal evening match up here. Excuse me, sir…(*Ben stops a large Lansanan wearing a white suit with a red and white (Real Botae) bow tie.*) Zephon Television, London. How did you feel this evening went – talking about the night as a whole?

**<u>Real Botae Director:</u>**

Not so good. Botae needed the winning tonight. It was
owing to the people of the town, the team let them down.
*(Goes to move on.)*

**<u>Ben Maddox:</u>**

But for players and spectators, were you right to stage the
match so soon after the tragedy? Was it a hard decision to
take, with the town in mourning?

**<u>Real Botae Director:</u>**

*(Shrugs)* I'm not knowing. Before, thinking we win, we have no
doubts, no, not a hard decision, sir. Now...well, it was
a game of football only. And we lost. *(He moves on)*.

*The camera focus changes to pick up others coming along the
corridor – and concentrates on the bald-head of a white man
further back.*

**<u>Ben Maddox:</u>**

And there's Eamonn Reilly, the old Spurs and Republic of
Ireland player. Mr Reilly, a sombre night, but a bright talent
to lift the evening?

*Eamonn Reilly ignores the camera and the question, walks on past
as if reporter and cameraman don't exist.*

**<u>Eamonn Reilly (out of vision) gratingly:</u>**

Turn that scabbin' thing off! There's no cameras allowed up
here.
*Cut*

Ben felt a tap on his shoulder – and knew that Jonny had done as the man asked. Within five minutes, though, Eamonn Reilly was all smiles as he brought beer to the round aluminium table in the stadium lounge.

'Something secret going on?' Jonny asked him, direct and professional. He didn't take kindly to being told to stop shooting, not even by a boyhood hero.

'Whenever isn't there?' the Irishman replied. 'Jee-sus, whether it's on account of Aer Lingus stewardesses or tappers from other clubs, I've needed spy-holes on my hotel doors for ever, especially from people like yourselves...'

'So what's the secret out here?' Ben asked him, although he and Jonny both knew what it was.

'You saw him tonight, eh? The young bucko.'

'Mujiba Kalala?'

'That's the item.' Like any dedicated whiskey man Eamonn Reilly didn't touch his own beer – they didn't serve such gold here. Instead, his eyes flicked from one to the other of the Zephon men.

'For which club, you saw him?' Jonny asked. 'The Lilywhites, Spurs?'

The old Irish international picked his nose with his thumb. Thinking time, Ben knew, like one of his own sneezes. But he could see the glaze of disenchantment harden over Jonny's eyes: football heroes were for the live pitch where there were no close-ups.

'If I should tell you, and promise on the memory of the aul wan to give you the world exclusive, will you cut me out of that little crowd scene there?' Reilly jerked his head to where they'd been shooting out in the corridor.

'You have any problem with that?' Jonny asked Ben. 'I don't.'

Ben thought about it. The man had just revealed a weakness, wanted to do a deal: which meant that Zephon had the upper hand. *You don't waste positions of strength,* he could hear Kath Lewis saying it.

'Would your exclusive include a full interview, with a commentary against live action, of why you're interested in Kalala?' he asked.

Eamonn Reilly's eyes told Ben that he knew he wasn't dealing with a Spurs or Ireland fan but a pro reporter. 'Within reason,' he said tersely, and now he did take a gulp from his glass.

'It wouldn't be other than Tottenham, would it?' Jonny asked. 'Twenty years, I watched you at the Lane...'

Eamonn Reilly laughed. 'Love Our Lady, am I that dossin' *auld*?'

'Spurs, not Liffey Athletic?' Ben stilletoed in, to catch the man mid-laugh, semi-relaxed, half-winning.

'What the holy heck do you know of that shambolic little outfit?' Reilly demanded. 'You brought a "Who's-flamin'-Who" in your knapsack?'

Suddenly Ben felt like a north London Arsenal fan who'd wiled his way into the White Hart Lane players' lounge. 'We get our research done,' he said.

'Routine, research is routine in this job,' Jonny interceded. 'Like your own scouting notes...'

'Liffey Pathetic? Charity,' Eamonn Reilly chose to tell them. 'I come from the god-forsaken place. I sit on their board so's my name can sit on their beggin' notepaper.'

'That's what we reckoned,' Ben came back. 'Didn't we?' Jonny nodded. 'So we take it, it *is* Spurs?'

'Surely it is.' Eamonn Reilly reached into his shirt pocket. 'And to show you my great good nature, I'll give you a look at this.' He pulled out a folded sheet of paper, azure, with the Atlantic View Hotel crest upon it. 'My scouting notes.' He laid it on the table, nearer to Jonny than to Ben, and avoiding a pool of condensation off his glass. And as Jonny Aaranovitch picked it up to read it, the Irishman laid down his terms for a deal – avoiding any blurry misinterpretations.

'When the signing's in the bag – or when the moment fits otherwise – I'll be lettin' you know, and we'll set up a session with Lansan TV. Studio, run the footage, exclusive to your good selves…' He was looking at Jonny who was reading his report on Muj Kal, but his attention was on Ben.

'What "fitting moment otherwise" might there be?' Ben asked him.

Eamonn Reilly leaned back, opened his arm to let amateur Ben in on a professional secret. 'Oh, the seller comin' over all reluctant, or an over-valuing agent. Letting the press know about your shenanigans can sometimes force a move in your own good self's direction. It sort of lights your way home…'

'Okay.'

'But Eamonn Reilly's not out here, all right? Until I say he is, he's a million miles from Lansana.'

'Fair enough.'

'Now,' Reilly relaxed, actually drank some of his beer. 'Do you go along with me about young bucko?' he asked Jonny Aaranovitch. 'You know the Spurs style – it's never really changed, except under George Graham…' And his eyes followed Jonny's down onto the sheet of paper, his scouting notes.

'Not that that's what we're here for,' Ben muttered darkly into his glass.

## ATLANTIC VIEW HOTEL
## BAY ROAD, JOHNSTOWN, LANSANA

Scouting report on
Muj Kal, Sikakok Arsenal – 27 April
Versus Real Botae

Blue shirt, no.23    Started match, seen him
before as sub at Johnstown.

Natural ball player. Flair. Takes chances but
mostly paying off.

First half: positioning good, anticipates the likely
ball.
Not great with head but got Georgie Best feet.
Needs to work on this.
Not too tall, low centre of grav. Swerves, runs,
looks about him.
No real chance to show out this half.

2nd half
Set out his stall and took the game on. Not
greedy but took his chances. Skills galore, bit of
Eusebeo about him, good first touch, dribbling – ball
always under control. Balance like a wire walker.

Basics: throw-ins, making himself available, fitness
– all good.
Decent young pro – looks healthy – will need
good medical (lot of AIDS, TB around)

Scored exceptional goal – match winner – involved foresight, skill, surprise, chance-taking, <u>bravery</u>.

<u>Over-all</u> Bit slight, needs building up.
Wd fit in well with Spurs' set-up. Paxton Road would love the boy.
Got Hoddle's style with Greavsie's finish.

<u>Recommend Spurs makes an opening offer.</u>

EReilly


Jonny passed the paper to Ben, who'd already read it, upside down. 'Fair enough,' Ben said. He'd somehow thought that a scouts' report would be more technical – anyone in the stadium could have written most of this.

'These points,' Jonny asked, 'your professional assessment, you'd make them in an interview?'

'If he scribbles his name on the contract. You can have an exclusive interview with him ahead of a Spurs' press conference – that's a cinch of a promise.'

'And if he doesn't sign in the end?' Ben asked.

'None of it's news, anyway, then! Not worth the satellite time filing it. The story's him, not me.' Eamonn Reilly picked up his report and put it back in his pocket. 'I'm auld history, brother, not news.'

But as the three of them shook hands on the secrecy-for-now deal, Ben couldn't help but wonder how far that statement was true...

# Joyce Avoka's story –
## written up by R. A. – part 6

General Lakle was as close to looking contented as Joyce had seen him, and she had seen plenty of the Red Fire leader. He wasn't remote, he was among the tents a lot, more often the boys' than the girls' – but then there were more of them to keep on their toes. When he had a lieutenant with him he would swoop to inspect in unusual places. Sergeant Six made sure the sleeping tents were tidy – but General Lakle would march into the mess tent, roll up his sleeves, and delve his hands into sacks of rice, or flour. In the chemical latrine area with its chipped enamel pans, he would have his lieutenant prod and poke with a stick for anything more solid than human waste. Like every revolutionary leader ever, he was a prime target for a traitorous attack.

Today, though, he called a parade of the Botae raiding party to debrief them on their night's work: not only the men of the manganese mine bombing platoon, but the young soldier ants who had terrified the township outskirts. There they all sat, shivering under the open-sided canopy, cross-legged, arms folded at the correct angles. Had they pleased him? Was he in a happy mood, or foul?

The general entered and showed his soldiers' teeth in a smile. 'The Botae mission was well done,' he told them. 'Yusa will be pleased with you. You are the troops upon whose backs our independence from Lansana will be built. You – and others like you – will carry us like the biggest, strongest, fieriest swarm of courageous soldier ants ever to tread this earth.' He looked around the faces, nodding as he spoke, as if he was aware of the colourful words he was deliberately using for these troops to quote later. 'No hitches going and coming, no losses, manganese mining halted, and a Lansan township living in holy fear of us.' He stood to attention as he spoke. Despite his words he wasn't a performing speaker; but he always had his troops' attention, he had no need to try to hold it through stage-craft.

'Where next?' he growled. 'Every Lansan town in the north is asking this question. Because every Lansan town in the north is expecting to *be* the next to be attacked. Yoori Red Fire has claimed responsibility, these people know who we are, our cause is known, we can squeeze their fear in the grip of our hands.' He paused and took a sip of water from the table behind him. 'But now it is Yoori people who need to know more clearly that Red Fire is the only effective cause for the Yoori clan. In Yusa's name. And we shall attend to that: no one Yoori will be above being Yoori.'

Joyce Forty-five sat listening with the rest, her breathing perhaps more shallow, less whole-hearted than the others, because she was here being thanked for doing something that she had failed to do.

'For the present,' General Lakle went on, 'swell your hearts with your parts in our struggle, especially our first-time recruits. You discharged your duties well. Yusa and Yoori generations in heaven are proud of you. We wait for delivery of the "big one" that will bring our final victory, but until that day, we can count on you!' There were frowns from the sergeants at the mention of some 'big one', but abruptly, the Red Fire leader turned smartly on his heel and marched from the canopy, as his lieutenant led the regulation twenty seconds of clapping.

On Sergeant Six's commands, Joyce's tent stood up from their crossed-legged position, one movement, like gymnasts. Just in front of them, a tent of boys had already been commanded to stand by their own sergeant. But with the general gone, the atmosphere under the canopy relaxed, and the heady air of congratulation from the leader hung all around like swung incense. So Joyce was not surprised when the boy in front of her turned to look over his shoulder. It was her partner from the alley, the boy who had carried the grenade when she had carried a rock.

'Yusa sees everything!' the boy muttered at her. Joyce stared into his eyes. 'Everything!' he said, before his tent was marched off.

And a terrified emptiness dropped into the Joyce's stomach, as she and her tent of soldier ants was marched back to their lines – past the hanging rope that swung for traitors on its high crossbar.

# MEMORANDUM OF AGREEMENT

## GENERAL OUTLINE PRECEDING FULL
## AND LEGALLY BINDING CONTRACT

BETWEEN THE LEGAL GUARDIAN OF MUJIBA KALALA
(HEREAFTER REFERRED TO AS 'THE CLIENT') AND
GERALD ABOWA (HEREAFTER REFERRED TO AS 'THE AGENT')

IN WHICH THE AGENT AGREES TO REPRESENT THE CLIENT'S INTERESTS
AGAINST THOSE OF ANY THIRD PARTY (REGISTERED FOOTBALL CLUB AND/OR
SPORTING ASSOCIATION AND/OR MEDIA/ADVERTISING INTEREST), SUBJECT TO
THE FULL AND INFORMED WISHES OF THE SAID CLIENT.

Clause 1: the agent in representing the client does so at his/her own expense, such expense to include travel, accommodation, staffing, inconvenience, etc.

Clause 2: at all times the agent puts first the best professional and personal interests of the client.

Clause 3: in respect of the foregoing, the client agrees to pay to the agent 15 % (fifteen per cent) of his/her weekly, monthly, annual remuneration – including one-off payments and 'benefits' – before the deduction of tax where applicable and of any expenses.

Clause 4: in respect also of clause 2, the client agrees to pay to the agent 25% (twenty-five percent) of any negotiated signing-on or transfer fee.

Clause 5: so far as the client's personal terms are concerned, the agent will negotiate on the client's behalf, remuneration to be paid to the agent of 15% (fifteen per cent) of the monetary value of such personal terms (eg, value of house(s), car(s), medical insurance, etc.)

Clause 6: any disputed areas in clauses 2 and 5 will be subject to the ruling of the international governing body of the sport concerned, without prejudice to the client's or the agent's rights in law.

ON GENERAL AND TEMPORARILY NON-BINDING ACCEPTANCE OF THESE OUTLINE TERMS, A PROPERLY AUTHORISED AND LEGALLY BINDING CONTRACT WILL BE DRAWN UP BETWEEN THE PARTIES WITHIN FORTY-EIGHT HOURS, SUCH CONTRACT TO BE SIGNED AND WITNESSED WITHIN SEVENTY-TWO HOURS OF ITS RECEIPT.

Signed............................................................................................. *the client*

Signed............................................................................................. *witness*

Dated..................................................

Signed............................................................................................. *the agent*

Signed............................................................................................. *Witness*

Dated..................................................

## SIKAKOKO TOWNSHIP

Gerald Abowa laid the document in front of Muj's father as if it were a treaty of peace between two peoples, and with it, balanced on his soft palm, was his gold Mont Blanc fountain pen.

The Mercedes Benz had arrived outside Muj Kal's house before the footballer had left the Real Botae stadium. The distance between the towns was around seventy kilometres, and even had Golden Glasses been at the match it wouldn't have been the greatest of feats to beat the boy home.

There was an expectation at the house that Muj would be home from the match soon. He kept his bicycle at the Sikakoko ground, chained in the car park among other players' cars and, allowing for the team coach journey back from Botae, his parents knew within half-an-hour or so what time to expect his light to shine along the red clay road. They were anxious tonight, though, with their son going to Botae where there would be a ferment of resentment for what the Red Fire had done. But the Sikakoko club had its own security guards travelling with them, and a big police presence was promised. It was a deferential knock on the front screen, though, not the screech and skid of Muj coming in at the back that had Muj's parents' heads shooting up. Nokongolo Kalala had hurried to open the door.

'Gerald Abowa.' It was Golden Glasses, a smile gripping him as tightly as he gripped his crocodile skin briefcase.

'Did I telephone to you?' Muj's father asked – not rudely, but affecting a hazy sort of memory.

172

'You did not, sir.' Golden Glasses unzipped some more of his smile, till the stitching began to fray. 'But I have news for you...' He hovered there, doing the accepted thing of shutting the mosquito screen behind him.

'Come in.' Muj's father took a lingering look outside, but all he saw was the outline of the Mercedes Benz at the gate; and within five minutes he had been told the situation. A scout who had been tracking Mujiba had seen him play that night: because he – Gerald Abowa – had previously arranged with Mr George Chognon, the Sikakoko manager, to play Mujiba from the start of the game, to show him off. Mujiba had played well, and the scout had let both Sikakoko and himself know that he was interested in signing Mujiba for an English premiership club. *How about that?* Abowa's smile and wide arms asked the question of Muj's father.

'So, to be clear, what is your part in this?' Nokongola Kalalala's face was unchanged. Truly joyous news for him came from the word of Yusa in the Bible, and earthly good news tonight would be the safe return of his son.

The agreement form was quickly brought out of the briefcase. 'Players do not act alone, for themselves, Mr Kalala. They have agents...'

'And you are one of these people?'

'As I explained before. I act on the player's behalf.'

'And – without offence, sir – why you?' Nokongola's head was on one side, like testing Muj on his Bible study.

'Regard the document, if you please. Look particularly at clauses three and four.' Nokongolo Kalala wound his wire spectacles onto his face, and read. 'You will see that my percentages are of a good order; in short, I come cheaper for you than other agents...'

'Oh? Why should you do that?' Muj's father put the document down.

It was professional, the spiel. 'Because Mujiba is not well-known. For the international stars I represent–' and he named half a dozen, all African '–I take bigger commissions. But I make allowances for a new talent, a local boy...'

'You are from near here?'

'Near enough,' Gerald Abowa said. 'You can ask at Sikakoko, go to see the executives there, they will tell you.' He puffed out his lips, like a fat fish. 'I am well-regarded, sir. I am known to be a hard negotiator for my clients, but a fair one.' He slid his hand across the surface of the table in a wiping motion. 'Everything is always as it should be.'

Nokongolo Kalala handed back the draft agreement. 'And your client would be – ?'

The big man frowned. 'Would be you, sir, until Mujiba is of age. Eighteen.'

'It is I who signs any agreement?'

'Indeed.'

Muj's father nodded his understanding, but in an internal sort of way. 'Then Mujiba would have to sign a new agreement with you when he is eighteen...?' The question hung like a globule of honey, gathering before the drop.

'That would be customary.'

'On the same terms...for a local *eighteen year old* boy?'

'Ah. Well...'

Which was when Muj Kal himself screeched home to spill the news of his winning goal.

And at which Gerald Abowa was asked to return the following morning, after family discussion had been

174

held – leaving the draft agreement behind. He went, passing Muj on the veranda, with the sort of smile and bow at him that teachers give to pupils on Parents' Evenings.

Muj didn't know how he felt about the man; it was a mix of pride in being wanted as a client, and of apprehension at being tied to him. Everything in his life was as tangled as a lawyer vine plant. After spilling out his excitement at the scoring of the winning goal – praise Yusa – Muj read the draft agreement standing at the kitchen table; the percentages meaning little to him. But coming over him again was that same feeling of being an article, merchandise, of being goods of some value to someone. That winning goal had been worth a certain amount of money to his club, and he would be required to regularly prove his worth with many more. But this was not what bothered him, he could score his fair share, he knew that. His fear was that this contract was the legal paper work of a sort of sporting slavery.

Would he still be Mujiba Kalala? Or would he be an owned worker with a number on his back instead of a brand on his skin? And would he then be a club possession first, and a Yusa loving Yoori second?

Was that where he wanted his life to go?

# LANSANA SUN

## *Leadercomment*

## YOORI PRIDE!

**A YOUNG MAN** will have woken this morning to the prospect of being a new Yoori idol. Muj Kal, Sikakoko Arsenal's winning goal scorer last night represents the fresh, sporting face of Yoori youth – the sunshine dreams when Red Fire child soldiers are the dark Yoori nightmares.

**WHERE MUJ KAL GOES** in the next few years – and what Muj Kal does – could well be where his fellow youth would like to follow. He is an African role model – while kidnapped grenade throwing, bullet-belted indoctrinated 'soldier ants', who maim fellow Lansanans for a lost cause, are models for youth hatred and despair.

**LOOK UP** to the likes of Muj Kal, Yoori young, he is the new star in your sky.

# YOORI COUNTRY

It was a spooky meeting – as Ben knew that it would be. Interviews where there's a secret location and a lot of waiting, make for jumpy journalists. Rebel leaders are as patient as snakes in long grass, never showing themselves until they're certain there are no forked sticks waiting to pin them to the ground; and President Obed Abu's secret service must certainly have had Charles Henderson marked for 'accidental' execution if he set foot over the Kutuliza border into Lansana.

Ben and Jonny had got nowhere with the 'road accident' moderate's sister. She'd been grieving *sad* not grieving *angry,* and the interview they shot with her wasn't worth satellite time filing it 'down the line' to London. Even Ben's trying to provoke her – *Wasn't your brother selling the Yoori cause short by trying to do a deal with the president?* – drew only a slow shake of the head, and a 'no' said so quietly that the microphone didn't pick it up.

But this man should make better television. Rebekah Arens knew someone who knew someone else with Kutulizan connections who thought that Charles Henderson would talk to British television on the Yoori behalf, and as a 'fixer' she'd proved her worth by getting this meeting set up.

Its location was in an Ade mountain cave where prehistoric people had once lived. Above Sikakoko, in the valley of the dam, a line of weather-worn holes ran along a bluff like wartime shell damage. In the furthest of these, Ben and Jonny were told that they could set up and await the man, who would have come over the Kutuliza border. But they had to be alone.

If they were not alone, the man wouldn't show.

Ben read the map reference, putting his GCSE 'A' in Geography to some use, and with Jonny at the wheel of a hired Jeep they drove alone up the twisting road above the Ade Dam for twenty kilometres, and where a rotting signpost grew out of the scrub they found the track to the historic caves. After a further hour's drive the track ran out and they followed the contour line on foot to the east; and there they came to where a scree of fallen rocks formed rough steps to the line of ancient dwellings above.

A chill wind blew up here as they made the final clamber to the furthest cave, where a profound darkness came malevolently out at them. They approached like cats at a wolf den, edged inside, Ben's eyes taking some time to check the cave's size. It went back thirty or more metres into the mountain, narrowing to a low, dank, corner where water had once dripped. Jonny shone a camera light around, Ben expecting all the time to jump back at the sight of eyes, or the glint of teeth, or the sudden flash of an ambusher's weapon.

'No one here,' he confirmed in a sombre echo.

'No one comes, and J.S. Aaranovitch is wrapping this assignment, I tell you.'

For a few moments Ben saw only the retina memory of the switched-off light in his eyes. 'Up to you.' He deliberately edited his words; but his imprinted image of Jonny was no longer of the man he'd known before they came out to Lansana. Jonny seemed to have lost his edge – and Ben wasn't sure whether to blame Rebekah Arens for that, or Jonny's recent stint in the kibbutz. While Ben Maddox preferred the active life of a TV reporter over a quiet existence with Meera, Jonny

Aaranovitch suddenly seemed to want something else.

These rankling thoughts ate up some of the time – until after nearly two hours of waiting, when Ben's wide eyes could tell this dark cave wall from that dark cave wall, Jonny suddenly stiffened. He had heard something outside: shooting cameramen have the sharpest ears, being blind to everything not seen through their lenses.

'Is coming!' he said, all at once English seeming like his second language.

Ben stood ready, his eyes sharp on the cave entrance – which, he now noticed, was ominously shaped like a skull.

Two men came round its edges, one from either side. They were silhouetted in the entrance, so Ben couldn't see their features, but they were big, and the poke of their gun barrels was menacing. He held his breath as his heart-rate raced. What would they do? Spray their automatics all around the cave? Get rid of two British journalists who were nosing into Red Fire affairs? Was this a set-up, and Rebekah Arens had inadvertently fixed them for good?

The men came further into the cave, and were lost against the widening walls. Now was the moment for something to happen. Ben flashed the camera light. 'In here,' he said – probably the stupidest thing he'd ever said. Of course he and Jonny were in here, there was nowhere else for them to be.

The newcomers' eyes had acclimatized quickly. Sure-footed, they came deeper into the cave and moved to Ben and Jonny. Showing no teeth, they took one of them each and searched their bodies, roughly, expertly – Ben's man smelling of sweat that was even more offensive than his hands. The guy was burly, and youngish – younger than Ben.

'You wait!' Jonny's man said, and while the other covered them both with his matt-black Armalite, he went back to the cave entrance and beckoned the main man in.

Here he comes, Ben thought, the clean European hands that were going to justify a bloody African revolution. The Yoori spokesman.

'Charles Henderson,' the man said smoothly. 'And you're Maddox from Zephon Television.' He looked 'army', a square face, clipped moustache, hair cut short in the American colonel style.

'Ben Maddox,' said Ben, 'and Jonny Aaranovitch, my director.'

Jonny said nothing, but stooped to his camera case.

'So you fine fellows are going to let the Brits know what the Yoori are fighting for?'

Jonny came up, with his Sony DSR camera. 'If Zephon decides to broadcast it,' he said.

'Then you'll have to be very persuasive. The Yoori are the underdogs who need international support, some pressure on the Lansanan government from a country with influence like Britain. All your aid with African debt...'

'Could we save this for the interview?' Ben put in quickly, for a moment his fear of a flat piece overcoming his physical fear of the gunmen with this man.

'Very true.' Henderson spoke carefully, Ben noticed. He sounded all his consonants but fell down on his vowels, like a Londoner who's moved out to Surrey. 'You shoot me in the cave door, no recognisable peaks to show...'

Ben nodded.

'Won't people guess we're in Lansana somewhere?' Jonny asked. 'Those who know anything will know that you mustn't be seen to be in Kutuliza. You're a spokesman for the Yoori, that's all.'

'And that *is* all. "A spokesman for the Yoori".' He clearly knew the journalist code. *A source close to the Prime Minister* usually meant the Prime Minister themself. A *spokesman* could often be the same, like *a close friend of*: they all remained *unattributed,* anonymous: while *off the record* was meant not to be reported at all, simply given or 'spun' to a journalist as background information. 'I am the Yoori political wing, not speaking for Yoori Red Fire.'

'Here okay?' Jonny asked, where the edge of the cave entrance gave way to a distant horizon, creating a sense of depth and space, of remoteness, but not giving away where this man had chosen to be interviewed.

'That's my fellow,' Henderson replied, sounding every bit the old-fashioned white in a black country.

# ZEPHON TELEVISION

## Transcript of Interview with Charles Henderson

**APRIL 29 Yoori Ade Mountains,
north of Sikakoko, Lansana**

**PROGRAMME: ZT/JA/20/1**

**BEN MADDOX PRESENTING**

### EXTRACT

*Long shots of Ade mountain range, general, no caves or recognisable features*

#### Ben Maddox (voice over):

We're in the mountains that would be Yoori – here in the disputed north Lansana territory, belonging until 1918 to Kutuliza next door. Waters from these mountains feed Lansana's hydro-electric dynamo, not far from where I had a secret rendezvous with a man who would like these tribal lands to fit back into their historic part of the west African jigsaw. Back into Yoori Kutuliza.

*Shot of a powerful hydro-electric stream, dissolving into a medium close-up of Charles Henderson.*

#### Charles Henderson:

I am not a man of war, I am a man of peace, speaking for the Yoori people who want independence from Lansana, and the right to choose their country of paternity.

**Ben Maddox (off camera):**

Which you – they'd – like to be Kutuliza to the north, instead of Lansana?

**Charles Henderson:**

Perhaps. Maybe not. The Yoori people would do the choosing, a referendum, democratically run. This is all they ask for – a peaceful and democratic choice by local people…

**Ben Maddox (off camera):**

Then how do you square that with the recent Yoori Red Fire attack on Botae? Wasn't that an attempt at bullying Lansanans to say, 'good riddance!' to the Yoori North East Region, despite its water power wealth?

**Charles Henderson:**

Let me make this clear. I am not Red Fire. This is a mistake that many observers make. What I speak for is the political arm of Yoori Independence. And–

**Ben Maddox (off camera):**

Like Mbidi Renula, another moderate Yoori – but who died violently a month or so ago?

**Charles Henderson:**

In a road accident, as the police inquest found. But you can understand why the legitimate political wing needs to have its voice heard. Furthermore –

**Ben Maddox (off camera):**

Although your voice is not African, let alone Yoori?

**Charles Henderson (with cut-aways of Ben Maddox listening):**

I'm cool with that. Let me explain. My grandfather was Yoori who married out, to the daughter of an aid worker. I was not born Yoori but I have deliberately chosen to align myself with Yoori, which gives my status even greater strength, don't you think? We can't choose our parents, but we can choose our friends.

**Ben Maddox:**

So how will the Yoori get what they want, peacefully? And is there a time scale?

**Charles Henderson:**

By persuasion. By making people – by *helping* people see the justness of the Yoori cause. The Yoori are a people who once owned these lands, but after a war a hundred years ago – which was not their war – these lands were given to others. Germany lost that war, so the Yoori lost, too – where's the justice in that?

*Charles Henderson stops speaking, leaves a gap for Ben Maddox to speak, but BM remains silent.*

**Charles Henderson:**

We want influential people to champion our cause. On the international stage we want it raised at the United Nations. But nearer home, we want the young to see that their favourite bands, and singers, and sportsmen support the Yoori cause, to see that they are part of it. Sport the wristbands, wear the T-shirts, be proud. Make it cool to be Yoori. And the timescale? Events will determine how soon we achieve our aims.

*Shot of Ben Maddox looking sceptical.*

**Ben Maddox (off camera):**

Do you condemn blowing people up?

**Charles Henderson:**

I've told you, I'm not Red Fire. Please don't make the
mistake of confusing me with Red Fire. I am political,
they are militant. But you if you ask about time-scale – I regret
to say that the Red Fire methods might be quicker than mine.

**Ben Maddox (off camera):**

And deaths. You accept Red Fire effectiveness – but do you
condemn them for what they do?

**Charles Henderson:**

It's not for me to condemn or otherwise. I am an observer
of those violent events, like you. No more than that.

**Ben Maddox (into camera):**

But I condemn them. Wholeheartedly.

**Charles Henderson:**

Words. I prefer action. Peaceful, persuasive action.

**Ben Maddox (off camera, sceptical):**

Through popular music and sport? T-shirts and wrist bands?
Getting footballers on your marches?

**Charles Henderson (after a long pause):**

You make me sound trivial, Mr Maddox. And I am not trivial.
I mean business, believe me...

*Cut*  **END OF EXCERPT**

In London, Kath Lewis turned away from the television monitor. She called through to the news office for Bloom Ramsaran, who had been watching the package on her own screen.

'Good to hear his voice,' Bloom said, as she went into the news editor's office.

Kath Lewis gave her a long look. 'Just remind me never to put you and Maddox on an assignment together!'

'We'd be good for one another!'

'That man, Henderson–' Kath Lewis flicked a hand at the frozen screen '–he's definitely batting for the Yooris to be Kutulizan...'

'Cricket, there's a game I like...'

'I just wonder whether there could be other players on this pitch. Bigger.' Kath Lewis looked up at Bloom while she pouring herself a glass of Bordeaux.

'Like, who, bigger? Isn't this a local African conflict?'

Kath Lewis didn't answer, pursued her own thoughts. 'Probably. Just wondered who might have an interest in these African states? China, yet?'

Bloom watched Kath Lewis take something between a sip and a gulp of the red wine. 'You mean, who wants to sell them something?'

'Could be. Arms? Railway systems? Roads? Power stations?' Kath looked up at Bloom and raised her voice to lead-story level. 'Nuclear capability?'

'I'll do some research,' Bloom said, as calmly as an academic.

Kath Lewis turned her back on Bloom, moving on to something else now. Bloom went, got all the way to the door before she swung round to say, 'I'm reckoning those boys risked a lot for that interview.' And went.

These days I have good reason to be on the top of the world. The radio has talked about me, the television has shown my goal from Wednesday night, kids cycle past my house and nearly fall off, looking sideways for me. When the press gets hold of you they treat you like a favourite son, I guess until a younger brother comes along.

At the training ground I am always thrown the bib that puts me in with the senior players, a small club within the club, that talks easily to one another, internationals and me like a special gang who can jest and laugh. Since Wednesday — my goal, and what I said to Charlie Akrofi about not being his servant — means I am not the one who always has to run to get the over-kicked ball, the nearest one goes, World Cup player or not.

But I am not easy in my bed — at night alone when I am thinking about things. I see beyond the rope barrier where the scouts stand from other clubs who come to see the training sessions, and I feel like a racehorse being judged. Already I know that I am someone to be sold to the highest bidder. I know that if my father signs the contract with Mr Gerald Abowa, I will have no choice more than my ancestors had, those who were taken to the slave boats. No, that is too strong, I will not diminish THEM, I am very lucky — but I will be tied up by legal conditions, by a commitment to a big business football club with money people to please, profits to make.

By the light of my torch I read the Bible and look at the prophet Yusa's life. It's written, 'He laid aside the bags of gold, pushed from him the frankincense of flattery; yeah, he

trod a lonely, uphill path towards
the truths of heaven, and in his
heart he knew that this was the road
to God.' And Yusa has inspired our
Yoori people to worship him for his
goodness to the ancient Yoori Kings
and their Queen Mothers, never
failing to answer their prayers.
Which is the same life as my father
tries to lead, and which I know in a
perfect world for him he would want
for me to follow. But choosing the
life to lead is harder, not easier,
when fame is starting to walk beside
you, step by step.

**From:** k.lewis@zephontv.co.uk
**Sent: 30 April**    14:00
**To:** benmaddox@talktalk.net
**Subject:** Assigment

Hi, you two

We slipped in a two minute package of the Red Fire Botae attack, wrapped it with the Henderson interview.

We were right to put it at the bottom of the slate, not too much interest shown here in UK.

I thought there could be bigger players in this game, but I'm not sure now. Bloom's probably right, it is just a local conflict, and you could be risking your necks for next to nothing.

On the other hand the good news – the sports desk wants more on the football stuff, waiting for it, so you'd better be first, and it had better be good.

As a last throw on that story I'm also getting Bloom to do some more digging on the Irishman – her request, really.

But I'm nearly ready to call you back, annual leave starting to need cover. And there might be a snap election here. For God's sake try to get a fresh angle on the Yoori Independence fight. Can you get to some of those Red Fire kid soldiers? Advertisers pay top rates to slot-in with news bulletins of youth gone wrong.

Be good!

Kath Lewis

## SHERRIN'S HOTEL, SIKAKOKO

Ben and Jonny sat in the hotel bar, separated by the e-mail on the table. This hotel was a series of bungalow rooms in a small park, and the bar was in a building of its own – reached through a torrential downpour – which hadn't improved Jonny's liking for this assignment. These days, far from him being the director, the leader, Ben saw him more and more as a reluctant necessity. His own reporter's hopes from back in England had been dampened, and he was starting to wish he'd come alone, with a pick-up cameraman from Lansana TV in Johnstown.

Ben wiped his hair and face with his handkerchief and looked at the man who was reading Kath Lewis's e-mail with a frown. His last visit to his beloved kibbutz, and the work he talked to Rebekah Arens about, the film and photography course for young Israeli talent, were the only subjects that got him animated right now. Well, he'd chosen a bad time to want to hit the comfort zone; because Ben Maddox still had a long way that he wanted to go in the job he'd chosen for developing his own young talent.

Jonny pushed the e-mail aside to lean a wet elbow on the table. He waved to the girl at the bar. 'Stupid Kath Lewis!' he moaned. And, 'Three beers!' to the bar girl. Rebekah Arens would be joining them when the rain laid off a bit. 'Umbrella – you got one?' he asked Ben.

'Would a man this wet have an umbrella somewhere?' Ben said. He wanted to ask why Jonny thought Kath Lewis was stupid, but that would have sounded too 'head prefect'. He needed to get talking fast, though, before

Rebekah came. If he and Jonny were going to have a row, the worst of it was best kept between the two of them.

'I think we give it our best last shot,' Ben said. 'I hear what you say about the dangerous streets of Kutuliza – but let's get up there and see what we can dig out on the Red Fire from the other side. That's where their funding is, their lines of communication, and Charlie Henderson…'

Jonny eyed him, and didn't shift his focus as the beers came. 'You really are that ambitious, aren't you?'

'Why not? We're on a story—'

'Two stories, with the football. And I like the football better…'

'Sure – I don't take away from that. But the African political story's going to blow up bigger, really big, either this year or next. And it looks like we've got no competition, no BBC, no Sky News – not yet. When it does all go off, the Yoori lands will start being talked about like Angola, Zimbabwe, big stuff – and we'll be the guys who alerted the world. They'll all be paying to show the package we've sent, as background to their own stuff.' There was only one pair of eyes in the world for Ben right now, and they were Jonny's. 'If that's being ambitious, Jonny, I'm ambitious. But I'd prefer to say I'm just a jobbing newsman doing a newsman's job.'

'Nice, Ben, I like it!' Rebekah had run in through the rain to drip her words over Ben.

Jonny got up, sat her down, and in doing so he folded Kath Lewis's e-mail away into his shirt pocket. 'So,' he told Rebekah, 'there's a cool, wet beer for you; in return for which, it looks like Mr Maddox and I want two air tickets into Kutuliza. Is that a problem?'

Rebekah sat and sipped at her beer, then suddenly threw it back in her throat. 'Whatever,' she said. 'That's the sort of thing I'm paid to fix.'

Ben stared into his glass. Back in Paris he'd laid out for Meera his determination to carry on doing his go-getting, sometimes dangerous, journalist job. And, *good*, he thought now. *So Jonny does know where his duty lies.*

# WILL ARSENAL GO TOP ON SUNDAY?

**Graphic report: Michael Kasea**

Muj Kal, Sikakoko Arsenal's winner of the Real Botae game, is named in the squad for the 'six point' game at Mfinimfini on Sunday. Whoever wins this top-of-the-table clash will sit three points clear of the nearest rivals, and open a five point gap between the top two and the third placed team, Johnstown Lions.

But will the young, fast, and tricky midfielder, who enjoys his role sitting just behind the front line of attack, be in the starting line-up for this big game?

Manager George Chognon wasn't saying at yesterday's press conference, but he wasn't ruling it out. 'Is it right for a manager to give away his tactics to the other side?' he wanted to know.

Sticking with a winning team is an old adage in football – and managers don't come much older than George Chognon.

The Botae game and its Lansan/Yoori circumstances put Sikakoko Arsenal's next home fixture high on the TV news schedules, and claimed extra space in the newspapers. Carried with it was the growing interest in Sikakoko's emerging new star, Muj Kal – he was right up there with the big names, even though he still hadn't signed any deal with an agent. But what no one had got hold of, not even the 'inside track' Lansana sports press, was the possibility of a Spurs offer for the boy. Eamonn Reilly was managing to keep his activities very quiet.

Muj Kal's first surprise – after the elation of being on the squad sheet again – was being told not to cycle to the training ground on the Sunday. After some light exercise he would go in the team coach to the stadium, which was the normal arrangement; but on this Sunday he would first be picked up from home by a club car, like the senior players who didn't like to drive. And at the end of the match, after the warm-down back at the training ground, he would be driven home in the same car. Muj Kal's car! It was as if he was going to be a star, and stars aren't allowed to be jostled off their bikes by the kids who wait at the gates of training grounds.

It was all building up. The strong wind that sometimes blew south from the Sahara was blowing him further in the direction he was already taking, like a sand buggy gathering speed. And whatever the turmoil of his feelings and thoughts about better serving Yusa and the Yoori, it was hard to put on the brakes.

So, for now, for Sunday, he had to let himself be blown full speed, and do what he was doing more brilliantly than ever, in the name of the prophet.

# ZEPHON TELEVISION

## WORLD MONITORING UNIT

**PROGRAMME: SA/TV/32X**
**SOCCER SALOON**
**DAY/TIME: 20.30 LOCAL TIME**
**SUNDAY 01 MAY**

## BACKGROUND

*A panel of three ex-footballers from the English Premiership are seated on bar stools in a studio 'bar': Johnnie Taylor, Pieter van Heflin, and Scott Paterson – all well-groomed in suits and ties.*

*The 'barman' is Terry Hales, a younger, professional sports presenter with South Africa TV.*

*The plasma wall behind Hales shows the background to the bar – bottles, glasses, with arched across it the location, SOCCER SALOON. On cues for the showing of action clips from that day's games, the plasma wall changes to show them. The panel is discussing that day's Sikakoko Arsenal home game against Mfinimfini.*

### Terry Hales:

So, what did you make of this young Mujiba Kalala – to give him his full name – the new boy wonder, Muj Kal?

### Scott Paterson (brooking no argument, speaking with Scottish certainty):

He's terrific. He's got all the skills, he's young, and he can only get better. The new Pele, for my money.

**Johnnie Taylor:**

They was missin' this lad in the Africa Cup, wasn't they?
God, he would've brung a splash of the old sunshine to that
competition, eh? Phenomenal!

**Pieter van Heflin (with a pronounced Scandinavian accent):**

Which is a very long word for you – so we can say that he has
to be good!

*(General laughs)*
*The plasma screen changes to show an action clip from the first
half of the Sikakoko/Mfinimfini match.*

**Terry Hales:**

This first goal. How about that? Scott?

*Action of Muj Kal on the right side of the field receiving a ball on
his left foot, twisting to run at a Mfinimfini defender down the
right wing. Scott Paterson – leading on this segment – speaks
voice over*

**Scott Paterson (off camera):**

He's taken that ball on his left foot – arguably his weakest –
and straight off he's fooled the defender.  He was expecting
it to be the outside of the right boot, so he's wrong-footed
already – an' see that double step-over!  Magic!  Now they're
all thinking he's going to hug the wing, but watch this – he
cuts inside, he changes pace, and he lets go that rocket of
a shot.  Goal all the way!

**Johnnie Taylor:**

Bobbie Charlton!  Wayne Rooney!

**Scott Paterson:**

Never! No comparisons! This boy's himself. He's the first Muj Kal.

*As the goalkeeper scoops the ball out of the Mfinimfini net, the plasma screen reverts to the 'Soccer Saloon' background.*

**Pieter van Heflin:**

Are you related, or something? Yes, he's good...

**Scott Paterson:**

He's very, very good, make no mistake about that!

**Terry Hales:**

And he made no mistake setting up the second Arsenal goal...

*The plasma screen now changes to a clip from the second half, play running the other way*

**Scott Paterson (voice over the action):**

Terrific. Look at this. Totally different aspect of his game.

*Muj Kal, in the Mfinimfini penalty area, his back to the goal, receives the ball and shields it from the defender who is coming in behind him.*

**Scott Paterson (voice over):**

See, he knows he'll get a penalty if that man puts a foot wrong; he's got to be so careful. Now, see what Kal does. He looks up, he knows exactly where Charlie Akrofi is. And he goes the other way, makes himself the space, and cool as you like, flicks up the ball...and does that bicycle kick – sweet onto the head of Akrofi. Goal! Simple!

**Johnnie Taylor:**

Dreamboat!

**Scott Paterson:**

And there's your newspaper headlines tomorrow. There's your new young talent who'll have every club in Europe chasing after him!

**Pieter van Heflin:**

I have to admit he was quite good!

*More laughs.*

**Terry Hales (to camera):**

Well, there you have it. And we're going to take a break there – be back with more action in a moment. Don't go away!

**Scott Paterson (off camera):**

Muj Kal won't, that's for sure!

# LIFFEY ATHLETIC

# AND FOOTBALL CLUB

### FIXTURE LIST – THIRD XI

**Wed. 25 Aug.  H  Port Lough**

**Wed. 1 Sept.  A  Dells**

**Wed. 2 Feb.  A  Kilwell**

**Wed. 8 Sept.  H  Sheevan**

**Wed. 9 Feb.  H  Loscommon**

**Wed. 15 Sept.  A  Ballymount**

**Wed. 16 Feb.  A  Cork III  (IFL CUP 2)**

**Wed. 22 Sept.  H  Waterhill**

**Wed. 23 Feb.  H  Claregar**

**Wed. 29 Sept.  A  Claregar**

**Wed. 2 Mar.  A  Bardon**

**Wed. 6 Oct.  H  Drummore**

**Wed. 9 Mar.  H  Dells  (IFL CUP 3)**

**Wed. 13 Oct.  A  Carrickhill**

**Wed. 16 Mar.  A  Lister**

**Wed. 20 Oct.  H  Cork III**

**Wed. 23 Mar.  H  Basky**

**Wed. 27 Oct.  A  Basky**

**Wed. 30 Mar.  A  Rathstown**

**Wed. 3 Nov.  H  Bardon**

**Wed. 6 Apr.  H  Ballydalk**

Wed. 10 Nov.  A  Loscommon

Wed. 13 Apr.  A  Drummore

Wed. 17 Nov.  H  Kilwel

Wed. 20 Apr.  H  Ballymount

Wed.  1 Dec.  A  Ballydalk


Sat.  23 Apr.     IFL CUP QTR-FINAL


Wed. 8 Dec.  H  Lister

Wed. 27 Apr.  A  Port Lough

Wed. 15 Dec.  A  Dirr


Sat. 7 May     IFL CUP SEMI-FINAL


Wed.  22 Dec.  H  Rathstown

Wed.  4 May  H  Clare Hills

Sat. 1 Jan.  H  Carrickhill


Sat. 7 May     IFL CUP FINAL


Wed. 5 Jan.  A  Clare Hills

Wed. 11 May  A  Sheevan

Wed. 12 Jan.  IFL CUP (1)

Wed. 18 May  H  Cloughtown

Wed. 19 Jan.  A  Cloughtown

Wed. 25 May  A  Waterhill

## SOUTH BANK, SE1

Bloom Ramsaran looked carefully at the Liffey Athletic Third Eleven fixture list. The First Eleven away fixtures, kicking off on Saturday afternoons, were played in the bigger towns. But none of these better-known and tourist-visited places had cross-referenced with other newsworthy bits of her knowledge of the Republic of Ireland. The Second and Third Elevens played on Wednesdays, the Seconds in a league with the reserve teams of the other clubs in the bigger towns, but the Thirds were on a circuit of their own – mostly smaller places. And some of these smaller places rang bells for Bloom.

Bloom had started at Zephon at the same time as Ben, but instead of the political team, Kath Lewis had assigned her to the ethnic, royal and arts scene – the desk that Bloom called *Queen Paints Black Man*. Except that Kath had recently thrown these couple of jobs at her: finding out which countries had business activities in west Africa – like China selling railways, or Russia selling nuclear know-how – and, now, telling her to dig deeper on Eamonn Reilly. She'd got nowhere near on the first – failed, in fact – because those countries covered their tracks better than MI6, and Kath had flapped a hand and said, *Never mind!* in her writing-off voice.

But Bloom had her book of contacts the way that Ben had, which she guarded closer than her credit cards. It would go with her from job to job during her career – and right now it was open at the letter 'I', for Ireland. She pushed her keyboard aside, and on her desk she spread a one-and-a-half-miles-to-the-inch map of the Republic of Ireland.

'Now then, Mr Eamonn Reilly, let's see where you travel to cheer on your Liffey third team...'

On the map she found Port Lough and circled it, then Dells. And her eyes started to widen as she found Sheevan and Ballymount.

'Fits the pattern!' she muttered aloud.

'Talking to yourself, Bloom?' Kath Lewis was passing through the newsroom on the way to her office.

'Sure. When I talk to myself, I always get a polite reply.' But Bloom edged the map to cover her private contacts book.

'Well, don't ring *him*, he's out of touch!'

'Who's out of touch?'

'Top of the page you've just covered. That civil servant from Paddy O'Neill's Law and Order office. He makes the coffee at Stormount these days.' Kath Lewis's executive eyes missed nothing. She went on into her office and Bloom's silent reply to her departing back was far from polite. She pulled her book from under the map and put a question mark against the demoted civil servant's name. But as her eye went down the page, she saw someone else who could confirm or deny a journalist's best guess, and this man she rang.

## SIKAKOKO TOWNSHIP

Charles Henderson sat in the front of the second-hand car with the local number plate. When he was in Lansana he rarely travelled in the same car two days running, and none of his vehicles stood out in any way. Nor did he ever go directly to his destination, but took long detours, and always sat with a newspaper ready to bring up to his face for stops at traffic lights. Diesel fuel and spent time had to be cheaper than his life.

He had bank accounts under various names in several foreign cities, and today he was on a visit to the Barclays Bank in Sikakoko to talk to its Yoori manager about the possible transfer of some funds into a Swiss bank account in someone else's name. A large amount. But as his driver stopped at lights, and street kids pestered with cheap pens and packets of tissues, he put up the barrier of his *Lansana Sun*, and saw something that delayed his plans for a while.

'Drive me around for a bit,' he told his driver. The lights changed and as the car pulled away, he opened the glove compartment and reached in for a taxi-style radio.

# LANSANA INTERNAL SECURITY SERVICE

## TRANSCRIPT OF RADIO TRAFFIC, SHORT WAVE DX 177909

### 02 May. 11.19 hrs.

**Voice One (believed to be Charles Henderson):**
Rockface to Island. Over

**Voice Two (unknown):**
Island receivin'. Over.

**Voice One:**
Rockface to speak to Wolf. Over.

**Voice Two:**
Wolf ain't here, Rockface.
Any message, you got? Over.

**Voice One:**
Tell Wolf to contact Rockface,
soonest. Subject, 'Target'.
Use scrambled line to Rockface base,
suggest 14.00. Over.

**Voice Two:**
Message copied. Over.

**Voice One:**
And out.

**Voice Two:**
Yeah, an' out.

Duration 31 secs.

Outgoing strength, strong - poss.
Sikakoko area.
Responding strength, moderate, broken
up - mountains?

Comment: Typical Henderson/Red Fire
communication, like before. Some
targeted action being planned? Suggest
alert North East Region police.
Standby Northern Battalion, Lansanan
army.

Code: AMBER.


The Duty Listening Officer at Desk Three of the government building in Mfinimfini first saved the report and then forwarded it through to her superior's computer, before printing a LIVE TRAFFIC sheet and putting it in the 'Action' tray for the capital. But the phones stayed in her ears, and the digital recording went on, endlessly. It was professional practice – although she mouthed an unprofessional profanity as she glanced back at that latest transcript. Something was definitely being planned.

## SIKAKOKO TOWNSHIP

Police raids on houses usually happen just before dawn, the time of surest sleep, when suspected criminals are tangled in their sleeping shorts and their deeper dreams, unready for fight or flight. But housebreakers hit their targets an hour or so earlier, before the streaks of light in the sky can pick them out of the shadows. Logic, and experience. And that unlawful hour was when a unit of General Lakle's Red Fire brigade hit Muj Kal's house in Sikakoko Township.

Their instructions were very clear. 'You make no noise! You make no fast get-away like the Sahara Rally! You do not wake the dogs! You do not wake the parents! An' you leave behind a Yoori Liberation manifesto – not in front of the eyes, but to be found when people search. It must be as if he has thought of Yoori matters, and he has decided this is how his life must go. For Yoori independence.'

The three men understood. This was the first kidnap of a named person that they had carried out. Usually, these raids were in less skilled hands, when it was any Yoori youth that they took, kids old enough to carry guns and obey strict orders, and young enough to be brainwashed. All the hit squads needed for them was a plan of the village or the district, where targeted children's houses were marked by the reconnaissance men. But tonight's raid was specific. A watch had been kept. Yoori religious people who knew Nokongolo Kalala had been spoken to discreetly by Red Fire sympathisers, which resulted in a diagram of the road and the position of Muj's house, and the layout of the rooms inside, even marked with who slept where.

So at 03.00 hours a silent black BMW hatchback came into the road, its lights extinguished. It turned, and parked ready to leave with the tailgate up, like an undertaker's hearse outside a bereaved house. But this house was two back from Muj's, and nearer to the main road out of Sikakoko. The driver stayed with the vehicle, dressed like the others in a black T-shirt, black trousers, and black Korean trainers. From the car's interior, he quietly let down the back seat, making the flat luggage-space coffin long. His two companions, mouths shut tight, drifted through the fronts of the bungalow properties in the road – sure-footed, as if they knew where dogs were chained and fences could be breached. These were skilled men, trained in guerrilla warfare, crouching, giving hand signals above their heads. The first man sprayed before him with a small garden syringe filled with the odours of the gerbera daisies and acacias that grew in these grounds – this would mask human smells from a wakeful dog, where a knifed or poisoned animal would give the lie to Muj Kal going off of his own free will. Such a dog would have to be taken with them, 'run off'.

Child kidnap was always a Yoori danger. Where parents could afford it, doors were dead-locked and windows grilled, which was why so many Red Fire recruits were taken from the poorer places. These better-off districts didn't feel so threatened; but no bedroom doors were left unlocked, and parents slept with hunting guns or long knives by their beds. The weakness in Nokongolo Kalala's defences, though, was the twenty centimetre gap between the tops of the walls of the rooms and the roof, where air could circulate – and where a trained guerrilla fighter could circulate also. Once inside the house, and balancing on the width of a breeze-block, such a man could move between rooms as easily as a lizard.

In his bedroom, Muj Kal was deeply asleep. For an hour or so he had lain awake, wondering what his future held. His life was in a sort of limbo. On arriving home in the club car, his father had told him that Mr Gerald Abowa had been in touch by telephone and was having some firm clauses for the future inserted into his agent's contract; these would satisfy everybody greatly. Muj Kal was pleased. Training with the top professionals had gone well, he'd felt good – and all the time he was a footballer he wanted to enjoy that. The senior players had been working on their own with the coach for an extra hour, trying out moves, and practising set pieces for Sunday's away game versus Apuei Hotshots; and Muj had again been involved in that. At the end he had been elated by the kids at the gates, waving at him, the new hero, and stopping him for an autograph before he was driven away. Now, in sleep, if a fair part of Muj's head had not been filled with love of Yusa, that head might well have lain swollen on the pillow, except that his last, drowsy thoughts, were about the need for some decision about his life. His spirit was working up to it, but he wanted it to be *his* decision, not *theirs*. He wanted to have the choice, the responsibility for deciding where his life was going. He needed to weigh his success against that lumpish feeling of being goods to be sold. So he went to sleep asking the question, *which route do I take? A*nd he was woken roughly to an answer.

Security is an African industry. In Lansana, grills and locks were locally made along the sides of the roads leading into the towns, but the Red Fire had most of the common keys. And Red Fire knew that the raid on

Muj's house had to be a key job – a hacksawed grill would be no good, it would give the lie to the boy running away in the night.

They got in through the main door at the front, coming up from under the veranda like rats. The back door would be bolted, while this front door was of a modern security design with mortise locks: an easy entry to someone with the right keys. A 'feeler' was put into the lock first, a pliable polystyrene strip that gave a general impression of what 'series' the lock and key would be in. With that known, it was the seventh oiled key that turned the cylinders – while the Yale was as easy as whispering *Open!* From the clip on his belt, the first man took a key-ring torch with a patch of red plastic taped across the bulb, and showing a low glim, he let them both in.

Inside the narrow hallway, with the second man making a hand-and-shoulder ladder, the leader pulled himself up to the top of the internal wall. He wriggled himself stealthily to lie full-length along it, from where he could see the different rooms of the bungalow, like opened drawers below him.

The sleeping quarters were at the back, but they were off the main corridor, a straight slither along the air-circulating space; and within three silent minutes, the man could see Muj Kal lying asleep below him. Sheetless, with a leg drawn up, the boy's body made a still pirouette in the hot night. Carefully, so as not to crinkle a poster or clatter a picture, the intruder let himself down into Muj's room, and silently unlocked the door. With a flash of his glim he alerted his partner, who opened the front door and came along the corridor to the boy's bedroom.

One of Muj's sisters turned in her sleep, and ground her

teeth. Someone sighed in the parents' bedroom. The night stood still, and held its breath for nearly a minute.

Now, from a pouch around his neck, the second intruder took a small plastic syringe and bared the needle. A few millilitres of Pentothal had been carefully prepared, and the arm arched in slumber above Muj's head lay as convenient as a patient's on a trolley. Without the accuracy of targeting a vein in the back of the hand, the drug would take fifteen to twenty seconds to work; twenty vital seconds while the boy had to be held still, and silent.

The first man slipped the folded Yoori Independence Manifesto into a bedside drawer, and on a prearranged one-two-three signal with his head, the boy's abduction began. One Red Fire clamped his hand over Muj's mouth while he pressed the boy's body down onto the bed, spreading his own frame flat on top – and the second stuck the needle into the boy's arm. There was a jerk, a try at pushing against the weight on top of him, a fighting for breath, a spasm while the anaesthetic did its job – and by the count of ten, Mujiba Kalala was lying there unconscious.

The rest was practised and efficient. The boy's limp body was hoisted over the first man's shoulder, while the other tidied the bed, grabbed some clothing from the wardrobe, and followed through the bungalow to quietly shut the front door, using the Yale key – not so much as a click. And like undertakers in the night, the two men put Muj Kal into the open hatchback further down the road, closed its doors gently, and glided away into the sunrise.

Muj Kal's decision had been made for him. He would be a fighter for Yoori independence, an influential young man who would appear to have chosen tribal ideals over personal fame and fortune.

# LANSANA NATIONAL RADIO

—And now the sports news. Word is coming in that the young footballer Mujiba Kalala – Sikakoko Arsenal's exciting striker and new teenage icon – has chosen tribal allegiance over football. Sources close to the Yoori Red Fire Independence movement claim that the young man has turned his back on a professional sporting career in order to work and fight for Yoori independence. They say that he is disgusted at the treatment of Yooris by the Obed Abu government.

His manager, George Chognon, is shocked by the news.

<u>George Chognon:</u>

This is a big surprise to me. At training he is normal yesterday, he works with the senior players, he seems happy. Now, he goes. We must wait and see if he makes a change of his mind perhaps. He is young, and I hope he sees good sense. There is a big career for him ahead in football, and he is influential to young home-grown boys with football talents. This is a big surprise, and a big blow.

—Other sports news: the Johnstown Lions' veteran goalkeeper, Simon Favula, is to retire at the end of the season…

# TOP SECRET

## BRIEFING: ORIGINATOR
## CAPTAIN 'AZURE'

## LANSANA MILITARY INTELLIGENCE

Suspected location of 'Camp Vodi',
Kutuliza: see marked map.

From Kutuliza capital, KRAFT, follow route marked
'A' south-east to dividing fork 'B'. Follow only the
Western fork, the eastern fork being the
Lansana/Kutuliza road, patrolled its length to the
Lansana border, with a strong border presence. This
eastern fork runs through a steep-sided valley and
deviation into surrounding countryside is impossible.
AVOID THIS ROAD.

The western fork is also patrolled, but covertly. It
leads to the generally mountainous area where best
intelligence suggests Camp Vodi is emplaced.
A location high at the head of the Amoa Valley
which could be attacked only by air through
Kutulizan air space needs confirmation.

Suggest you pose as tourists, light hand-held tourist
digital camera — military can provide — and carry

no Press passes. Military can also provide tourist visas and passports in false names, and pocket satellite navigation system. If a 'fix' can be confirmed on Camp Vodi, Lansana military can take further action as determined by government if Kutulizan situation escalates.

SECURELY SHRED THIS BRIEFING AND MAP. Mark your own map with symbols for possible sightings of aardvark and jackal as code for military map markings.

Jonny Aaranovitch spun three-sixty degrees in one direction and three-sixty in the other before regaining his balance and staring angrily at Ben.

'Working for Lansan intelligence? This is not Johan Aaranovitch! This is not any part of the code as a member of the international press corps! When we say *press* we claim neutrality, *don't shoot!* So all that we throw away, and take on false names, carry false passports and visas? A Geneva Convention for press spies doesn't exist!' With furious hands he folded the military briefings and threw them across his hotel bed at Rebekah Arens, who was sitting tense on a wicker chair.

Her body turned to iron. 'You wanted "in" at the top level, Jonny, I get you in! This took some doing, I can tell you!'

Ben stood with his hands in his pockets. He knew that Jonny was right. The press shouldn't expect to have its cake and eat it. If they want the bullets not to fly at them when they wave their press passes, they mustn't devalue being press by posing as something else. Ben looked from one to the other, knew that Jonny and Rebekah had got some kibbutz thing going between them – and yet as a journalist Rebekah had pulled all sorts of strings to give them this option. He leant against the door jamb. *But was Jonny altogether right?* Wasn't this briefing exactly what undercover, investigative journalism was all about? He thought of the reporter who joins the football hooligans for the inside story; the writer who trains to be a policeman to expose racism in the force; the spurious kitchen assistant who's only there to photograph the vermin in a Michelin star restaurant. Wasn't all that sort of thing part of the job, too?

Jonny was seeping his anger out by checking his recharging battery levels. The silence in the room was focused on a small orange-flashing light on a power-pack. His eyes flickered again, as if in response to what Ben was thinking.

'Foreign correspondent, home correspondent – these are different. In your own country, deception's always on to get to the bigger truth. Pretending your story is to make a big political fish bigger – when what you want to do is reveal how much that fish stinks. But abroad such deception is different – it's meddling in another country's affairs – and this we do not do! This is how to get imprisoned, shot, hanged, *fatwa'd!*'

Ben nodded. He understood, agreed. But there *was* an excitement about being Secret Service, briefed in the heat of a tribal, political, international conflict. And what would stop them being briefed by Kutuliza on the other side if they got to the right people? What a news item that would be! He took a long drink of cold, bottled water. No, that was a stupid idea! He was getting carried away.

And then he had it. 'How famous are you?' he asked Jonny.

Jonny stared at him, and shrugged. 'A BAFTA nomination for documentary camera work. Very, very, very famous – in my house.'

'Right. And how many people in Kutuliza watch Ben Maddox presenting Zephon *World View*?'

'How many hands I'm allowed to use?'

'So.' It seemed so obvious to Ben now. 'We go, but as ourselves. You're Jonny Aaranovitch, I'm Ben Maddox, no deception.' He turned to Rebekah. 'You're Rebekah Arens – but we all leave our press passes here. "Purpose of visit?" – "tourism". Easy! We just take care on the streets, watch each other's backs: the tourists who get mugged or shot are the tourists who aren't *expecting* to get mugged or shot... We've got the home Sony – even journalists can be tourists from time to time, shoot holiday videos, can't they?'

Jonny took in a deep breath, and blew it out over what seemed like a string of long thoughts. 'With a pocket satellite navigation system in our rucksacks?' he asked, finally.

'If we get some clear African nights, I know something about the stars...'

'The boy wonder, I'm with! But why? Why can't we agree that this is a story for spiking, until the fighting starts?' He looked at Ben as if he was sorry for being about to give some fatherly advice, a shrug and an apologetic palm of the hand. 'It's a good journalist who knows when a story's a turkey. Who cares about all this on Zephon News? We should be going home, not into Kutuliza.'

But Ben bristled. 'You're thinking audience ratings, are you? Is that the job we're in?'

'In truth, yes, partly. You start forgetting that, Benjamin, and you're back on the "Gravesend Reporter"!'

'Oh, cut this soul-searching crap!' Rebekah Arens suddenly shouted, standing up and leaving her wicker chair creaking. 'Go to your BAFTA for this debate!' Her outrage threw water on both their fires; two mouths opened at once in defence. But she was going on. 'I don't like this one bit, but it's got to be said, boys – you're both missing the big story, you know that? The human interest reason for not stopping now: the back page item they're printing on the front page: the sports story that's at the top of the news bulletin! Could go international?'

Now two pairs of eyes asked *What's that?*

She threw the *Echo* onto the bed.

# NEW FOOTBALLER STAR WON'T SHINE

'Muj Kal!' she said. 'Your two stories coming together. Eamonn Reilly! Spurs! New sporting hero, the new Pele, who defects to be a Yoori freedom fighter. How much would the agencies pay to air an interview with him from wherever he is?'

Ben and Jonny looked at one another yet again, then at

the piece that Rebekah had been saving to show them since she'd come into the room.

'Shit! There goes our exclusive with Eamonn Reilly!' Jonny moaned.

'That's why we do this stupid thing and go to Kutuliza!' she said. 'We get near to this kids' terrorist camp and shoot pictures of the track leading to where this sports hero is living – tyre tracks, boot prints, signs of militia – even the camp itself – what he's given up his career for.' She paused, lowered her voice, 'Or seems to have given it up. But what if it was taken from him – if he was kidnapped, like hundreds of kids a year?' and for a moment she sounded just like Kath Lewis. 'Whatever, follow the story, boys – believe me, this one's a biggie!'

**Eamonn Reilly**

**From:** ereilly@irl.com
**Sent:** 06 May          10:00
**To:** royjones@spurs.co.uk
**Subject:** Re:  Our Spurs hopes

Our boyo has done a bunko. His next-to-nearly agent
Gerald Abowa says he's left both home and club to be
a political player in local tribal affairs. I'll hang around for
half a week in case he comes to his senses and runs
home to ma for tea. But I'm not hopeful. I sure as hell
thought it was in the bag. I could offer bills galore and
the best club in the land, but I couldn't tout him a cause
to die for.
E. Reilly

The what-a-damned-shame tone of Eamonn Reilly's e-mail
to the Spurs director of football was not maintained for the
phone call he made immediately after he'd sent it. He
flipped open the cheaper of his two mobile phones – the
one that he paid as he went, no printed bills – and nailed
in a Kutuliza number. From his tone, he was speaking to an
answering machine – or to a person of very few words.

'You know who this is. My reason for being where I am
has just gone bye-bye out the door. I can hang on here for
another week, top whack, so I need a final answer on the
price. If that answer's not "yes" my people are in no mood
to negotiate – all deals are off, okay? I'll expect to hear from
you on this number.'

And he swore, and turned and lobbed the mobile phone
like a grenade onto the hotel bed.

## SIKAKOKO/KRAFT ROAD

Muj Kal opened his eyes to the darkness, and to the sensation that his bed was moving. His mouth was dry, his limbs felt like logs, and when he put out his hand there was no wall by the side of his bed. But there was a person next to him. His mother? Was he ill? Had a cousin come to stay?

'Keep calm!' a deep voice said in the Yoori dialect.

'What is it? Who are you?' Muj was pushing to get up, his head whoozy almost to sickness, like a skull filled with marzipan. He rolled in the other direction, away from the deep voice, and he hit his nose on something hard. Now he could hear an engine, feel the rumble of the wheels on a rocky road. He was in a car.

'You're Yoori now, Kalala! You're Red Fire! You're fighting for independence, boy!'

The voice was strong, but somehow reassuring, too. And before Muj drifted off to a secondary sleep on the after-effects of the anaesthetic, echoing in his brain he heard his own reply.

*Am I? Is that what I decided?*

# FOR THE ATTENTION OF KATH LEWIS

## MESSAGES

*Bloom Ramsaran working from home – phoned at 13.35.*
*Please phone her a.s.a.p.*
*DBA*

# ZEPHON TELEVISION

## Telephone Transcript Service for files

### 09 May  Time:15.03

### KATH LEWIS EXTENSION TO 079519331264

**Kath Lewis:**

Bloom?

**Bloom:**

Kath?

**Kath Lewis:**

Can't a woman get taken out to lunch without
coming back to urgencies?  What have you got?

**Bloom:**

Jerk chicken roll.

**Kath Lewis:**

(Very pointedly.) What have you got for me – to phone you a.s.a.p.? A-S-A-P – which usually means As Significant As Poo.

**Bloom:**

Listen to this.
*(Click)*

**Bloom (via recording machine):**

...So are you confirming what I'm saying?

**Southern Irish male voice (recording):**

Yes, I am confirming it.

**Bloom (recording):**

Just to be very clear – your intelligence confirms that the towns and villages I mentioned, at least ten of them, are where the Provisionals kept arsenals of arms…?

**S. Irish male voice (recording):**

As certain as we can be.

**Bloom (recording):**

Stuff that wasn't destroyed under the Good Friday Agreement?

**S. Irish male voice (recording):**

Stuff that was moved – and could have been taken to be destroyed, to be fair. Or hijacked by a third party.

**Bloom (recording) (insistent):**

But wasn't necessarily destroyed?

**S. Irish male voice (recording):**

Certainly. Not necessarily. Who was it who counted it all, as independent witnesses – two priests? They wouldn't know an incendiary-device from an incense-waver.

**Bloom (recording):**

So, where's your best guess that the stuff is now?
If it wasn't destroyed...?

**S. Irish male voice (recording):**

Got to be on a ship going somewhere.
For sure, they wouldn't bury it again in Ireland.

**Bloom (recording):**

A ship going to...?

**S. Irish male voice (recording):**

Now, that's your problem. As long as it's off our turf...

**Bloom (recording):**

Before you go – what would we be looking for, on this ship?

**S. Irish male voice (recording):**

Come on, you can guess. Kalashnikovs, Armalites, Webleys, machine guns, sniper rifles, rocket launchers, detonators, Semtex explosive: the usual shopping basket for a revolution.

**Bloom (recording):**

Can you say all that a bit slower?

**S. Irish male voice (recording):**

Try to fool the fairies! You're recording this, or I'm Lenny the Leprechaun. Run it back. But thanks for the fellah's name.

**Bloom (recording):**

My pleasure.
*(Click)*

**Kath Lewis:**

So, that's what Eamonn Reilly's been up to! Legendary footballer, my Aunt Fanny!

Kath Lewis put down the phone, screwed up her memo, and called for someone to bring her a list of shipping departures from Irish ports in the past three weeks. And not a word of thanks to Bloom for a great piece of 'overlapping': using what she had filed away on one story to bring to bear on another.

But Bloom didn't expect congratulation. Men like Ben got praised to the sky for what they did, but girls had it harder. All the same, she was pleased with herself, and pleased with the way that the little towns of Dirr and Dells had sounded slightly comical to her when she'd seen them on two separate, unconnected occasions – and put those two and two together...

# Joyce Avoka's story –

## written up by R. A. – part 7

Joyce – she still couldn't think of herself as Forty-five – had been tormented for the past few days by the knowledge that her failure to be a good soldier ant had been seen by the boy. In the raid on Botae he had thrown his grenade with determination and hatred – and she had ducked out from throwing even a rock. So, since then – and especially when she was in his view – she had marched with an extra stamp to her feet, and acclaimed the Yoori fight in the loudest voice. She somehow found the courage to stare that boy in the eyes as if she could burn out his image of her betrayal. It was the only thing she could do, and to do it she thought of her father's face when he faced a black-backed jackal, or a rock python. Meanwhile, in Yoori talks and Yusa readings, there was chilling emphasis by the sergeants on the need to stay strong, to make sure that no one person was a weak link in Red Fire's strong armour: they were all encouraged to expose the traitors, for the sake of Yusa. So her blood ran thin every morning as she woke: could this be the day when the boy decided to reveal her shame? And she knew that when the next chance came to go on a mission, she would have to be the greatest terrorist of them all. She would have to strangle babies, if need be.

But would that chance come in time? On a clear morning after the raid, General Lakle ordered a parade under the canopy. It was a rare thing for their leader to call them all together, and Forty-five's heart was beating fast as he strode into the front of the ranks of soldier ants.

'Today, I have someone special to single out!' he barked, even before he reached the centre, scowling at their faces as he strode. 'Today I have someone to stand before you who, until the arrival of the "big one", could make a difference to our success or failure in the great Yoori fight!'

Forty-five's eyes went blurry. Had the boy at last given her away? Was she going to be held up as a bad example, an enemy of the battle for independence – her ultimate punishment intended to make them all brave? Suddenly, she felt weak and empty, as if she hadn't eaten; and sitting there she knew the feeling of the traitor whose neck is about to be put into the noose.

'Bring him in!'

She looked around. The boy who would give her away was sitting with his tent behind her – he would not have to be brought in, he would be stood up. So it wasn't him, and therefore it wasn't her! She almost fell sideways with relief.

'Mujiba Kalala!'

Someone was being led under the canopy. It was a boy dressed not in the soldier ant uniform but in a track-suit; and on his feet were white trainers, not the issued black. He was new – standing there looking around him as if he didn't know where he was, but managing to hold his head up and his eyes steady. Joyce had never heard the name just given – so she didn't know whether he was going to be hanged, or praised up to high heaven. How would this boy affect the Yoori fight?

'This person is now very famous in Lansana,' General Lakle went on. 'Young people all over the country who know sport know who he is. He is influential. He is a new football star, he is Yoori, and there will be others like him to follow, from the world of Yoori bands and singers, models and film stars!'

Joyce could sense the boys behind her appraising this person at the front, this Mujiba Kalala. Here in Vodi Camp they were all isolated from television and the news, except for the newspaper cuttings that were pinned to notice boards at the end of successful raids – and the boys, not knowing of him, were making little throat-clicking, disparaging noises, too quiet to be heard at the front. But the girls along Joyce's line sat up with even straighter backs.

'We shall show Lansana that the Yoori people they most admire are all part of our struggle! With people like Mujiba Kalala at the forefront – boys, girls, men and women all renouncing fame and high earnings to fight for Yusa and the Yoori – we shall show the strength of our cause – and we shall win!' General Lakle used his voice to work up to the shouting of those last words; and the whole canopy of soldier ants did what was expected of them; they cheered.

And as they cheered, and the sergeants whipped them up to continue the cheering, Mujiba Kalala suddenly raised an arm, and waved at them.

So, this famous boy certainly was Red Fire.

# KUTULIZA

Ben, Jonny and Rebekah looked every bit the tourists. Being younger, Ben wore the baseball cap, T-shirt and pockety trousers, while Jonny had gone for the panama hat with safari shirt and linen slacks. Rebekah was the gypsy traveller: her headscarf had little medallions hanging from it, and her flowing silk blouse and skirt gave her a Bohemian swish. With rucksacks, a digital SLR Nikon camera prominent around Jonny's neck, and white, sunscreened noses, they set out to be conspicuous visitors.

They had flown first to Accra, the capital of nearby Ghana, where Ben and Jonny applied for Kutuliza visas through the British Embassy: Ben as a 'writer' and Jonny as an 'artist'. Rebekah's newspaper office had sorted hers, and Ben didn't ask how – what wasn't in his cup he couldn't spill – but he suspected that those military connections had helped her to get something that would take close scrutiny.

The three of them were held at Kutuliza's Kraft Airport in a long queue made up mostly of black Africans, although Ben spotted a group of middle-aged white men, looking like ex-pat engineers, who had flown in on a Moscow flight. Israelis in Lansana, Russians in Kutuliza – it seemed that the bigger nations couldn't leave these small states alone. *Aid, or help-yourself?*

Whatever any of them were here for, the whole queue was spied on through wicker screens; but Ben, Jonny and Rebekah kept up a lively conversation as they shuffled forward – about animals, and shutter speeds, and the relative merits of the sleeping bags that were rolled up on top of their rucksacks. Jonny nearly over-did things by wanting to get out his sketchbook, but when they came to the Immigration Desk and showed their passports and visas, they were let through after a very careful study of the photographs.

Two of them, that was. With UK passports, Ben and Jonny had no problem; but Rebekah, with a Lansanan passport, was questioned closely.

'We're friends from way back, in London,' Rebekah told the Immigration Officer, waving at Jonny and Ben, 'I'm showing them my Africa – Ghana, Lansana, Cote d'Ivoire, Mashariki, Kutuliza. I'm proud of it...'

'Tourist?'

'Of course, tourist. Would you work with a romance-novel writer, and an artist who sleeps with his models?'

The Immigration Officer wasn't sure that he wouldn't – and with a flick of her passport as he returned it, he waved her through.

Their entry permit had had to show a hotel address – the 'Berlin' in Kraft, but they'd left nothing there but three locked, reserved rooms. Today, after negotiating the gun-happy streets, Ben was driving a rented four-wheel-drive along the western branch of the mountain road south, where, of course, they hoped to find and photograph jackal. They had driven out of the city and taken the right-hand fork where the road divided – with no road signs – and journeyed on for three or more hours, their eyes everywhere, looking for the Red Fire patrols that they'd been warned about. But they saw nothing, no spirals of dust, no birds suddenly flying up, no smoke.

There had been rain, and after a short and bad-tempered storm-burst with flashes of lightning and rolling, thunder, the skies had cleared. *So clean!* Ben thought, breathing in the rarefied air as they drove higher and higher, up and up the hairpin bends. What a very special, unspoilt, place to be! If only it didn't have to be shared somewhere further on with people not transfixed by the beauty of the earth, but filled with the need to cause political change by warlike means, and bent on death and destruction. Although if they could get that close it would be secret shots of the hidden camp that would pay for this trip: and there was no excitement like the journalist's excitement on a dangerous mission.

### Eamonn Reillly

**From:** royjones@spurs.co.uk
**Sent:** 09 May          12:35
**To:** ereilly@irl.com
**Subject:** Re:  Travel

Sorry about the Mujiba Kalala disappointment. Do not prolong your stay – such kids get fanatical, we'll forget him. Return now, or remain at your own expense beyond Sunday next.

Roy

Eamonn Reilly read his e-mail message and said an unpleasant Gallic word.  But glowing on the side table in his room was his mobile phone with its most recent incoming text still lit up.

**S.S. Cape Fontwell
arriving Abidjan,
Cote D'Ivoire, Friday.
Shipment on board
including the big one.
Your payment rec'd
so will be unloaded.**

His bags were already packed. His car was arriving in twenty minutes, and he would be driven south to Johnstown, and from there he would fly to Abidjan, the capital and main port of Cote D'Ivoire, the country next door, to arrange the transportation of the special shipment north to Banfora. Here an armourer he'd worked with before would check the goods and make the final settings. The crates would then go on to Kutuliza: and by the time Charles Henderson's money transfer – the asking price paid in full – was starting to earn interest in his own Swiss bank account, the crates would no doubt be being impatiently unpacked by those who would use the contents with deadly effect. Especially the 'big one'…

Reilly checked his bathroom and his bedroom drawers to ensure that he'd left nothing behind, wiping door handles, taps and surfaces with a handkerchief as he went. He especially made sure that he took with him the Gideon Bible that Charles Henderson had made important, which would have his DNA within its pages. And as he stood up from searching under the bed, he suddenly guffawed, a laugh without humour, and said aloud: 'Unpacked perhaps even by bucko Muj Kal…'

All my other writings are hidden in my room. Not lost, perhaps they will be found, and my parents will understand how divided I have been in two directions for so long. Too long. Now I have no reason for figuring out my doubts - the big decision has been made for me. I am in the Red Fire camp, and I am a Yoori boy who loves Yusa.

Today they stood me in front of everyone and proclaimed how I am going to influence the Yoori youth to follow me. Because I am a footballer I am valuable to Red Fire, for a little while. I raised my arm in salute to that - which was a shameful and big-headed thing to do - but I will be soon forgotten in Lansana and Sikakoko except in my family home, and my worth will be no more than any of the others in this tent.

The boys here say that until then the leaders will not employ me on a raid, in case I run away. No one goes on raids until they are true believers. But I am a true believer, although not in this warlike way. My father is not warlike, although he loves Yusa as much as any of these. So mine has been a wasted life, caught between two ways of living it, ending up not pleasing him

*and not pleasing myself as a sportsman.*
*I dithered too long, and I am nothing*
*now...*

Muj Kal read what he had written – disguised in his study
of the Bible they all had to read nightly, learning the
passages about Jozea – or Yusa – the Prophet. Some of the
boys who could write were allowed to copy them out to
help their learning, and in this way Muj had written those
final words of doubt, and depression. Now he looked at
this pathetic sheet, already stained with salty spots from
secret tears, and he ripped it up, as if he knew the words in
the Bible – which he did, anyway. *And Jozea went on his
way saying, 'There shall come a mighty scourge across the
land, and, yeah, the righteous lashes of the scourge shall be
with God, the everlasting'.*

This would be his training from now on: religious and
military, not fitting into a 'four-four-two' for the home
stadium or the 'diamond' formation for an 'away' game.
And his number would not be that on his Sikakoko Arsenal
shirt – twenty-three – but the 'last three' of 1634 that the
Red Fire had that afternoon tattooed on his arm.

And as he rubbed the itching, lumped-up skin, he
suddenly realised that now that he was here, he hadn't even
got a name anymore.

## THE KUTULIZA MOUNTAINS

It was a clear, starry night, the sort that so many travel agents try to sell to Europeans. But up here in the Kutuliza mountains it was rarer to have clear skies than in many other parts of Africa. What Lansana profited from with its hydro-electricity plant, was the rain that fell so frequently in these mountains; although to Ben tonight the heavens looked as stellar pinpricked as a perfect page of astronomy in an encyclopaedia; and he felt that he could lift a hand and almost run his fingers across the sky's smoothness.

Lying there, he saw the constellations of Andromeda, Pegasus and Aquarius shining above him in a line from northwest to southeast; while moving in from the periphery as he gazed was Pisces, appearing to be in the path of the half moon – although the constellation was millions of miles beyond it. At such times, Ben the non-believer always felt that he had to believe in *something* having created these wonders; but it wouldn't be a sandy-toed prophet or some spirit in the minds of men and women; it would be a force of immense, indescribable proportions – too huge and wonderful for his small brain to understand.

He heard a quiet whistle. Jonny was lying somewhere near, awed by this, too. The difference between them was that Ben could claim to fix this stellar pattern in his head, and knowing the time and date, should be able to pinpoint where they were. For Jonny it had to be sheer wonder, perhaps something for his camera, to file in the next package sent back to Zephon.

Already, as they'd eaten their cold rations – and as they'd shivered in the mountain night without the dare of a fire – Ben had outlined what sort of place he thought the Red Fire would have chosen for its camp. He'd scribbled it on paper, and shared it with the others, before Rebekah had gone off to a small waterfall to wash.

1. Has to have easy access to the main, eastern Lansana / Kutuliza track. This has to be the main route down to Lansana for raids like the one on Botae.

2. A well-drained site – or above the level of the rain clouds. Mud and mosquitoes would otherwise make the place untenable.

3. Fairly flat – and if there isn't more than one site, big enough to accommodate a small army in tents or huts.

4. Surrounded by higher mountain peaks – probably high in a narrow valley – preventing radar and reconnaissance from picking it out. Well camouflaged.

5. Sited conveniently near enough to the less used western road for supplies to be brought in from Kutuliza – more or less the route we've taken.

6. Permanent. Unlike Al Quaida's in Afghanistan, these people are sited securely enough not to have to keep on the move. Al Quaida consists of small cells of terrorists, but this is a camped army like Hannibal's before he crossed the Alps.

He left Jonny wherever he was and went back down to the four-wheel drive which was camouflaged into a gulley, near to rapids that would thrill the wetsuit off a white-water rafter. Already the valley was filling from the east with a dense white cloud, approaching up it fast like a great, silent animal. Mountains could change in seconds. He pulled out the large scale map provided by the military and photocopied by Rebekah with their navigational references cleverly replaced by tourist markings – *jackals, mountain lion sited*. With the aid of a low-powered torch he found his present location and marked it, and studied the contour lines in their sector for the sort of site they might be looking for. He needed to identify a small plateau – which would be shown by the lines widening out at some point, something in the shape of an eye – and which was surrounded by contour lines as dense as fingerprints, to signify an enclave in steep mountains.

And there it was! Ben was sure that there it was – and well within the area that the military had identified. On the map were two plateaus that looked big enough to encamp a small army – without much to choose between them; except that one was lower, and the other higher; and, looking at the fast disappearing tree line all around him – with shrubs, bushes and scraggy grass nourished by the rainfall – he knew that a good commander would go for the higher. Tonight's clear sky would have to be rare around here, normally the place would be cold, clinging wet. Washed-out troops living like pigs in mud would be dejected troops, so a drier, protected site within narrow surrounding peaks would be preferable. And if the site were on the Kutuliza side, which it would be, then Lansanan planes over-flying it would be in contravention of the United Nations charter, whichever way they came in. While if the camouflage were good – and Ben had seen the Royal Artillery virtually disappear on Woolwich Common – then there wouldn't be much joy even from satellite spying.

And he was disappearing fast himself. The cloud had come swiftly up the valley, and already his visibility was down to metres. Goodbye night sky! But he'd had time to pinpoint where they were right now – and he was certain that he'd found a likely camp site. A fingernail count across the map told him that it would be roughly fifty metres higher up, and perhaps two kilometres on along a valley ridge that ran off the western Kutuliza/Lansana road. It would be ideally placed for supplies from Kutuliza, and near enough – further along that valley – to be in fair reach of the other, main eastern 'raiding' road down into Lansana.

This would be where General Benjamin Maddox would set up his camp, anyway.

He climbed back to the shelf where he had looked at the heavens, near to where Jonny was. It seemed a different place, here in the cling of the cloud, with no stars overhead, just the dark. 'Jonny!' he hissed.

To get no reply.

*'Jonny!'*

Jonny couldn't have been lying more than ten metres away, Ben had heard him whistle at the beauty of the sky. But he wasn't there now. Perhaps, like Rebekah, he'd gone to perform some private function, but he should have said something...

Ben inched his way back to the overhung niche where their three sleeping bags were unrolled, Rebekah deep in hers already.

'Rebekah!'

'Oy?'

'Where's Jonny?'

'With you!'

'No, he's not.'

'Gone to wash his hands.'

'You were in the cloakroom. Did you see him down there?'

'No.'

'He'd have passed you – here, or on the way down.'

'Well, he didn't.'

The same went for going back to the jeep near the perilous rapids; Rebekah would have seen him.

'Then where the hell is he?'

Jonny's rucksack lay in his sleeping space as a headrest, and behind it, neatly stashed, was the Nikon camera and the case containing the Sony digital camcorder. Everything to do with Jonny was there – except Jonny. Ben picked up the camcorder case. It was light – and empty. As he'd thought, Jonny must have gone to get some shots of that spectacular sky; and, since he was nowhere else, he must have climbed to the peak above their overhang to get above these clouds. 'I'll find him – stay there. He's shooting background for the next package.'

Ben re-climbed to where he'd looked at the stars, and up beyond it to what seemed a likely spot for photography, where Jonny would have had a three-sixty panorama of the African night and the sky.

'*Jonny!*'

But there was no Jonny there. Ben thought of flashing his torch as a signal – but this area could be patrolled by Red Fire, and the 'tourists' had been very careful not to give their position away so far. He crouched, and, shielding the torch, looked at the ground. If Jonny had been here filming, his suede tourist boots would have left their marks on the roughened ridge.

And what he saw suddenly turned his stomach. There were his own marks, clear enough, and what could have been Jonny's under an overprinting of footfall, but there were more marks there than the two of them would have made, ridged, and scuffed up with movement. And at the edge, quite obvious to the eye, was a footprint belonging quite obviously to neither of them – a sole print with a distinct design that seemed familiar to Ben: a zigzag motif that he'd seen before.

He shuffled along to crouch by it; and as he stared down in close up, he remembered where he'd seen that design before. It was the same pattern footprint that Jonny had filmed in the trees near where the Yoori moderate had had his fatal car crash.

*Whoever had done something to Mbidi Renula had done something to Jonny Aaranovitch!*

Jonny had been taken: by Red Fire guerrillas in the mist.

She saw the white man brought in. It was early morning, and the misted cobwebs were still shimmering across between the tents as she went to the canvas washing lines. Two Red Fire patrol soldiers – rifles slung – pushed him before them through the alleys beneath the net of camouflage. He looked as if he had been roughed up, his forehead was bleeding from a likely rifle butt, and his light jacket was torn and dirty. His face was set in a defiant scowl, and he dragged a foot as if he had been kicked and dead-legged on the march back to camp.

These men, she knew, were one of the look-out patrols from below them along the mountain passes, guarding the camp twenty-four hours a day. The first guard had a radio walkie-talkie, and if this prisoner had been leading an assault unit against the Red Fire, he would have radioed in and the whole camp would have been turned out in defence: every soldier ant knew the drill for that. So for these two to bring the prisoner in alone, he must have been a lone traveller, or a spy, caught on the track leading here.

Joyce should have gone on with her washing, but something made her want to see what happened to this man. She was still nervous of the boy who could report that she wasn't a good, true, Yoori fighter, and she had a painful fascination over what happened to people who went against General Lakle.

She crept along to the end of the line of tents, keeping the soldiers and the prisoner in view. There weren't many people about this early in the morning – Joyce slept as lightly as traitors do until she could prove herself in the next raid – so there was no taunting crowd, no jeering and spitting, as the man was brought in. She ran into a guy rope, scorching her cheek as she hurried to see his fate, and came to a canvas corner that was the mess tent. She peered around it.

'What's going on?'

She spun to the sudden voice. She had been too intrigued with what she was watching to notice anyone near. Was that threatening boy following her, keeping an eye on her? But it was the boy who had been brought into Camp Vodi the week before: the boy who had been held up as a hero for Yoori independence. He was different, in uniform now, partly – he had only the shirt and the black trainers, the tracksuit bottoms were still his own.

'They've brought someone in.'

'Who?' The boy looked around the canvas corner with her.

'Don't know.'

'Was he trying to escape?'

'How, escape?' That seemed a funny thing to say. Why would the boy be thinking 'escape'? This man was white, there were very few Red Fire who weren't black, only that smart white boss who sometimes came but never stayed – the prisoner had to have come from outside.

The pair of them watched as the guards pushed the stumbling man before them towards the headquarters area where General Lakle slept.

'What's that, hanging from his belt?' Joyce asked the boy. She meant the belt of the second soldier, which had some piece of black equipment dangling from it.

'Camera,' the boy said. 'Camcorder, or something.'

Joyce didn't know what a camcorder was, but she understood 'camera'.

'He's been spying, then.' The boy drew in his breath. 'Don't think they'll like it when they look at the pictures on that!'

'No.' Joyce turned to look at him. 'I know you,' she said, 'from when you came in.' She felt the need to say something personal, human. The boy looked at her, good-looking, but tired-eyed. 'I'm Forty-five,' she told him.

'I'm Six-three-four.' Then, 'What's your real name?' he asked, looking at her again, after the man was pushed into the general's tent.

'Joyce.' She whispered it as if it was the vilest word. 'And yours?' She was ashamed to have forgotten what they'd been told – this boy was famous and very important to General Lakle.

'Mujiba. Have you been here long?' he asked.

Joyce took a long time to answer – but as she did so, her whole body suddenly shivered with the dangerous thrill of what she said. 'Too long!'

She looked at him for his reaction, as the boy nodded, and sighed, and gave her a despondent pat on the shoulder – although she saw that his eyes had shone at the honesty of her reply – one that could lead to her being treated as badly as that man in General Lakle's tent, if this Mujiba couldn't be trusted.

Although, somehow, she thought that he could, because, 'We'll keep that secret,' he said. 'Ours. Yes?'

# CAMP VODI

It had been an inevitable decision, now that he was here –
not that it would change anything. For two nights Muj had
hardly slept, once the after-effects of the anaesthetic had
worn off: he had turned over and over in the night until his
thin mattress had become chaff. Some of the boys with
whom he shared a tent were killers; but, almost worse to
live with in the small space, was the swearing,
blaspheming, and foul noises from their rank bodies.
Their shirts and underclothes stank on them as if they
hadn't been changed in weeks, and the special black
trainers that everyone wore gave off a sweaty, rubbery
odour that made him want to gag. And the others didn't
like him. They had been here too long to know about his
football skills and the attention in the press that he had
had, and they resented him being held up before them as a
Yoori star. Who was he, when they had done things to get
themselves hanged, if they were taken prisoner?

'When you've blown up your first Lansanans you can
talk to me!' the tent leader had said. 'Cut me some fingers
to count, or dig out an eyeball to roll – till then, keep your
body out o' my way!' Mujiba was forced to be last in the
food queue, and on his first morning he'd been detailed by
the tent leader for latrine duties, emptying the enamel
buckets into the water-course that ran down the mountain.

This wasn't worshiping Yusa, this had nothing to do
with Yoori pride. This camp and these people in it were no
more than a pack of terrorists and bullied street kids, who
trained and raided instead of stealing, and scavenging
around the rubbish tips of Sikakoko. And while they'd all
had to learn by heart the words of Jozea from the Bible,

they had learnt it only by head; none of the Yoori here embraced the deep meaning of the prophet when he said in a chapter Muj's father had taught him:

'*"And excepting those times when thou are called to action, thou shalt live thy life even as a dove. What is inside a man is of more worth to God than the clashing of cymbals and the throwing of spears, for holiness is a fount that springs from within." So spake Jozea.*'

There was nothing in this camp of the true spirit of Yusa, nor of the Lord God, Mujiba thought.

And as he went back to straighten his sleeping space in the foulness of his tent, he found that his eyes were watering – with the memory of only two days before, when he had thrown back his top sheet, hooked back his mosquito net, and run out to the car that was waiting to take him to football training.

Another life.

**Ben Maddox**

From: klewis@zephontv.co.uk
Sent: 10 May          14:00
To: benmaddox@talktalk.net.
Subject: Re: Jonny Aaranovitch

Terrible news about Jonny. We're sitting on this until
the situation is clearer. Talks ongoing with Foreign
Office, International Press Corps, etc.
You are to get down to Johnstown and take
the next available flight back to UK.
Keep in touch.
Kath Lewis

Back in the Kutuliza capital's Berlin Hotel, Ben and
Rebekah had to pretend to the management that nothing
had happened; they were simply back sooner than
expected, and Mr Aaranovitch was meeting up with them
later. But Ben was choked, and Rebekah distraught. They
both knew that Jonny wasn't simply 'missing' in the mist.
From the footprints on that remote ledge it was obvious
that he had been taken by people wearing the same trainers
as the killers of Mbidi Renula.

And the tragedy of it was, Jonny had been a reluctant
hero. He hadn't wanted to go north into Kutuliza, he
hadn't been driven by Ben's charged determination to
come out of Africa with a story worth showing on British
television. Jonny's new world seemed to be his kibbutz,
and he had just found some sort of companionship with
Rebekah Arens; at least, he'd spent more time with her
than he had with Ben. It had been as if he was making it

clear that he was ready for a quieter life. In his younger days he'd been a brave war photographer, covering bloody conflicts all over the world. His film of orphaned children from a Kurdish school for the blind, running in confusion out of the shelled building, was still a classic twenty seconds of archive material. If he'd been freelance, its continued use whenever atrocity was discussed would have paid him a decent pension.

But on this assignment his attitude seemed to have changed, he was looking forward to a different future – and now he was dead, or being held hostage wearing a blindfold, with a kitchen knife at his throat. Yet Dr Abu Obed and the Lansanan government would never give in to hostage-takers' demands, any more than strong governments ever do. No way would Jonny's life be exchanged for Yoori independence.

Hardened journalist as she was, Rebekah's eyes permanently glistened with tears, and her words were all recrimination, recrimination, recrimination. *It was her fault!* she pounded into a cushion: she had colluded with the Lansana military intelligence to direct them into Kutuliza; she had tempted Jonny and Ben with the two-stories-in-one pitch of Mujiba Kalala apparently going over to the Red Fire rather than playing for Spurs. 'I thought it would be our *thing*, Jonny's and mine, the great on-the-road story we did together. Two oldies telling the kids—' which was when her voice failed her, the strangled words accompanied by a two-fisted beating of her chest like a mourner at a Lebanese funeral.

That first night back Ben had slept in her room, just to be someone with her, lying in his sleeping bag on the floor and staring up at the slow revolving blades of the electric fan: no starry sky that night. Now she was on the bed in his room, dozing fitfully while he packed – when his mobile phone suddenly bleeped.

'New text message from Meera', it announced. He opened it.

**Hi Ben. Kath told me. Come home now, next plane. Thank God u'r safe. Please marry me. Yes! I mean it. And u don't have 2 change ur life. Reely! I luv u. Meera xxxx**

Ben lifted his head, the texted words glowing in his palm. *Meera would marry him!* He had proposed to her in Paris, and she had said 'no', not while he did the job that he did. Now she had changed her mind; now she was saying that she wanted him, on his terms. Instead of driving her further one way, what had happened to Jonny had somehow driven her the other way – although she was urging him to come home.

He stared again at the message until the phone backlight switched off, so he thumbed it on again to keep seeing the words, taking in their full meaning. These were for carving on stone, not texting on plasma.

And even as he stared, the phone bleeped again, and a new message was signalled: 'from Bloom'.

With great hesitation he opened it.

**Go to it, Ben. Ignore Kath. Stay.
Bring that story back for J's
sake. It's big. E. Reilly is
running IRA arms to Kutuliza.
Rt now shipment on road north
thro Ivory Coast. If Kath sacks
u I'll cum with u somewhere
else. BBC? Sky? Take our
chances. Eh? Luv Bloom**

Oh, God! Ben couldn't switch off the message fast enough. 'Oh, my good God!' he said aloud.

'What's happened? News? Bad news? Something definite?' Rebekah was sitting upright on the bed.

'No, it's not Jonny,' Ben said. 'Just personal stuff, from London.'

Rebekah stared at him. 'Lucky to have it, *personal*!' she told him. But she was suddenly off the bed, coming round it to him. 'Benjamin, I'm sorry, that was out of order. Anyway– ' she stared him in the face '–that's enough mooning over Jonny…' Now it was Ben doing the staring. 'His story's going to bloody well get told! Rebekah Arens is going to let the world know what's happened to her man, *bugger* mooning!' She was suddenly no longer the grieving girlfriend. Her eyes were wide, and her auburn hair seemed burnished under the light. 'If I blow it out to the world, stop keeping it a secret, our beloved president will *have* to do something drastic about Red Fire! They all dread foreign journalists getting taken, it becomes international…'

But Ben laid cautious hands on her shoulders. 'Won't that just make sure Jonny gets killed?'

Rebekah's sudden sneer turned her face ugly. 'Who are you kidding, Ben Maddox? You know, and I know, that he's dead already! Tortured, and dead. So let's get his last story out to the world!'

## SIKAKOKO TOWNSHIP

They drove south to Sikakoko. They kept the four-wheel drive for the journey, down the eastern Kutuliza/Lansana road, through the border, past the Ade Dam, and into Sikakoko below it. Here they returned the Hertz hired vehicle to a local dealership and met Richard, who had come north from Johnstown in the car – whom Ben instructed, straight off, to take them to the home of Mujiba Kalala.

The bungalow was grieving quiet, and it was some time before the door was opened by Muj's mother. Had Muj seen her, he would have been shocked by her appearance. Already, she looked a generation older, her hair flat and lifeless, her eyes tired, and her body frail within her dress.

First off, Rebekah did the talking; direct and to the point: doors get slammed very quickly on journalists who don't pitch quickly.

'I've got a friend who has been taken by Red Fire,' she said. 'He must be in the same camp as your son...'

*What a pro!* Ben thought. Her voice didn't betray her real thoughts about the fate of Jonny.

'Oh, yes?' Muj's mother's voice was of the graveside.

'I'm from the Johnstown *Graphic*, and this is Ben Maddox from Zephon British Television.'

Ben smiled briefly at the woman as, behind her, Muj Kal's father appeared; snappier, bearing things better, it seemed.

'I think we have said all that we want to on this matter,' he told the two. 'We wish to be left in peace.' He put his hand over his wife's shoulder to grip the door, ready to shut it.

Rebekah picked up on the hand. 'Your son unlocked this door and came out through here?' she asked him.

'That has all been investigated, and reported,' Muj's father insisted.

249

'So he did go voluntarily?' Ben asked.

Nokongolo Kalala just stared 'no comment' back at him, his knuckles whitening on the door as he went to push it closed.

But Muj's mother wasn't finished. 'No, he didn't!' she said. 'I'm his mother – I know!'

Rebekah grunted, Ben took in a breath, Muj's father looked at his feet. For the first time in Lansana, Ben suddenly thought that there was an advantage to being foreign – being white. He and Rebekah didn't look as if they were tied-in to the tribal politics of the Lansanans; the woman seemed to feel that she could speak to them.

'Please!' Nokongolo Kalala said, but Ben knew that their feet were in the door now; Muj's mother was going to have her say. The same as in many west African countries, where, in days of old, it was queen mothers who chose the kings, the Lansanan woman's voice had to be respected.

Within moments, the four of them were standing in Muj Kal's bedroom. Ben looked around the walls. This was any boy's bedroom from practically anywhere in the world: pictures of international footballers, and a band, an iPod on the table, and a radio; with one exception – a Biblical figure hung on the wall above        the        bed,        engraved        within a silver frame, with a matching framed text beneath it.

'Yusa,' Nokongolo Kalala said, as Ben peered closer at it. 'Written as Jozea in the Bible, the prophet of the Yoori.'

Ben read the text.

**What is inside a man is of more worth to God than the clashing of cymbals and the throwing of spears, for holiness is a fount that springs from within**

'Our son was torn, he was always in two minds,' Muj's mother said, pulling open a drawer and taking out a school notebook in which were several sheets of neat handwriting. 'He wrote his thoughts, he was divided between being a religious man like his father, and being a footballer...'

'May I?' Rebekah took the book and started reading Muj's writing.

'...But he was not violent, a fire-brand. He would never go to join the terrorists!' Eni Kalala sat on her son's bed. 'They chant only the warlike texts, from Yusa's early life.'

'They live by such words.' Now Muj's father seemed to be losing his resistance to the journalists. 'We found this in the same drawer.' He showed them a Yoori Independence pamphlet, all raised arms clutching weapons. Across the front was printed in large letters:

**'JOZEA PROCLAIMS 'THERE SHALL BE A MIGHTY SCOURGE ACROSS THE LAXFUL LAND, AND QUESTION NOT, THE JUST LASHES OF THE SCOURGE SHALL DWELL WITH GOD, THE KING EVERLASTING.'**

'They say it all the time. The Red Fire are the lashes, and they will be with God at the finish. This is what they preach – it is their mantra, what you call...their slogan.'

'He had this pamphlet?' Ben asked. 'So couldn't he have been a secret supporter – perhaps he wouldn't want to upset his mother?'

Nokongolo Kalala kept his tone even. 'I did not say he had this; I said that this was in his drawer after he had gone...'

'Put there!' Eni Kalala raised her voice as she stood up from the bed and stepped across to open Muj's small wardrobe. She ran her hand lovingly among the garments. 'See these shirts and tracksuit tops! All clean, all fresh, I wash and iron every day.' She turned to them. 'He was a fastidious boy, clean everything, every morning.' She dropped her voice, almost growling as she seemed to gain strength from telling these journalists her theory, *'He would not go to some new life in sweaty training clothes!'*

There was a moment's silence in the room.

'He would not do that to his mother!' she finished.

Rebekah went to hand back Muj's notebook to the woman. 'So, you think this was an abduction, just like the other children, but dressed up to look like a voluntary act?'

Muj's father intercepted the writing as it was being handed over, and held it close, folded in his grip. 'We think but we do not say! We ask you, we plead with you that we do not say!' Ben and Rebekah both looked at the suddenly impassioned father. 'If Red Fire thinks that we think that, if that is made public, then as surely as Yusa walked this earth, our son will be killed...'

And the journalists had to go along with that. They both strongly believed that journalists have no lesser duty to personal safety than anyone else. It should never be the story at all costs...

MINISTRY OF DEFENCE AND STATE SECURITY

# REPUBLIC OF LANSANA

# VISITOR PASS

## RESTRICTED TO AREA ONE ONLY
## OCEAN ROAD BUILDING

NAME: Benjamin Maddox

DATE: 16 May

### THIS PASS TO BE HANDED-IN
### UPON DEPARTURE.

### FAILURE TO DO SO WILL RESULT IN
### PROSECUTION UNDER THE LANSANA
### OFFICIAL SECRETS ACT OF 1995

Ben had made up his mind. There had been no agonizing. That first text message – from Meera – had put his head into turmoil. The second – surprisingly – had calmed it. After the initial shock of what Bloom had said, there had been no great debate within his head. With the Mujiba Kalala story fuelling his journalist's thoughts, and Jonny's fate burning his conscience, he knew that he wasn't going home yet, whatever Meera or Kath Lewis told him. Meera was very dear to him, he loved her, didn't he? But the excitement, the thrill, the real fizz had come when he had read that message from Bloom – carry on! Do your thing!

So now he was defying Meera and his boss and walking into the official headquarters of the Lansana Secret Service.

The building was of the old 'colonial' style: the entrance was through twin pillars between which heavy iron railings had been emplaced, with armed soldiers at a single gate. He showed his pass and was taken into a portakabin in the courtyard, where he was body-searched thoroughly, and his miniaturized voice recorder taken from him; but his journalist training had been good – he knew shorthand – although he wasn't here today for an interview.

In a short while a rickety lift had taken him to the fourth floor, overlooking the harbour and the Atlantic beyond, and he was being unsmilingly greeted by two Lansanans in dark suits, one of them a woman of about fifty, the other a younger man. The woman was black, otherwise there were uncomfortable similarities with Kath Lewis; she was definitely in charge, and she was mean with her smiles.

'You sit here.'

Ben sat at one side of a wide table facing the secret service pair, a mug of hot water and a Nescafé sachet suddenly before him, as the woman – who was never named – slid a paper across the table.

'Our radio traffic has picked up on this,' she said, 'an Irish voice saying the alphabet – reciting groups of letters.'

Ben looked at the sheet, and up at the woman. 'Eamonn Reilly?' he asked.

She didn't answer.

Ben prodded further. 'We know Eamonn Reilly's involved in something out here. My office knows the whereabouts of the arms he's selling to Kutuliza…'

'Us, we are also thinking Eamonn Reilly,' the woman conceded.

'This thing sent to whom? Do you know?'

The woman simply stared at him.

'We think we know,' the man said, with the voice of a cool, smooth-headed operative. But then he clammed up as tight as his boss.

Immediately, Ben got up. These two were playing at being secretive: they had to be a different department from the army people who'd briefed him with marked maps. 'Well, I'll say goodbye, and thank you for the Nescafé,' he said, turning to the door. But he guessed that they wouldn't let him get far. It was a journalist's trick to pretend to switch off the camera, put away his voice recorder – and they knew that he could pinpoint where Jonny had been captured. From which location the Red Fire camp had to be within walking distance: he had heard no vehicle. These people needed him.

'You sit down, please,' the woman said. 'This has only just come in, we're still assessing its security level, but we don't think it's important. You can have a look at it.' She suddenly smiled, soon gone. 'It was on a wavelength we're monitoring for a man called Charles Henderson – but a lot of what is sent is not relevant to Red Fire, he has many dubious interests.'

'I've met Charles Henderson.' Ben sat again. 'I've interviewed him, in a cave in the Ade mountains. We ran the piece in Britain.'

If the woman was surprised, she covered it well. 'So, do you make anything of it?' She was nodding at the paper.

Ben looked at the paper properly now. It was not a full sheet of A4 but a piece sliced across at top and bottom, with no headings or signings.

| | | |
|---|---|---|
| ZEADL | ZYANH | JUXTA |
| ENHWF | LSTLV | UEHLR |
| CTFWW | TJSKX | FBGRS |
| BQAUQ | PFBWS | DOTAF |
| UANXX | FBGMC | BSAXL |
| KLVAB | PJCBN | XAILH |
| EJTHQ | JSSQG | FLSSP |
| SEBBE | ULDMJ | MBMCB |
| XFBGB | AAHEQ | JZFAU |
| ASYAZ | FULXZ | LFKEW |
| VBTLH | JUHZA | |

'Five-letter groups,' he said. 'A common pattern – you must know this sort of code.'

'Surely,' the woman said. 'The new PINs and security numbers, possible references to bank accounts. We'll monitor for a reply before we start taking too much time on this...'

'May I take it? I've played with these before.'

The woman's face said, *why not?* Ben slipped the paper

into his pocket. She went on, 'More important, you say you could take us to where your colleague was lifted? The Kutuliza mountains are a very big place…'

'We were lucky – and your army people briefed us to get pretty near.'

The woman looked surprised, and Ben could see her resisting the temptation to shoot a look at the man beside her. The military and the Secret Service seldom shared all of each others' secrets, in whatever country you found yourself.

'If you've got a star chart on your computer, I can feed in the date and let you know pretty tight to where we were that night…'

'And from there, you've worked out a likely location for the Red Fire camp?'

Ben put both his hands on the table before him, like a gambler laying down his cards. 'On certain assurances,' he said. 'That you don't attack the camp by force, and that I come with you. Force will kill everyone there indiscriminately…'

'We can't attack by force. It must be easy to defend, this place – and we can't go in by air…'

'Because?' Although Ben knew the 'because'; he wanted it confirmed.

'…Because the only way in – if it's roughly where we think it is – is up the valley coming in through Kutulizan air space. And Kutuliza officially condemns Red Fire. They say they're as much against them as we are. So we would be violating the air space of a friendly state.'

Ben already knew that this was the fix Lansana was in, fighting an enemy that was masquerading as a friend. Meanwhile, it was the small people who suffered…

'Mujiba Kalala, the young star footballer, is there against his will, he didn't defect, he was taken,' Ben said. 'That's not to be made public for his own security, but if you can bring him out and present him on television denouncing Red Fire and Yoori Independence, you'll have a public relations coup, I tell you. Worth a hell of a lot of military and diplomatic action. It would speak to the young Yooris, and do Red Fire a mega-ton of damage.'

'We understand that. But why should you come with us on such a raid?'

There was no hesitation from Ben, only determination. 'Because my friend is there, and if he's still alive, I want to bring him out, without starting another war.'

'Bring him out without force?'

'The British SAS could mount such an operation. Why can't you? There must be a lot of kids like Kalala there who'd be blown to smithereens if you went in by force.'

There was a long silence, longer than was comfortable. Ben seemed to have put them on their mettle. But when the door opened behind him, he suddenly realised why they had been holding fire.

He turned to see the president, Dr Obed Abu, standing there. The other two in the room stood up, and Ben followed swiftly. So, the president had been listening-in!

'I like your thinking, Ben!' he said, stepping forward and shaking Ben's hand. 'Covert. No troops to be sacrificed storming a hard-to-take position; no international conflict with a neighbouring country. A "Dirty Dozen/Hogan's Heroes" sort of operation.' He nodded, and smiled. 'The sort they'll make films about one day...'

'A news story putting Lansana in a good light, Dr President,' Ben interposed. 'The rescue of a sporting hero would have lots of space, plenty of air time…'

'Sure. And pictures of Mujiba Kalala and me together – good TV! The world sees what Lansana is capable of doing peacefully, the Lansanans see the lies the Yooris tell about this boy – and my government is praised for trying to protect its misguided, kidnapped children…'

Ben nodded, went along with that. 'But could I ask you a question, Dr President?' He was riding his luck on the back of Obed Abu's enthusiasm, and this could be useful stuff for his story. 'Why haven't you gone in before – mounted a covert operation to do something like infect the camp's water, or plant explosives…?'

'You think like a warrior!' Dr Abu clapped Ben on the shoulder. 'We have, sir. But our men were captured and killed, we presume. They were never seen again…'

Ben kept his face looking calm. And this was the sort of mission he wanted to be on?

'…And then they moved the camp.'

'Their radio traffic told us,' the woman put in. 'They moved the camp to a higher and drier location, to better conditions…'

'Ah.'

'So we need to confirm this new location,' the president added.

But Ben wanted to know whether or not he would be going north with the government guerrillas, which, despite the track record of the last foray, he still wanted to do. Which was a question that the president answered for him.

'And you must go!' he told Ben. 'First, to confirm position; second, if we succeed in a covert attack, your presence will take the public eye away from my crack squad.' But going back to the door, he added. 'And if it all goes pear-shape, we shall say that the squad was hired by you, a private army to rescue your colleague.' He showed Ben two clean hands.

To which Ben nodded, a condition he was prepared to accept – if it meant having a crack at getting Jonny Aaranovitch out of hell or, more realistically, of getting the facts that would bring life to telling the man's tragic story.

# LANSANA INTERNAL SECURITY SERVICE

### TRANSCRIPT OF RADIO
### TRAFFIC, SPECIAL HIGH FREQUENCY
### OPERATIVE TO SECURITY SERVICE BASE

### 15 May. 17.00 hrs.

<u>Rockface (believed to be Charles Henderson):</u>
Rockface to Island. Over

<u>Island (believed to be Red Fire Camp):</u>
Island receiving. Over.

<u>Rockface:</u>
Put me through to Wolf. Over.

<u>Island:</u>
Wolf ain't right here, Rockface. Operational. Over.

<u>Rockface:</u>
Right, take this down, man, report to Wolf: big one's primed and timed. You got that? Big one's primed and timed. Over.

<u>Island:</u>
Big one's primed an' timed. Yeah, I got that. Over.

Rockface:
Now, get this. Take your man
with you. Got that? That's
'Take your man with you'.
Over.

Island:
'Take your man with you'. Over.

Rockface:
Tell him he's known to me,
dead at the scene, he's a
smokescreen. Over.

Island:
What?

Rockface:
He's known to me, dead at the
scene, he's a smokescreen. Got
that? It's easy enough! Over.

Island:
Yeah, man, I got it. Over.

Rockface:
Get that to Wolf a.s.a.p.
Over.

Island:
Will do. Over.

<u>Rockface,</u>
Over - and out.

<u>Island,</u>
An' out.

# THE ROAD NORTH

**Ben Maddox**
**From:** klewis@zephontv.co.uk
**Sent:** 16 May   09.05
**To:** benmaddox@talktalk.net
**Subject:** Re: My Instructions

I absolutely insist that you return to London without
delay. Rebekah Arens' office reports that you are not
in local difficulty. You are not to act alone. Foreign
Office is on to this.
E-mail me if there are problems getting a flight –
otherwise, acknowledge this e-mail and return to UK.
K. Lewis

Ben turned the paper over and read the e-mail again. She'd
dropped the 'Kath' for 'K': he wasn't her golden boy any
longer. Meanwhile he was using the handy back of the e-
mail for his own purposes. Even with Richard's driving
skill in the pouring rain, the going was slow, but Ben's time
was not being wasted.

'How're you doing?' Rebekah asked him. 'I was never
any good at codes – except "A equals one", that sort of
thing.'

Ben had gone back to blocking out certain letters from
the groups of five.

'I dunno. I've seen these grouped letters things before,
and I'm no Enigma machine, but then I don't reckon
Eamonn Reilly is either!'

| | | |
|---|---|---|
| /EADL | Z/AUH | JU/TA |
| ENH/F | LSTL/ | /EHLR |
| C/FWW | TJ/KX | FBG/S |
| BQAU/ | /FBWS | D/TAF |
| UA/XX | FBG/C | BSAX/ |
| /LVAB | P/CBN | XA/LH |
| EJT/Q | JSSQ/ | /LSSP |
| S/BBE | UL/MJ | MBM/B |
| XFBG/ | /AHEQ | J/FAU |
| AS/AZ | FUL/Z | LFKE/ |
| /BTLH | J/HZA | |

'I'm trying the obvious first. Cancel out the first letter of the first group, the second letter of the second group, the third letter of the third group...'

'An' the fourth letter of the fourth group,' Richard smiled from the front.

'Exactly. Cancel the fifth in the fifth, and start again.'

'Clever boy!' from Rebekah.

'Could be. Or it's Eamonn Reilly not such a clever boy – because he's given it away himself.'

'Yeah?'

'His dummy letters are in a pattern. He could have picked letters at random, but he's used the alphabet backwards – starting with "Z". "Z" is the first letter of the first group, "Y" is the second letter of the second group...'

'And "A" is the dummy letter in the twenty-sixth group.' Richard swerved round a pothole. 'This ain't just a brilliant driver sitting here...'

'So, what have you got?' Rebekah wanted to know.

'I've written it out – but not in best!'

```
E A D L Z A U H J U T A E N H
F L S T L E H L R C F W W
T J K X F B G S B G A U F B W S
D T A F U A X X F B G C
B S A X L V A B P C B N X A L H
E J T G J S S G L S S P S
B B E U L M J M B M B X F B G
A H E G J F A U A S A Z
F U L Z L F K E B T L H J H Z A
```

Ben frowned. 'But it's not so much what I've got as what I haven't got. Because with the simple thing Reilly's done with the dummies, he's got to have been cleverer with the code. Cocky, almost…'

'You mean it's not "A" equals "C" along the alphabet?' Richard asked. 'In a pattern?'

'Nope.' Ben stared down at the alphabet that he'd written out across the bottom of the page – his 'working'. 'He'll have chosen a line from a book, or a saying, which Charles Henderson already knows. You write that out above the alphabet, and you've cracked it.'

'Which could be anything in the world!' said Richard.

Rebekah turned round to Ben from the front. 'Well, keep on going, boy! We've got another four hours' driving before we rendezvous with the "Pompiers" in Botae.'

*Pompiers* – which was another code: for the small force,

named after the French fire brigade, that was aiming to turn their hoses on Red Fire, and bring out Mujiba Kalala – and perhaps Jonny Aaranovitch – alive.

Although, Ben knew, the chances of the first were brighter than the chances of the second, for the simple reason that no hostage-taker demands had been made. Which meant that Jonny wasn't a bargaining tool – he had to be dead already.

# ZEPHON TELEVISION

## TRANSCRIPT OF ZEPHON NEWS

### BROADCAST – EXTRACT AT 27' 30"
### May 16 22.00 bulletin

### NEWSREADER: ADRIAN LEMAR

**Item 31**

### Adrian Lemar (to camera):

Finally, some breaking news received from sources in Lansana,
West Africa. The award-winning Zephon Television film
cameraman Jonny Aaranovitch is reported missing while on
holiday in the country's North East Region.

### Lemar (voice over a photograph of Jonny Aaranovitch, head and shoulders, smiling):

Jonny was last seen north of Sikakoko, on a photographic hunt
for jackal and the said-to-be-extinct African hunting dog. His
camera equipment has been found near his four-wheel drive,
but there has been no sign of Jonny for thirty-six hours.

### Adrian Lemar (to camera):

Jonny lives alone in North London – but our hopes and
prayers are with him and his close colleagues.

### Lemar (voice over the weather map):

Now – the weather…

**EXTRACT ENDS**

# Joyce Avoka's story –
## written up by R. A. – part 9

It was the hardest physical work that Joyce had done since coming to the camp, and on the poor diet they were given, it tired her quickly. Back at home she had been used to doing everything her parents did, but with her father's hunting skills they didn't go short of roebuck meat.

Here, everything came in on the backs of pack animals – mules and donkeys and oxen – but the special consignment that had come in over the past two days was heavy, awkward – and dangerous. It was weapons, and explosives. This new consignment came up the narrow pass from the road, the animals led by the Red Fire men. As Joyce understood it, the lorries drove down from the Kutuliza capital to the nearest point to the camp, the same way that the food, bedding, clothing, and latrine chemicals did. From there the pack animals were led up the pass and along the tracks to the camp, where it was unstrapped from the animals' backs by the men, and carried into the munitions dump by the young soldier ants.

There were over a hundred rifles of different sorts, with machine guns, crates of revolvers, rocket launchers, boxes of detonators, belts and belts of ammunition rounds in sacks, and explosives in two-kilo cans. But weapons and explosive are denser than food and clothing, and the animals – like the soldier ants – buckled under the weight on their backs. Death comes heavier than life. And the heaviest item, slung on industrial wires between two single-file oxen, was a canister bomb, the size of a half-barrel of oil.

The soldier ants started in squads, tents of boys and tents

of girls, each unit under their sergeant; but as the laborious hours went by, they soon became a jumbled column – just like real ants – carrying loads one way and returning along the line for more. So it wasn't hard for Joyce to find herself working in the line just in front of Mujiba Kalala, who hadn't spoken to her since the morning when the white prisoner had been brought in.

No one in the shuffling column had much breath for talk – but a whisper can ride on an exhausted gasp.

'This is going to kill a lot of people!' Mujiba hissed.

'This – and us!' whispered Joyce.

Which was all that either could manage for a further half hour of carrying.

'Come on! One more rifle, two! You ain't weak, you're Yoori soldiers!' The sergeants kept the line moving, hitting out at ants who dropped anything to the rocky ground. 'That's money – an' life! You bend that canister out o' shape an' one of us is dead, you master?'

Hopes! Hopes! thought Joyce, if it's you! Which were bolstered when she was close enough to Mujiba again.

'Any hopes of getting away from here?' he said quietly into her ear, when the line stopped in a small clot. 'Run for it – back the way the animals came?'

'They will shoot! Or you would die – we're nowhere, us, on a big, bare, mountain!'

But the line carrying the weapons was two-way – and who had to be passing with an armful of rifles but the leader from Mujiba's tent? 'You think the girls will like you, footbally boy?' he sneered. 'Sporty-man, you are nothing!' And he made a scornful gesture with a little finger.

The boy following a few behind him snorted, his face

pressed into rifle butts. 'She don't count! She'll drop anything!' he said as he passed. It was Joyce's side-street partner from the raiding party, when she'd dropped her rock instead of throwing it. He shuffled on. 'I keep this wide-awake eye on that chickenshit!' And as he passed, he cold-stared her in the face.

'What was all that?' Mujiba asked her in a low voice when they next found themselves together.

Joyce told him as she struggled under an armful of rifles: she felt that she could really trust this boy. 'I didn't do my duty – I tried not to get township people killed. I am not a good Red Fire...'

'We can be good Yoori without being good Red Fire!'

'They will kill me in the end, I know – because I don't think I can kill for them...'

With the rest, they laboured on, until they had one more passing moment.

'I admire you!' Mujiba said. 'Some people know their own minds, don't obey wrong orders. That's good, not bad.'

'Are you like me?' Joyce whispered, bending to place a box of M16 cartridges.

Mujiba nodded. 'And I know that Yusa would not want to see us killed...' he said.

This gave Joyce a strange sort of comfort. Being out of step with everyone in the camp was frightening; now to find another of like mind brought the first smile to her face for weeks.

And as Mujiba turned from placing a crate of spare parts where a sergeant pointed, he saw the smile, and whispered, 'My sister! You smile like my sister!' And she saw that there were tears in his eyes.

The sergeant snapped round. 'Get on, you! Or you'll feel this belt!'

After which, no more was said that day between Joyce and Mujiba, but the exchanges had somehow given Joyce a glimmer of hope – for her soul, if not for her body.

# NORTH LANSANA

They were the elite: a small squad of trained trackers, reconnaissance and survival experts and, Ben suspected, assassins, if need be. They had arrived at the rendezvous in Botae's busy market-place in civilian clothes, could have been a football squad, but once the mission started and they hit the western road, they all wore the Vietnamese-inspired 'black pyjamas' – which Ben was given to wear as well.

Their leader, known only as 'Pomp One', briefed them straight off. 'This mission, we go in quick and get out fast! Garrottes an' silencers – I don' want no noise!'

There were only six of them, crouching with Ben by the roadside near to where he'd parked the Jeep the night Jonny had disappeared. Before coming, Ben had studied the star chart on the Secret Service computer and, helped by the Pompiers' satellite navigation, brought them to the spot that he recognised. The difference tonight was that after their transport had left them, the area around had been 'swept' by four of the Pompiers, and pronounced 'clean' of Red Fire patrols.

The black-clad squad, almost invisible at night, had come up the western less well-used Lansana to Kutuliza road hiding in the clean tank of a new Shell oil lorry which regularly served the generators of remote goat and sheep farmers: with its more flourishing economy, Lansanan Shell oil was cheaper than Kutuliza's own. From here they were going to climb above the road to the point where Ben, Rebekah and Jonny had prepared to sleep that other night, and then head on to Ben's best estimate of the Red Fire camp location.

But the plan relied on them finding a Red Fire patrol, and taking it by surprise. This was essential. The Red Fire was known to wear uniforms, which the Pompiers needed for a couple of them to move around the enemy camp without raising the alarm. Already, one of the Pompiers carried a Smith and Wesson Mark 22S, a 0.9 millimetre handgun with a sub-sonic round, known as the 'Hush Puppy' on account of its use on enemy guard dogs. And in case they were challenged, the Pompiers needed to know Red Fire passwords for that night – the likely spilling of which Ben hadn't questioned for a moment: he was with very persuasive men.

And it was this thought that pulled Ben up short. What the hell was he doing here with this ruthless unit? He was not a war reporter embedded with a NATO patrol. He had disobeyed Kath Lewis's Zephon orders, was probably out of a job – but he would always be a journalist sniffing out a story, and deep down he knew that this would make a dramatic report for someone, when the time came.

Which was shameful thinking – because the real reason for him being here had to be his fraternal attempt to get Jonny Aaranovitch out of Red Fire hands. Anything else would only be a bonus, and if he got paid for it, the money would go direct to Jonny's kibbutz.

With his large-scale map illuminated by a night-vision torch, and the help of Pomp Five, Ben navigated the way through the dense cloud layer that enveloped the unit; not at the front of the column, but third, while Pomp One and Pomp Two checked the track for loose rocks and booby-traps. It was slow going, the Ade Mountains were huge, and Ben knew from the map and its scale that they were going to be two or three nights getting to the camp. And it was cold. After Jonny's disappearance from the mountain, Ben and Rebekah had driven straight out, but Ben had discovered how the temperature dipped at night, especially when the weather was wet. So beneath his black pyjamas, Ben had clothed himself warmly, and he wore a black balaclava over his head.

All night they followed the goat paths along the valley side, across the screes and onwards up the trail that they made for themselves; and at dawn they rested up.

'Don' move about!' Ben was told. 'Eat Ration One an' get into your bag for sleep. No washin'! An' if you got to pass stuff from your body, you keep close for doin' it, jus' cover it when we leave. We're not here for smellin' good!'

Their rations were light and roughage-free – and after eating his hard-tack, Ben knelt to pee, all he needed to do, and pushed himself into his insulated sleeping bag, zipping it up high over his face. But sleep was hard to come. His mind was too active, and his legs wanted to jerk and kick with the strain of the march in his muscles: he wasn't as trained and fit as these men.

He thought about Jonny, and wondered what the poor guy might have gone through before he died: thoughts which led him on to thinking of Jonny's kid-like wish to meet Eamonn Reilly – and from Reilly to the code that was worrying his brain. The map reading had kept his intellect busy during the night trek, but now, as the sky lightened above the enveloping cloud and he tried to stay in the darkness of his sleeping bag, the problem of the code came back to deny him sleep.

He'd cracked the first level – discounting certain letters from the groups of five. Now, crucially, he needed to superimpose onto the twenty-six letters of the English alphabet a pre-determined phrase or saying or line from a book. That's how it worked, he was sure. He'd explained it to Rebekah.

'Like, if the phrase is, The quick brown fox jumped over the lazy dog' – the old keyboard exercise using every letter in the alphabet – '"a" is going to be "t", and "b" is going to be "h", and "c"'ll be "e", because they're the letters of the first word, "the": a, b, c equals t, h, e.'

'I can follow that!'

'Then, when a letter gets repeated in the phrase or saying, if it comes up twice like the "o"s in "brown" and "fox", the second "o" gets struck out, ignored.'

'So we only need the right saying to lay against the alphabet…'

'That's all! Which could be anything!'

'And I thought you could set the *Graphic* crossword!' Rebekah was definitely keeping her head up these days.

Now, wide awake in his sleeping bag, Ben's mind went to Eamonn Reilly's Spurs connection, which he was certain was no longer active – a club like that would have no truck with arms dealing – and he thought around it. What might Reilly have come up with? What was the Spurs motto?

He recalled it, saw it running across beneath the cockerel on the famous club shield before they dropped it. Audere-est-facere – 'to dare is to do'. Very appropriate, he thought, but not long enough, there weren't sufficient different letters in it. Or what about an Irish song?

In Dublin's fair city,

Where the girls are so pretty,

I first set my eyes on sweet Molly Malone…

He ran the words of the verses through – but this was

getting silly, and he needed something with some x's and z's in. He definitely couldn't rule out Reilly's need to use those rarer letters.

He lay there and thought for maybe an hour. Peeking out at the sky, he saw an eagle with its impressive wing-span wheeling above him, and he hoped that the bird of prey wouldn't take an interest in them and give their position away. But the Pompiers were all as still as mountain-old rocks, probably trained to sleep on demand, and after a while the creature flew off to hunt above another peak.

So, where had he got? But Ben knew he had to stop puzzling out the code – he had to get some sleep or he'd be useless navigating the trek that night. The Lansanan secret service didn't think it was very important, anyway. He zipped up again and lay inhaling his own breath – that often helped sleep to come – and with his eyes shut tight, his mind went to Mujiba Kalala, who'd been taken from his fit footballer's sleep to be a Red Fire advocate. Most nights the boy had slept easy, one might think: exercise, achievement, a straight-forward life. But had he? Ben thought of the boy's real interests, of which he might dream: the band on his wall, and the English premiership players who were his heroes. But what about his outpourings in the student notebook? He'd been torn two ways, hadn't he? That must have kept him awake some nights, the poor kid…

And eventually sleep came to Ben Maddox. But his subconscious brain went on working its computer-like connections to try to give him a solution to his problem, the way brains do: so that when he awoke, he might have it.

If he was lucky, and his brain was up to it…

# LANSANA INTERNAL SECURITY SERVICE

## TRANSCRIPT OF RADIO
## TRAFFIC, SPECIAL HIGH FREQUENCY
## OPERATIVE TO SECURITY SERVICE BASE

### 20 May. 05.30 hrs.

**Pomp One,**
Pomp One to Base. Over.

**Base Operator,**
Receiving. Over.

**Pomp One,**
Reporting unit in position. Laying up in hours of daylight, ready for assault tonight. Over.

**Base Operator,**
I'm transferring you to 'Oversee'. Over.

**Pomp One,**
Holding. Over.

**Oversee (female voice),**
Pomp One, you're there? Any casualties? Over.

**Pomp One,**
Negative. Unit in place. Location

found. Two uniforms an' password in
our possession. If needed. Over.

Oversee:
Bodies? Over.

Pomp One:
Two. Covered with rocks an' stones.
Won't be found till operation's all
over. Over.

Oversee:
Can you confirm position for us? Over.

Pomp One:
Not right now. Guy says tonight. No
clouds up here, he's gonna fix us by the
stars. Over.

Oversee:
Understood. Don't move in till you get
the word from us. Over.

Pomp One:
Back up? Over.

Oversee:
Negative. And out.

Pomp One:
An' out.
TRANSMISSION ENDS

## KUTULIZA MOUNTAINS

They were there! Lying in a crevice thirty metres from the ridge of the valley, Ben could see the camp. It was brilliantly camouflaged, would be absolutely invisible from the air, but using binoculars from two hundred metres above it, he could see the swirls of black, brown and green on the netting – and, from time to time, the movement of people through it.

Getting the Pompiers here hadn't been straightforward. He'd had to hold his nerve when the leader thought they were going too high, when, far too soon, the man had wanted to send a reconnaissance scout off on his own along a likely track. But back in Secret Service HQ, Ben had overlaid onto the large scale map the star pattern he'd seen on the night of Jonny's disappearance, pinpointing where they had camped, and he knew that Pomp One's likely track was not his.

Then luck had struck. On the second morning, as dawn broke they had come across animal tracks on what looked like a well-worn trail. There were tramples of them, with droppings along the way. And these weren't goats or sheep, these were big, heavy creatures – and not just of one variety. The Pompiers had good tracking skills, they could tell mule from donkey from oxen; and mixed like this, the beasts had to be a means of transport, the only possible sort on this remote mountain-side.

So three Pompiers had laid up near to the trail, while the others, with Ben, had gone higher to get some daytime sleep. And within four hours, the splinter three had ambushed a Red Fire patrol. They called it an 'opportunity' ambush: different from a planned one, where the enemy has been reconnoitred beforehand. On the trail where the pack animals had toiled, the Red Fire patrol had strung along, fairly relaxed on this routine route. From their conversation they were heading for their hide-out – noisy talk which gave the alert.

All Ben was told was that they'd been easily jumped, and within seconds of stripping himself of his uniform, one was dead with his throat cut, and the other was being promised life if he gave the information the Pompiers wanted. And the guy had spilled the camp password, and the radio frequency, and the call-in time of 18.00 hours every day. And then he had had his own blood spilled – for being in the wrong place at the wrong time.

All of which Ben learned later. Because when Ben first woke in the late afternoon, high in the crevice above the camp, his mind was fixed on a single thought.

Was it there? The code? The likely phrase or saying that was the key – had he got it? Had his sleeping brain really done its job? As he stretched his aching calves and rubbed his eyes, he knew that there was just a possibility, anyhow.

Pomp Four was on watch, his non-reflective binoculars circling in a constant sweep of the opposite side of the valley, of the camp plateau, and of the mountain-side below and above them.

Lying still, Ben spoke softly to him; so low that it could have been a breath of gentle breeze. 'You got a Bible?' he asked.

The man neither stopped his sweep, nor blinked. 'Pomp One – he's the Bible man,' he said; 'for burials on active duties.'

Ben nodded, zipped up again. Then he would have to wait until Pomp One woke, to see if he'd cracked the code, or not.

He was patient, and within the hour he had the Bible from Pomp One, finding among the books of the prophets the same text that was hanging from Mujiba Kalala's wall:

**What is inside a man is of more worth to God than the clashing of cymbals and the throwing of spears, for holiness is a fount that springs from within**

But he was sure this wasn't it: what he was looking for was something more warlike, the words that had been printed across the front of the Yoori Independence pamphlet that had been placed in Mujiba's bedside drawer. And turning back the tissue-thin pages of the Bible, he found what he wanted, the exact quotation – which was vital to have.

10. Have we not all one father? Has not one God created us? Why then are we faithless to one another, profaning the covenant of our fathers?

11. Judah has been faithless, and abomination has been committed in Israel and in Jerusalem.

12. May the Lord cut off from the tents of Jacob the man who does this, as he will save any who witness or answer for righteousness, or bring an offering to the Lord of hosts!

13. Jozea proclaims, "There shall come a mighty scourge across the laxful land, and question not, the just lashes of the scourge shall dwell with God, the King everlasting.

14. Has not the one God made and sustained for us the spirit of life? This shall be granted to those who scourge in his name."

15. Thus says the Lord of hosts: If you will walk in my ways and keep my charge, then you shall rule my house, and I will give you the right of access among those who are standing here.

There it was: verse thirteen: Jozea proclaims, "There shall come a mighty scourge across the laxful land, and question not, the just lashes of the scourge shall dwell with God, the King everlasting."

Wouldn't that be more the sort of phrase Charles Henderson and Red Fire would choose as the key to a code? Now, lying as still as he could in the lip of his sleeping bag, he shuffled between the Bible and the back of Kath Lewis's e-mail, looked at the alphabet he had written out and carefully, very carefully, he wrote above the alphabet the 'scourging' text from the Bible, the Red Fire mantra, skipping those letters in the text that were repeats.

```
J O Z E   A   P R O C L A  I M S
A B C D   E   F G   H I    J K L

T H E R E  S H A L L  B E
M N                    O

A  M I G H T Y  S C O U R G E
        P   Q          R

A C R O S S  T H E  L A X F U L
                          S T

L A N D  A N D  Q U E S T I O N
    U     V      W

N O T  T H E  J U S T  L A S H E S

O F  T H E  S C O U R G E

S H A L L  D W E L L  W I T H
                X

G O D  T H E  K I N G
            Y

E V E R L A S T I N G
  Z
```

Now, if he was right, Ben could substitute the letters of the English alphabet for those in the code – hoping two things: that he'd hit on the right key to the code in the Yusa text – and that Eamonn Reilly would have used English and not Akan, Ga, or Swahili for his message.

He dug out his small pocket notebook from the depths of his black pyjamas, and set to work. First, Reilly's coded message, without the dummy letters from the groups of five.

```
E A D L Z A U H J U T A E N H
F L S T L E H L R C F W W T J K X F
B G S B G A U F B W S D T A F U
A X X F B G C B S A X L V A B P C
B N X A L H E J T G J S S G L S S
P S B B E U L M J M B M B X F B
G A H E G J F A U A S A Z F U L
Z L F K E B T L H J H Z A
```

Then, carefully, very carefully, he started – or hoped that he had started – to decode the message. Which would keep him occupied until dark. But in keeping busy doing this, what he kept telling himself he hadn't to forget, was why he was here. For these people, he had led them to this spot so that they could go down into the camp below him and lift Mujiba Kalala. And for himself, to find out the fate of his Zephon colleague and friend, Jonny Aaranovitch.

# LANSANA INTERNAL SECURITY SERVICE

## TRANSCRIPT OF RADIO TRAFFIC,SPECIAL HIGH FREQUENCY SECURITY SERVICE BASE TO POMP ONE

### 20 May. 18.00 hrs.

Oversee:
Oversee to Pomp One. Over.

Pomp One (whispered voice, barely discernable):
Pomp One receivin', Oversee. Over.

Oversee:
Can you confirm position?  Over.

Pomp One:
2.5 degrees, 36 minutes by 13.6 degrees, 22 minutes. Over.

Oversee:
Is this your confirmed position of target? Over.

Pomp One:
Positive. Ready to move in tonight. Over.

Oversee:
Negative. That's a negative. Over.

**Pomp One:**
Uh? Negative? You're sayin' negative to tonight? Over.

**Oversee:**
The command from above is negative - period. Tonight and every night. Instructions are to return to base. Over.

**Pomp One:**
We're not goin' in? Not bringing out the boy? Over.

**Oversee:**
Positive. I mean, that's positive on the negative. You're not going in. Get that straight. Over.

**Pomp One:**
But we're here! Ready to move! Over.

**Oversee:**
Understood. But your mission has established target location for the future. Your instructions from the very top - you're hearing, the very top? - are to return immediately to base. You read?
Over, and out.

**Pomp One:**
I read. Over, an' out.

## KUTULIZA MOUNTAINS

Ben heard the news on a held breath: a breath he'd taken in for saying something vital himself. They weren't going in? After all this, they weren't going in – not for Muj Kal, and not, on the small chance that he was still alive, for Jonny Aaranovitch? Well, that was rubbish, and outdated, because they were going to have to go in, for the reason he was anxious to tell to Pomp One.

'Confirmation, that's all they wanted,' the commando said. 'We've been comin' to make the camp position right for the president – that it's more or less where his people thought they was hiding up. Mr President-man's waitin' for when Kutuliza does some big act that gives the "go" for bombing...'

These hard, military facts were hissed at Ben as if they were soft breaths at a spider's web: all within the code of quietness.

'Because he don't want to stop all this!' Pomp Five cut in. He was the quieter, man-of-the-map with Ben, a co-navigator. 'This killing, and abducting of kids– ' he waved an arm at the camp below them '–keep all that going, he says, what's a few dead and missing if it keeps the fires stoked against the Yoori Independence? He can live with a war-that-ain't-a-full-scale-war. War presidents gets remembered. Peace presidents has to work a hell of a lot harder to get their names in the history books...'

'So long as he knows where this place is for sure,' Pomp One said, 'for when Kutuliza takes their gloves off...'

'Well, you listen!' Ben grated at Pomp One. Whatever the president's selfish motives, this paper he was holding was going to change the Lansanan's minds. 'Look at this!'

He showed Pomp One what he'd been working on, folded in half.

'What you got there?'

'A coded message, and I've cracked it.'

D e v    I c e    v n a r m e d v
E A D    L    Z    A N H J U T A E N
n t    I l    m I d n I g h t    x x
H F L S T L E H    L    R C F    W W

m a y s t o p    l o w    e r    t o    x
T J K X F    B G S B G A U F B W
l v    m e    t r    e s    s t o p
S D T A    F U A X    X F B G C

h o    l    e s    I z e    o f    h o v
B S A    X    L V A    B P C B    N X A    Hs
S e    I n d    a m w a l l    w I l l
L    J T    G J S    S G L S S P S

f l o o d s I    k a k o    k o    s t
B B E U L    M J M B M B    X F B G
p e    n d w a t e r    e l e c
A H E G J F    A U A S A Z

t r    I c    I t y    d o m I n
F U L Z    L F K    E B T L H
a n c e
J H Z A

'I'm readin' the top line?' There was just enough light in the sky to read the lines of letters.

'Try this.' Ben unfolded the paper to show the decoded message with the breaks between the words.

*Device unarmed until midnight XX May. Lower to XLV metres. Hole size of house in dam wall will flood Sikakoko. End water electricity dominance.*

'He's using roman numerals for the figures – so it's the twentieth of May, and the depth for lowering the device is forty-five metres...'

'Je-sus! So, what we're sayin—'

Ben took back the paper. 'What we're saying is that tonight, in about seven hours' time, Charles Henderson is going to blow the dam! Reilly's told him when, and how...'

'Reilly? Charles...? Who's this Charles Henderson?'

'Kutuliza, in league with Red Fire. He says he's not, but he is. And this lot down here, these are the boys who are going to do it.'

'Je-sus!' Pomp One repeated. 'Flood Sikakoko!'

Pomp Five whistled, softly. 'It'll wipe the town – and all the mountain villages.'

And Pomp Three hissed, softly, 'With kids, and all my people!'

'Dev-a-station!' said Pomp Two. 'But Sikakoko's a Yoori township! They'll flood their own—?'

Pomp One was fishing up his radio. 'That's nothin' in the greater plan of things: it'll show ol' President what they're up to doin'. An' they'll be getting' down to the dam right now!' He spread the map of the mountains.

'Look an' see how they'll go.'

Ben looked hard at the contours; this army map was a good one, and he felt that it could be trusted. 'If they've got a big enough device to blow the dam, they'll have to have gone down on the road. Must have, there's no route from the camp to the dam for anything heavy or bulky – just a possible trail here.' He ran his fingernail a couple of centimetres down the map. 'If they slid down the screes and found their way through the forest towards the water-courses which...' he checked the gradient '...have got to be rapids.'

Meanwhile, one eye still on the map, Pomp One was alerting Oversee in Johnstown. He read over the decoded message, word for word, and listened to their reaction before he shut down.

'They're scrambling helicopters but they don't reckon they can get infantry in position in time.'

'Why not?' Ben wanted to know.

'You can't parachute men into these mountains. The altitude'll freeze 'em comin' out of the aircraft. An' they'd need oxygen tanks, plus they'd get picked off comin' down in such a narrow arc.'

Pomp Three was shaking his head, but agreeing. 'An' the ones who do survive would break their necks landing onto rocks...'

Which was true. Parachuting needed some sort of flat space for the roll, especially carrying weapons.

'The Northern Battalion's basing at Botae, but they can't get no one up to the dam by midnight...'

Ben blew out his cheeks. So, they were failing all round. Even if the president changed his mind and let the Pompiers go down to infiltrate the camp, six of them couldn't capture the place – their sham mission had been only to get Mujiba Kalala out. And what then, anyway, if the target was the dam? Ben looked down at the camp and the plateau below them, and checked with the map.

'Which gives us one chance!' he suddenly said. 'To get down to the dam by twenty-four hundred. There's one way, according to the map – if we're lucky.'

'Yeah?' Pomp One didn't sound convinced.

But Pomp Three, with family in Sikakoko was more urgent. 'What?' he asked. 'We got to take any chance!'

'We can't skirt the camp. There's no time to go all the way round the camp plateau, not on foot; but if we go down into the camp as planned, work our way through it as a short cut towards the south-east, where it slopes towards this steep valley...' Ben showed them on the map. '...And we follow these contour lines east to here; we can pick up this water-course running down here.' He pointed to it...and looked up at the élite fighting force, crouching around the map. 'Which looks as if we could white-water raft down to round about here...'

'Raft?'

'Could do...'

'Not over no falls?'

'Not if I've read this map right.' Ben skewed the map towards Pomp Five for an expert opinion. 'It looks about ...three in ten most of the way, slicing along these contour lines. It's ledged, sedimentary rock...'

'If we had a raft!' said Pomp One.

'Man, that's what we get from the camp!' Pomp Two suddenly put in. 'Saw or axe, some tent canvas, guy ropes – and logs we'll cut local, down there. Me, I'm water-survival trained...'

There was no opposition to that. No alternative. They had all been prepared to go down into the camp, until that radio contact with Oversee at base now the incursion was on again.

But first there had to be radio contact of another sort: Pomp One reporting that all was well from the dead Red Fire patrol to the camp.

## SHORTWAVE DX 17907

Red Fire Patrol Six Radio (Pomp One) 'Hyena':
Hyena to Island.  Over.

Island:
Island to Hyena.  Over.

Pomp One:
Hyena reporting all clear an' well. Over.

Island:
You both okay?  Over.

Pomp One:
No problems.

Island:
Get on, then, confirm position - we're busy up here.
You know the drill. Over.

Pomp One:
Sure I know the drill. It's just -

<u>Island:</u>
So give us your location code.  Come on,
man…  Over.

<u>Pomp One:</u>
OK, sure.

*Pomp One was turning to the others,*
*holding out the ear-piece of the radio.*

<u>Pomp One:</u>
You want tonight's… ? Over.

<u>Island:</u>
Yeah, Hyena, the normal …
You been at the funny herbs down there?
Over.

*Pomp One laughs, makes it last for a few*
*seconds.*

From crouching listening, Pomp Three suddenly leant over
and grabbed the mouthpiece from Pomp One: and with his
mouth almost chewing on it, he gave out a long, curling,
low-moving-to-high sound, like radio interference. He took
a breath, came away from the mouthpiece, and spoke,
doing a fair imitation of his unit leader.

<u>Pomp Three:</u>
Sor'...we're...int'...'ence...call...
'gain...'idnight...'Ver.

293

And he did another howling and curdling into the mouthpiece – gesturing urgently for Pomp One to switch the radio off.  They all looked at one another.

'Let's hope they didn't get a fix on that!' said Ben.

Pomp One slapped a congratulation on Pomp Three's back. 'They won't bother, not if we're radioin' in again at midnight.'

Which everyone hoped would be the case: knowing that a missing radio call from 'Hyena' to 'Island' was the least of the problems that midnight on the twentieth of May was going to bring.

**FILE NAME: Dell Computer Notebook
Ben Maddox / Pompiers
Notes for possible script –
Red Fire Camp and Ade Dam**

Left position soon as sun set, reckoned safe to move despite last light in sky. P1 in one of the Red Fire uniforms, incl. black trainers. Other uniform worn by P3 – man who knew what was wanted for raft making. Rest of us in 'black pyjamas' & balaclavas.

Too high for tree or vegetation cover, but rocks and boulders. With these trained guys in the dark not too difficult to descend 100 metres in quick time. Problem being not to start rock-slide, but P1 skilled at knowing which way to lead; took pains to move anything in our path that might give. Got eyes made for night-vision, without gadgets, real lynx.

My face blackened with mud carried especially from water-course lower down. Felt ready to be in vain President's film!

Camp perimeter poorly protected & patrolled. We came v. cautiously down final drop to plateau, but no razor wire nor men on picket duty: camp suddenly opened into ragged lines of winter tents. Why? My guess – with patrols out & remoteness of place, attack from above reckoned impossible. Not that we're attacking: we're infiltrating.

P1 ducked & ran under strung camouflage netting into first break between lines, signalled us to wait – us lying flat on ridged rock-tops at edge of plateau. P1 stood & looked around, real 'command' about him, every bit as if he belonged. He could hear what we could hear, talking in tents, voices of boys & girls; meant we were on side of camp where kids were. Looking v. hard, could see glim of low lights as tent flaps opened.

P1 suddenly spins around, his back to us. Someone coming along lines of tents, ducking head into each like school prefect, wearing three sergeant stripes. & coming towards P1 Straight off, P2 had his silenced 'Hush Puppy' up & trained on target. Strained ears.

P1 first to speak: always seems less suspicious: 'Everythin' smooth?' All radio stuff had been in English.
'Smooth, man! All mastered. What's your business over this side?' Sergeant surprised to find this other soldier there.
Nasty silence. Instantly, P3 makes back for P2 to take aim. P2 drew deep snipers' breath to let out slowly as prepared to shoot.
'What d'you think I'm here for?' P1 says as if there's always some furtive activity going on behind lines of a camp.
'Girls' lines?' Sergeant speaking.
'That's my top posho.'
Did Sgt. smile or pull face? Couldn't see. But turned on heels, checked one last tent, made off down line.
P1 called us in; 6 of us, stooping, running across space into lines of tents.
Moon rising, clear sky; clouds below us; glow cast eerie light through camouflage netting.

Knew which way to go, getting across camp to south-east side. Tent lines ran east to west, us at north-east side; so had to follow line of Andromeda as it lines up with Perseus;

gave us bearing, lined up compasses on it. P1 ready to go.
'Us in uniforms go first; others lie low beside the tents.
Watch for signals to come on.'
All slapped his arm to say OK. Had to make speed through
camp, had to be slick, had to get down to dam and do best
to stop detonation of some big device that would flood S.
township. But us still in lines of tents.

Boy came running out of tent, unstrapping belt, must be
heading for latrines – urgent.  Sight froze us, two in uniforms
standing, rest crouching agnst tent wall. Sudden thought.
Hissed at P1: 'Stop him, ask for Mujiba Kalala.' Couldn't
forget my story.  P1 shook head, but had to stand ground for
the boy.
As boy passed, I asked him, from behind P1. 'Mujiba Kalala,
which tent, boy?' In dark and boy's rush, could've been P1
talking.
Boy said: 'Footballer boy?'
P1 had to nod, say: 'Affirmative.'
'Next to mine. This side.' Boy ran on about his business.
No time for argument. Talk had quietened nearest tent.
Said: 'You go on!  I'll follow.' Didn't wait for reply, half
expected 'Hush Puppy' bullet in back, ran doubled-over
along line to tent next to lav boy's, stood by door flap. Heard
voice inside reading aloud from Bible. Looked around to
check line of retreat, away from tents towards south-east.

Suddenly knew how stupid this was. Mujiba Kalala not the
story any more – but dam. World's press wd headline on
township horror, economic disaster, stoked-up African war
between Lnsna and Ktliza.  Even poor Jonny small fry
against big turn in African history.

But I was here now. Could run and follow Pompiers, or give one last shot to Kalala business. Cd still be story, if dam saved!

Pulled back balaclava to stick blackened face into tent if had to. Called into tent in deep voice like Sergeant, 'Mujiba Kalala! Outside!'

'Mu-jiba!' Bible reader's voice, scornful, teasing. 'Tell Sergeant your rightful number when he's done with you!' Laughs from other boys.

Sound of movement inside tent. Snap: 'Come on!'

Tent flap moved, & Mujiba Kalala there, still dressed, notebook in hand.

Pulled him out, fast, clamped hand over mouth, told him, 'Not a word! I'm from Nokongolgo and Eni! Come on!' Ran him across 2-metre break between tents, and threw to ground just as sergeant marches back down line shouting for lights out, & silence.

Got him! But what now?

**SAVE AS BEN'S DOCUMENTS AND FLASHSTICK**

# Joyce Avoka's story –
## written up by R. A. – part 10

The rustle at the tent door-flap had everyone lying still on their thin straw beds. The sergeant had just been down the boys' lines shouting for silence and lights-out, but that wasn't always the end of night-time happenings. A girl would creep out – and not always to the latrines – or a soldier would come for someone he'd fancied from the last parade: to which there was no not-going. You went, and you kept your mouth shut.

Joyce had been lucky. No such thing had happened to her yet; she wasn't one of those bigger girls who took the eyes of the men; but there could always be a first time...

The flap opened, and a face came poking through it. Someone inside the tent shone a light at it, but not directly into the face, a soldier could slap you around for such outrage. But it wasn't a sergeant or one of the men, it was a soldier ant from the male lines: it was Mujiba Kalala, the football boy.

The girls pretended to pull up their blankets in modesty; except one, who asked, 'Me? You come calling for me?' at which everyone laughed.

'No. Shut up!' the boy hissed. 'Forty-five, wanted outside.'

It was Joyce, who wasn't totally surprised to be the one picked from the tent by Mujiba – but shocked that he had come in such a way.

She went, anyway. She had only partially undressed, the nights were always cold, and despite the winter tents and the uniforms, most nights were spent shivering. So, even in the dark, it took her no time to pull on her uniform trousers and trainers – against the tent's sniping and filthy remarks. She went to the tent flap, and slipped cautiously outside.

There was a man in black standing with Mujiba Kalala. 'Come on,' Mujiba said, 'I can't go and leave you to this!'

'Where? Why?'

'Ssssh!' hissed the man in black. 'Out of here. Follow, and don't trip.'

He led them dodging through the lines of tents. In the mess tent, the sergeants were drinking and laughing, and one of them came to its doorway and threw out a glassful of beer. 'Dregs!' he shouted in disgust, and went back inside.

There were pickets about, walking in ones and twos the way they always did, casually, concerned with law-and-order within the camp rather than with anyone coming in from outside, or anyone from inside going out. A kid on the run would soon be picked up, or would die on the harsh mountain.

And between dodging, and running, and throwing themselves flat, Joyce, Mujiba and the man in black came to the southern edge of the Camp Vido plateau; where they met up with two soldiers and four other men also in black, carrying an axe, and a small bivouac from the stores compound.

As the others prepared to carry their stuff onward down the side of the mountain, the man who had fetched them asked them a question. 'A white man. Did they bring in a white man?'

Joyce nodded. They certainly had, and she had been waiting to see him hanging one day from the gallows, as she dreaded that she would, too.

'What happened to him?'

She shook her head.  She didn't know.  But Mujiba did.

'They took him out two days ago,' he reported.

'Alive?'

'Just.'

'Where, which way?'

'The way the ammunition came, down the pass.  Stupid, they took the big canister back the way it had come...'

'And the man went with them?'

'Yes.  About twenty Red Fire, and two mules with the canister slung between, and the man tied up and marched behind.'

But there was no more dwelling on that. The men in black and the other two were ready with loads on their back and their hands free, starting to descend from the camp plateau down a steep rock face, gripping, sliding, falling – with Mujiba and Joyce among them.

Going where? Joyce kept asking herself.

## FILE NAME: Dell Computer Notebook
## Ben Maddox / Pompiers
## Notes for possible script –
## Red Fire Camp and Ade Dam

Knew it would be hard, fast, going. Descending always more difficult than climbing: difficult fight against gravity, or you could take the really fast way down! But P1 led well, good eye for likeliest routes down slopes, took us stepping, running, jumping, sliding down towards tree line.

Then not easy in trees. Moon, arching through sky, same general direction, obscured by tall hardwoods – & trails hard to see by torch, beam too direct, ridges & indents can't be seen. But had compasses. P5 brill. navigation as we crashed down through forest – brought us to where water-course heard, knew we were on track.

P2 comes into his own. Muj and girl catch breath, water survival expert goes for it, with help.
'Gripper bar raft! Want five trunks, about fifteen centimetres diameter – ' throws axe at P3. 'Get chopping, no worry about neat ends, just all same length, two metres...'
Throws folding knife at me. 'Watch that blade – a man's only as sharp as his knife, an' I c'n shave with that!' (Good phrase!)
Catch knife. 'Four stakes, bit of bend, about a metre and half long.' Go into trees & find clump of striplings, start cutting. P1 comes with own knife – cuts 3 to my 1.
Trunks took longer to get – P1 looking at watch – me looking at water-course. Narrow here, this high up not running at great speed, but about full enough for buoyancy needed for raft & 7 men. Will face what

happens further down when come to it.

7 men. Only. P1 speaks to me, I tell kids. Tell them: 'This water-course runs into dam reservoir. We're going down quick way! You follow, fast as you can on foot – but take care! & when you get down, don't show till you know what's going on.' I stop. Thought not occurred till now. 'If we're not there – if the dam's not there – you're on your own!'

Mujiba shocked – poss. no dam?

'Don't think about it! Look to yourselves…'

5 tree trunks laid side by side at right angles on top of 2 flexible stakes, 1 at front, 1 at back. Trunks pushed tight to each other & two other stakes put across on top, to meet bottom ones, tied v. tightly with guy ropes, kept in position with notches made by P2. Saw now where name 'gripper raft' came from. 'Bars' gripped trunks between them, held them in place. Spare guy rope wound round & round raft, brought up to decking in loops for hand-holds.

Now got craft for rapids!

Long, stout, stake for steering, P2 oversaw raft being put into water, holding tight against flow – & with P2 kneeling and steering, self just in front of him hanging on like born survivor, push off.

White water ride, here we come!

Rough ride, & dangerous. Map said shouldn't suddenly shoot over falls, but no being abs. sure till each tight bend rounded & not flying thro' air. Thank G for moon, hard enough in broad daylight, but night-time makes decisions last minute. But enough light in sky for P2 to steer more or less in middle of rapids, raft up to heaven one moment, down to hell next,

303

swirling to port, twisting to starboard, turning 360 in eddies, us getting drenched, half drowned; craft bucking, stalling, crashing into rocks & splitting our trunks, just about holding, & suddenly rafting down into cloud. Hear roar – really fast stretches ahead, & even in night, could see silver-grey of spray rising in air. P2 did well, couldn't really steer – had pole not rudder – but went from side to side like tacking, zig-zagging, punting in shallows near banks; & when nothing else for it, being swept along too fast, got us into midstream, & with all clinging on, heads down, raft & river took us where it would.

Down! Till, riding crest round tight bend, hit bank with great thud & land wth boots & faces in mud. P2 just about held onto raft – starting to come apart now – but no time for repair. Choice is, get down to dam somehow, or have safer raft. No choice! Tighten what we can in seconds flat, climb on again. Now more room. ??? P3 not there! Gone – no one knows where, or when. Nothing to do ab't that: missing, presumed drowned.

Next stretch easier, but as slewed round bend, heard sound dreading the most. Crash of water-fall! Raft picking up speed to hell of a drop, but with mighty plant of pole, P2 spins us round, we kick legs into water, head for bank.
Reach bank somehow, cling to roots and branches. Wet weight of raft breaking backs, pull it out of water & carry, yank, slide raft down & round fall – 20 metres high, would def. sent us into space.
No knowing where were – map lost with P3 – but had to get on. Just knew this river ran down into Ade Dam.

Running repairs essential. Tighten wet ropes again, P2 grabbed trailing vines from undergrowth to strengthen; in minutes in river again, broader, slower for a bit – before suddenly narrowed into water spume of West Africa, fighting mist hanging over like huge ghost.

No warning – force of rapids hit us in back, took us in frothing, turbulent race, as much out of water as in, all shouting heads off, no one choking back fear. Rode it, somehow: scudded on surface, aqua-planed at terrific speed towards end of world – till sudd. river widened, water calmed. Flow slowed, & there in front was broad, shining expanse of dam reservoir, swirling anti-clockwise on the surface, force of the waters swelling it, reflecting moon-hazed clouds – any other time awesome sight. But signal for action.

'In!' P1 commands. 'Off the side!' Showed us what meant, as one all slid off disintegrating raft & clung to side. 'An' swim! 'Starboard!' Kicked feet, one hand for raft, other for swimming, headed for wall of dam. Us hard to see now, look at luminous watch.

23.20.
Now about 40 mins to stop Ade Dam being blown to kingdom come, Sikakoko drowned.
Me not fit for this. Not trained. Weak, exhausted, want to die. Want to be left, but P1 pushes me on.
So this is real war.

SAVE AS BEN'S DOCUMENTS AND FLASHSTICK

## ADE DAM

Ben and the Pompiers pulled themselves out of the freezing water and dripped themselves off as best they could. Ben lay on the parapet and took what seemed an age to recover his breath and find the strength to move his arms and legs. Which he willed himself to do, and with the others crouched low on the dam parapet, their heads kept down, while Pomp One took out his night vision binoculars and scanned around the walkway that topped the dam wall. He scanned from east to west, and back from west to east, but seemed unable to fix on anything: until, with a cluck in his throat and the briefest nod of head and binoculars, he leant forward and really started staring.

The Red Fire unit of saboteurs was in place for the final phase of the operation. The day before, General Lakle himself had led them down the mule track from the camp to the road, rendezvousing with the truck he'd used in the Botae raid, which then drove them down the Kutuliza stretch to the border, which was rarely manned – too vulnerable – although from now on there was the slim chance that they'd run into a Lansanan patrol. All the while, the 'big one', the canister packed with Semtex plastic explosive, was cradled and handled with surgical care. The road was bumpy, the explosive could be unstable: and when timing devices are set by others, the lives of the people planting a bomb are always in someone else's hands. This someone, who none of them knew, could send them to Yusa at the next tick of an alarm clock. That was the risk these Red Fires took as a result of

Charles Henderson, and the government for which he secretly worked, deciding to bring things to a head. And General Lakle had to go along with that, because if it failed, and he was back operating as before, Kutuliza would cut off funds to his Red Fire army.

It was the capture of the Jewish man that had triggered this final make-or-break decision, and after a secret meeting when Charles Henderson had come to interrogate the prisoner, the Red Fire general had finally understood what was happening – and got his head round it all by setting it out on paper.

The man Aaranovitch's body to be found with his genuine Israeli kibbutz address on him, plus planted ID papers to make him look like a member of Mossad (Israel's secret service). But he'll be dressed in Red Fire uniform.

So this looks as if it's Israel that's sabotaged the dam.

Is well known that Israel's trying to sell nuclear power stations to richer African countries. Will look like, with dam gone and no hydro-electric power any more, Lansana has to accept Israel's offer.

Truth is, Red Fire is pretending to be the Israelis pretending to be Red Fire!

With no dam to make Lansanans hold on to Ade Mountains, Yooris get independence from Lansana. (They

won't rebuild, they will go nuclear
then. Likely Lansana buys water
energy from Ghana in meantime.
But will sooner or later need
cheaper nuclear energy from
Kutuliza when its secret Russian
nuclear reactor is ready at Tumi -
selling energy to most countries
around.

Charles Henderson had stirred a tasty pot, with Kutuliza
staying in the clear. And General Lakle was up with all this,
he was an intelligent man. Right now, his prisoner was held
by two men at the eastern extremity of the dam, but as the
truck made its getaway just before the dam went up, he'd
be shot by a captured Lansan rifle.

The Red Fire men had kept a very low profile. With so
many countries, including Kutuliza, depending on the
energy generated by this dam, it wasn't brilliantly well
guarded because who would be its attackers? So without
too much trouble the lorry had dropped off the Red Fire
unit and hidden up, the unit making its way along the
parapet with the bomb and its forty-five metre wire wound
around a drum.

They had made their final move, a long trek to the centre
of the parapet, pulling the bomb on a trolley. Two men had
gone ahead, creeping up on three dam security men and
clubbing them into the water: because that's what an Israeli
Mossad attacker would do. The moon came and went
behind clouds and danced macabre shadows on the water
as the bomb was carried gently to the inner edge of the

concrete parapet, right in the middle of the dam, directly above the sluice. The length of the wire was crucial; at its extended length of forty-five metres it would hang the bomb just above this sluice – where the water from the reservoir gushed and powered through to spin the turbines. But this sluice was a hole in the wall – a potential weakness – and when the bomb went off near it, the explosion would have maximum impact – for the Lansanan water industry; and for Sikakoko, which was to be the Yoori sacrifice.

Now, with the clock at 23.38, the Red Fires were lowering the bomb over the parapet with great care, ten of them gripping the wire with thick-gloved hands to hold back its weight.

'You let this down till we get to the mark on the wire. We tie off the wire against the parapet – and get the hell out of here!'

Everyone was concentrating on lowering the deadly device with speed and accuracy – there wasn't a man there who wasn't watching either the bomb as it disappeared down into the waters, or the wire as it was paid out off the drum. The wire hummed on its large spindle: twenty, twenty-five, thirty metres. If the bomb were too high when it exploded only the top of the dam would be blown up: damaging enough, but not catastrophic.

Thirty-five, forty…

'Slow! Slow now!' The watch read 23.42 on the general's wrist. The run back to safety was timed at s even minutes. Right now, the lorry would be coming out of hiding, not overtly military but with a Sikakoko builder's name on the side, its occupants ready with the engine revving. This was when the prisoner would be being untied and held against a tree. The Lansanan bolt action rifle would be being armed…

Forty-one, forty-two, forty-three, forty-four – and the painted mark on the cable came into the first man's hands.

'Forty-five!' It was 23.44.

'Right, tie off!' While the ten men took the strain on the cable, the drum end of it was disentangled from its trolley and fed round the metal framework on top of the parapet. With great strength, two men tied it off with a hitch. Now the bomb couldn't drop lower, even if everyone lost hold of it.

'Okay! We get out of here!' which were General Lakle's last words.

Because this was the moment when the Pompier guerrillas struck.

They came at them by water, with the raft vital to their plans. Ben felt dead with exhaustion, but with the rest he followed the parapet from the west like a naval commando, only his head above the water. His heart raced – but as he swam in the lee of the dam wall, he suddenly wondered what the hell he was doing there! He could have stayed in safety back with Mujiba and the girl – what was he doing down here with these front line troops? This wasn't his conflict, he was a press man, and no way was he trained to fight – and kill. But there was no going back now, and as soon as he'd asked himself the question, he'd answered it. Jonny had been brought down to the dam for some reason, the girl had said so. And if he was still alive, if there was just the slightest chance that the Pompiers could stop him from being blown to kingdom come, then Ben was going to be part of it.

And not for a second did he think of Meera, or Zephon,

or London. This sort of danger concentrated the mind.

Ben's unit was out-numbered. There were ten Red Fire, the Pompiers were now six. But Ben knew that surprise counts for a lot, and these saboteurs had no idea that they were coming. Ben lifted an arm from the water to glance at his watch: it was fifteen minutes off detonation time. With the rest, he drifted the raft into the dam side, about twenty metres short of the Red Fire. Pomp One showed a hand to point to the parapet's metal framework – they had paid out a wire – presumably with the bomb on it – and were tying it off. Whatever was done had to be done quickly. Now everything was hand signals. As they'd planned, Ben was signalled to stay with the raft and hold it steady against the dam wall, so that he could swim with it round to the wire. The others silently slithered up out of the reservoir like water rats; and, within seconds, Pomp One was pointing the muzzle of his M16 down at the ground, drawing back the cocking handle, breaking the seal, and allowing the water to be shaken out. Now his weapon was primed. He raised it to his shoulder. Two of the others were kneeling beside him on the parapet. They could be seen now, if the Red Fire looked around, but Ben knew that everything was about to happen very fast.

'Double taps!' Pomp One had hissed, back in the water – two shots fired in quick succession – there's always a chance that a marksman will miss with only one round.

Kneeling there, each had his target – a man apiece with the first salvo – a quick re-focus on the night sights, and another man apiece within five seconds. Which should be six of the ten killed or wounded. Meanwhile, Ben watched, eyes above the surface like a crocodile, as the other two, pistols out in two-handed grips, crept round the parapet to get nearer to the Red Fire, but keeping out of their own men's M16 sights.

And, 'Yes!' Pomp One shouted, firing at his first target. The sudden crack of the weapons echoed off the water and shattered the night, all around the dam. The men with pistols ran yelling at the Red Fire, firing as they ran – while Pomp One and the M16 men ran in, firing too.

It was deafening, and bloody, a massacre. The Pompiers had been right, surprise had been everything. And it was an execution, sickening to Ben to see the surprise of death on the faces, their bodies spinning and collapsing, grotesque on twisted puppet legs. Ben wanted to throw up in the water. War up close was disgusting. But he knew he had his job to do. As the order was shouted, he kicked off from the dam wall and went in with the raft, propelling it like a beaver towards the wire. This had to work! There was no time for escape any more, the bomb would go up within minutes.

Shots were still ringing out on the parapet, singles, finishing-off bullets being pumped clinically into heads. But Ben's job was the raft, and he prayed that there were enough Pomp survivors to haul the bomb up from the depths. He kicked his final strokes and brought the raft in to where the wire was suspended – to be suddenly confronted by a frightening head shooting up out of the water beside him. The face scowled into Ben's, the teeth bared, the eyes wild – but dead, and ugly in that death. In a nightmare way, the body turned, and floated past him giving off blood like red ink in a basin of water.

And had he not been quite dead, Ben asked himself, could he have finished him off, held him under? He didn't know – survival is one thing, finishing-off another – although he knew that he would never forget that terrible face.

Ben looked up to the parapet side to see huge activity on the bomb wire. The Pompiers were hauling on it to bring its deadly weight up from the depths of the reservoir: no one shouting the time, they did it, or they didn't! No one there would be left to wonder by how many minutes and seconds they had failed.

Ben stayed in the water holding the raft – and suddenly, with the most gentle of ripples from this most lethal of devices, a canister broke the surface.

With panic – now that they could see it – the Pompiers somehow manoeuvred the bomb up onto the raft, and centred it as best they could, Ben steadying from down in the water, his hands on this thing that could destroy a township. From above, Pomp One took a deep breath and commanded, 'One, two, three!' and with strength and care, they pushed the raft off from the side of the dam.

They had all risked their lives on what would happen next. The strength of the rapids running into the reservoir caused the surface to swirl slowly anti-clockwise, and Ben saw with great relief that three metres out from the side of the parapet, the raft slowly started to move away in the circular flow, to the east.

Ben was pulled up out of the water, and ran with the rest back in the direction that they'd come, to the west – hoping like hell that the plan had worked. The bomb would have caused catastrophic damage down below the water – but on the surface, who knew? Would it blow their heads off?

He had never run so fast in all his life. He was an athlete at school, but then he'd been in training. Here he was in

313

the soggy, winter-weight 'black pyjamas', wearing a lot more than a singlet and a race number. But he ran for the prize of the rest of his life! He'd heard of super-human feats when a life is at stake. Now his depended on putting a distance between him and that big canister out there in the reservoir, and he reckoned he must have broken all Olympic records as he ran for the chance to survive.

And then it went! The air was suddenly sucked from the earth. Blast suddenly hit him – and he never remembered hearing any sound. A sudden, freak, hundred-kilometres-an-hour hurricane caught him sideways on, sending him crashing against the side of the parapet, as a mushroom of water spread up and out into the sky, fifty metres high. The walkway shook like a Richter Seven earthquake, and his legs and feet were no longer his own. He threw his arms up to protect his head, as he was blown like a twig in a gale along the kerb of the reservoir – with a huge wave coming roaring across its surface. There was no choice of what to do – he had to cling to the metalwork of the parapet railings, and take the deepest of breaths in God's earth.

The wave hit him: a crushing, tidal force that pinned him to the railings, swamping him in its wet power, forcing his gripping fingers to open, open, open, helpless in the pressure that would take him over the side of the hundred metre dam. But somehow he clung on. He thought his fingers were going to break, two seconds became ten… and then that first power went from the wave. And instead of receding and coming at him again, millions of litres of reservoir water went on over the dam side.

He was left like a stranded shark on the dam side, desperately trying to clear the water and the ringing from his ears, waiting for the dam to collapse any second and take him down with it.

Or had their physics been right?

It had. The dam wall held, the structure was safe. And with Pomp One and Pomp Two – there was no sign of the others – Ben retraced his steps beside a slowly calming reservoir, low on water now, and went east along the parapet.

To see if there was any sign of that dear man, Jonny Aaranovitch. Ben was in one piece – please God that Jonny was!

# Joyce Avoka's story –
**written up by R. A. – final part**

Joyce and Mujiba watched the raft disappear round the first bend of the water-course, the men sitting, kneeling, and clinging on desperately. One moment they were there in the moonlight, the next they were gone, and all that could be heard was the bare mountain sound of the ever-running water.

'We follow!' Mujiba said.

'Will we get caught? Will they come after us?' Joyce looked back up the mountain towards the camp.

'They don't know we've gone. They think we're both doing something secret behind the tents…'

Joyce lowered her head modestly.

They found that the layered sedimentary rock strata of the mountain, ledge below ledge below ledge, kept the water-course running down sideways rather than vertically, which made following it easier, since it didn't drop straight down in a succession of falls. But easier was still hard. Their trainers were good for this terrain, but there were times when they had to help each other, holding hands across stepping rocks, lifting and being lifted, and clinging to each other for balance. It was strenuous going, and after a while, as they came down into the trees, they took a short rest. They sat huddled by the water, cradling their knees in their arms, and shivering.

'You are a nice boy,' Joyce suddenly found the voice to say. 'You came for me.'

Mujiba said nothing, didn't look at her, but stared ahead harder, across the water and into the trees on the further side.

'I say, thank you.' Joyce again broke the silence between them.

Mujiba finally cleared his throat. 'Only because I wanted to,' he said. 'We are not soldiers, either of us, we are not for turning into Yoori killers...'

Joyce thought of the rock that she had dropped rather than throw that night in Botae. And instead of her past guilt, now she felt a new pride. This boy made her feel good, he gave her back her sense of rightness and wrongness.

'And did I say you look so much like my sister when you smile?.' He reached towards her and took her hand in his, holding it tight. 'Come on! Let's get down there!' And he pulled her to her feet. But, somehow, on the rest of the long way down the mountainside, there seemed to be more need than before for the two of them to cling to each other. And it was in such a moment, when they took another rest, standing by the side of the white-water rapids, that Mujiba turned to Joyce, and kissed her on the cheek.

'I'll always be a sister,' she said – as their bodies suddenly shook, and all at once the air was filled with the violence of a huge explosion. Earth and rocks flew, branches whipped, trunks were scarred as a powerful blast hurricaned up the mountainside. Their feet were taken from under them, their bodies thrown like rubbish into the foliage. They shouted each others' names, but there was no hearing anything, only the weird sound inside their heads of a dead sort of echo – except that suddenly they could see each other, and they crawled to where they huddled to the earth and clung to each other, fiercer than ever in their dangerous world.

317

'The bomb!'
'The dam!'
'Sikakoko!'

And with that ringing in their ears that would last for hours, they ran, jumped, and slithered down beside the water-course to find out what had happened at the Ade Dam.

## ADE DAM

The surface blast saved Jonny's life. Had the dam blown deep below, the explosion would have been directed away down the valley. But the blast blew out at ground level, evenly all around in concentric rings. The powerhouse building took some of it, but it was the surrounding trees and mountainside that took the real force.

Jonny Aaranovitch was being held by two Red Fire soldiers at a tree. It was a tried technique, the prisoner held in front of a tree with his arms behind him around the trunk, the guards gripping tight on a wrist each. It's for when the prisoner isn't tied, is going to be moved, because in that position the tree prevents the flexing of muscles. Not that this prisoner was in any shape for fighting someone off. Days ago, up in the camp, he had been stripped, searched, beaten, and kicked. He had been left in his own mess until decisions were made, and then he was told that he would be hanged, and photographed for leaflets in Johnstown.

But only hours before an evening execution in front of the camp, he had been cleaned up, pulled into a Red Fire shirt, and had his own wallet and other papers stuffed into his pockets. Like that, he had been force-marched under the gallows and out of the camp, pushed down a mule track, and thrown into a lorry, the one that had brought him down here to the dam.

He knew little except that there was an importance about midnight; there was talk and a jumpiness about zero hour. One after another, more and more frequently, the two guards took a hand off his wrist to look at their watches. Something final and deadly was going to happen. although why would a Red Fire be nervous about killing a prisoner?

Or perhaps the importance of midnight was to do with the canister that they'd carried down as if it were filled with nitro-glycerine...

One of the guards suddenly released him again and ran round to the front of the tree. This was different! He was lifting his rifle to take an almost casual aim at his head. Cameramen look down many gun barrels, but this gun was in deadly earnest. Jonny's freed fingers came to his lips and he uttered the first words of a Hebrew prayer. Just as the earth suddenly shook under him and a mighty explosion blasted the gunman off his feet and away into the trees, the pressure pinning Jonny against the front of the tree taking the force of it, his praying face distorted like a sucked balloon. Then, as the tree gave, he was spun off his feet and sent like a stave into the foliage of ripped-off branches.

His head was ringing, his body newly scratched and bleeding, weak beyond all weakness, but it was his chance. No one was holding him any more. Up on the road the lorry was on its side and someone was screaming in pain. So he tried to run – and somehow found some panic strength in his legs to put one foot in front of another and stumble away from the dam. Finally, he could stagger no further, and had to throw himself down behind thick blackthorn and, like a dying mole, dig furiously with his fingers into the earth for some sort of protection.

And he passed out – not for the first time since his capture. The meagre food and the constant beatings, he was in poor shape: but he was alive. Now he didn't hear any more firing, nor the shouts of Lansanan troops arriving. He was out, unconscious, oblivious to the trample of boots as a unit of reconnaissance men with heat-seeking equipment scoured the mountainside for Red Fire guerrillas – and found him cold, and apparently dead, a body in a Red Fire shirt.

But no making-sure bullet was put into him – he was white. And soon another white man was around, and even though this man's face was smeared with mud, Jonny Aaranovitch opened his eyes to recognise Ben Maddox.

They huddled, they cuddled, and Ben somehow kept the tears from coming.

'Can we use your radio?' Ben asked a Lansanan commando. 'Can we let people know he's okay?'

There was no denying him that. But, journalism still ruled. Before Ben put Jonny on to Rebekah, he told her to radio her editor to hold the front page, and to get a film cameraman up from Sikakoko. He wanted his Dell computer notebook, too, before he forgot details 'We've got to get this story down to the wire while it's still hot!' he said. 'And, God, what a story we've got!'

# NO DAM DESTRUCTION
## STAR FOOTBALLER FOUND

*On-the-spot report*
*by Rebekah Arens*

A vicious Red Fire attack on the country's vital Ade Dam in the mountains above Sikakoko – which would have threatened Sikakoko itself – was foiled at midnight yesterday by a crack force of Lansan military.

Acting on a tip-off, they ambushed the Yoori Independence terrorist brigade that was preparing to blow the dam wall. The bomb went off, but the courageous military had made sure that it caused only surface damage. The hydro-electric plant at Ade will not be prevented from producing its normal output today, although as the plant manager told me, 'We shall be inspecting the dam walls for cracks and fissures – and we've got a few broken windows to mend!'

Saving the dam means that Lansana can continue to sell low-priced, environmentally friendly fuel to neighbouring countries, thus preserving the strength of the economy.

President Obed Abu paid compliments to the military. 'It was a brave and daring raid-on-a-raid. It was the stuff of film and drama, a complicated plot. Unfortunately, three brave men were lost in this operation – they paid the ultimate human price for holding Lansana together.'

The Kutulizan ambassador denied any connection between his country and the Red Fire action. 'We support Yoori Independence,' he said, 'we do not deny that, but never through warlike action.'

An offshoot of the drama was the release from terrorist hands of the Sikakoko Arsenal footballer, Mujiba Kalala, whose Red Fire capture was intended to boost the Yoori Independence cause. With another escapee from the Red Fire camp high in the northern mountains, he met up with the commando force and later told the *Graphic*: 'We are Yoori, but we are peaceful. We wanted to get away from the camp, and we will help the Lansanan military to close it, and bring its leaders to justice.'

The heart-warming account of Mujiba's companion, Joyce Akana – a kidnapped Yoori girl's experiences in Red Fire hands – will be told exclusively in the *Graphic* next week. Look out on Monday for the first part of her moving story…

# JOZEA THE
# PROPHET HOSPITAL

Johnstown Road, Sikakoko

MEDICAL DISCHARGE REPORT

**PATIENT NAME** Johan Aaranovitch
**DATE OF BIRTH** 19.02.58
**ADDRESS** C/O Shervin's Hotel
Ade Valley Road
Sikakoko

## MEDICAL CONDITION TREATED

Broken ribs (2)
Severe bruising to body (left side and back
Contusions/lacerations to face, head, limbs
Wounds to face requiring 30 stitches (total)
Malnutrition / hypothermia

## DISCHARGING DOCTOR'S REPORT

Good recovery being made, patient able to
walk and function, further treatment (removal
of stitches, body repair checks and levels of
protein, with blood checks and liver function)
to be undertaken in country of residence
(UK).

PATIENT'S AGREEMENT TO CONDITIONS OF DISCHARGE (SIGNATURE)

*J. Aaranovitch*

MEDICAL AUTHORITY (SUPERVISING DOCTOR'S SIGNATURE)

*V. Amedina*

DATE 21 May

# ZEPHON TELEVISION
## TRANSCRIPT OF ZEPHON NEWS

### BROADCAST – EXTRACT AT 15' 10"
### May 12   22.00 bulletin

### NEWSREADER:  ADRIAN LEMAR

**Item 10**

**Adrian Lemar (to camera):**

Five nights ago we reported our star cameraman, Jonny Aaranovitch, missing in the North East Region of Lansana, West Africa.  You'll be pleased to hear that Jonny is alive – and fairly well.  Over to Ben Maddox, our reporter currently in Lansana.

PACKAGE 10

*Shots of Ade Dam with low water level, cut with broken windows in the plant building, and turbines running normally.*

**Ben Maddox (voice over):**

This is the Ade Dam, energy provider for much of West Africa. Here last night an attack on the dam was foiled by Lansanan government troops.

**Ben Maddox (to camera):**

The attack was here.

*Pull back to show Ben Maddox on dam parapet.*

A bomb had been lowered right below my feet, forty metres or so below the surface, with the intention of blowing a hole in the dam and flooding the towns and villages beneath it, *(looks over his shoulder to south)* principally Sikakoko, Lansana's major northern township. It was timed to explode at midnight. But a Lansanan reconnaissance force – that had been sent to free kidnapped children from the terrorist Red Fire camp north of here in the mountains – had wind of the attack, and foiled it.

### Adrian Lemar (to studio screen showing package):

Ben, how was Jonny Aaranovitch mixed up in this?

### Package 11

### Ben Maddox (to camera):

Innocently, in a story that we hope to tell at a later date. He was being held by the Red Fire rebels, but managed to escape when the explosion occurred, which—

*Pull back to show Ben Maddox on parapet again:*

—happened at surface level, and not below it, thus saving the dam wall, and thousands of lives, Lansanans and Yoori tribe Lansanans alike.

### Ben Maddox (to camera, close up):

The political implications, and the full story, have yet to emerge, but meanwhile my friend and colleague—

*Film of Jonny Aaranovitch in action in Iraq, shooting pictures after a suicide bomb atrocity*

**(Ben Maddox (voice over):**
—Jonny Aaranovitch – the great Jonny Aaranovitch – is alive.
He's coming home soon.

**Adrian Lemar (to studio screen):**
Ben Maddox, thank you.

**Lemar (to camera):**
And we'll ask Ben about the scratches on his own face
when we get him back to London. Now, after the break…

EXTRACT ENDS

Kath Lewis sat with Bloom Ramsaran in the studio control
room, watching the transmission. As the news went into
the commercial break, Bloom turned to Kath, but said
nothing, just looked.

'What do you want me to say, then?' Kath said to the
bank of monitors.

'Nothing,' Bloom replied. 'Speaks for itself, doesn't it?'
Kath nodded now.

'And there's more to come,' Bloom went on, 'as it
unfolds. Special Branch are looking for Reilly—'

'Safe in South America, I bet.' Kath's eyes were all
around now, nodding as the programme director called the
line-up of camera shots for the second segment, checked
the autocue operator, ready with Adrian Lemar's next
words on the screen.

'While Charles Henderson doesn't get what he
wanted…' Bloom said.

Kath Lewis turned to her. 'Do you know what that was?'

Bloom shook her head. 'Not precisely. Power and money, I bet.'

'Well, I've got a friend in the Foreign Office. Word is, he was going to be governor of Kutuliza's new Yoori province...'

Bloom snorted. 'Why aren't I surprised?'

Kath Lewis's eyes flicked to the Transmission monitor up on the top bank, where the commercial break was finishing. 'Because good journalists never let themselves be surprised,' she said.

Which brought a smile to Bloom's face. Praise, indeed!

And, 'Studio!' called the programme director.

Going home, Ben sat on the opposite side of the aisle from Jonny and Rebekah. How could he be a dog and sit close enough to hear their quiet Kibbutz conversation? He could respond when spoken to, but otherwise he kept himself to himself.

And he had his own thinking to do, too. He was going back to face Meera and explain to her why he had defied her wishes and not come home straight away to the marriage she'd promised him. The girl couldn't have given any more leeway than telling him he need not alter his life-style; to which he'd responded by deliberately making that life-style more dangerous than ever.

He looked along the seats to his left, to where a recovering Jonny was arm-in-arm now with Rebekah Arens – who was right then writing up her last story for the Johnstown *Graphic*: before going with Jonny to Israel on convalescent leave. And the sight of them filled Ben with envy. Those two were birds from the same flock, they rose in the same air currents, they fed off the same seed. Meanwhile, he and Meera would need great adjustments to live together when he was back at work, doing what he wanted, being a TV journalist. Give-and-take, they called it. But were either of them of the sort who could ever give enough?

Ben didn't know. And he thought of Mujiba Kalala and the girl, Joyce. They had been so happy in the transport down from the dam, proudly claiming a new kinship.

Suddenly, Jonny was thumping his arm. 'Look!' he said, waving a hand forwards.

Oh, no – not some other Spurs has-been, sitting up in Business!

But Jonny was waving at the line of television monitors suspended from the aircraft ceiling. News 24, the BBC's world outlet to airlines, was flashing a familiar face in an interview. The three of them grabbed up the headphones from their laps, and fixed their eyes up at the screens.

## BBC NEWS 24

*Cut away to:*
Action shots of Mujiba Kalala scoring the winning goal in the home game against Mfinimfini. Crowd cheering and player celebration.

### Studio Anchor (voice over):
—Mujiba Kalala.

*Cut to Mujiba Kalala standing outside the Sikakoko Arsenal ground. He is well-groomed and in smart casual wear. Inserted shot of the gaggle of photographers facing him.*

### Local interviewer (voice over):
Is it good to be back, Mujiba?

### Mujiba Kalala:
Good, very good. Coming home always is, yes?

### Second voice (voice over, shouting):
Were your parents pleased to see you?

### Third voice (voice over simultaneous):
How were you treated in the terrorist camp?

*Mujiba Kalala shakes his head, indicating 'not well' as he replies to the first question.*

**Mujiba Kalala:**

Sure, my parents were very pleased to see me.

**Second voice (voice over):**

So you won't be going away for a while?

**Mujiba Kalala:**

Yes. But only to away matches!

*General laughs*

**Local interviewer – the first voice (voice over, nearer, claiming 'ownership' of this interview):**

So, seriously, Mujiba Kalala – what about travel? What about these rumours of transfer to a European club? In England, or France? Wasn't your name once linked to Tottenham Hotspur?

**Mujiba Kalala (zoomed-in close-up):**

*(After a long pause)* I've been speaking to my manager, Mr Georges Chognon. We've had long talks…

**(First voice (voice over):**

He doesn't want you to go?

**Mujiba Kalala (still in close-up):**

Right, he doesn't want me to go. *(A couple of beats)* And I don't want to go.

*General reaction, reporters' voice calling out 'Why?' 'Whose decision?'
'How long will you stay?'*

## Mujiba Kalala (camera pulled back to medium shot showing the Sikakoko Arsenal stadium behind him):

I'm staying for good. While I am good – if I'm good at all...

*More general reaction to which Mujiba raises his hands*

## Mujiba Kalala (still medium shot, but zooming in slowly):

I'm proud of Lansana. I want to play for my country. I want to play in Africa Cups. I'm Yoori but I don't want divisions between these players and these players. There's too much division. I want to stay to play for African pride, for Lansanan pride. How good will our leagues ever be if we go like hired hands to play for other countries, just because they're richer? That way we always leave our own countries poorer. Let us be ourselves – Lansanan! Lansanan and Yoori, together! Yes.

*Package ends, with a freeze on Mujiba Kalala's defiant face*

## Studio anchor (voice over):

Mujiba Kalala – a young Lansanan who knows his own mind.

The three pairs of eyes in row nineteen came away from the screen, the earphones off from their heads. For a moment there was silence between them, until Jonny Aaranovitch spoke.

'Zephon,' he said, 'Zephon exclusive, that should have been, not BBC...'

Ben nodded. 'Yeah,' he said, 'we had it all set up with that skunk Eamonn Reilly, the old Spurs renegade...'

'Spurs, nothing-schmuthing!' Jonny said. 'Liffey Athletic! Small time, that's all! And finished.'

The three of them nodded, content with the verdict.

'Kath Lewis is still going to kill me!' Ben Maddox said. 'Such disobedience!'

'Not while I'm around,' Jonny told him, in a quiet voice.

'And will you be around?' Ben stared across at his colleague. There had to be so much shock to come out, nightmares and stress to deal with. What had happened to him in the Red Fire camp must have been both psychologically and physically damaging. The poor guy had been waiting for his own execution.

'Convalescence first!' Rebekah came up from her notebook, speaking to Ben's nodding agreement.

Beyond her, Jonny looked across at Ben. 'Would you want me to be around? Despite our professional differences?'

'Professional *discussions*,' Ben corrected. 'You know I would! What are you after, compliments?'

'Reassurance,' Jonny said. 'Because, do you know, Benjamin Maddoxstein, this camera eye seems to have got better in that hospital...' And he put his finger to it in a knowing way.

'That's good, then,' said Ben, 'because that Sikakoko cameraman couldn't keep me in focus.'

Jonny roared out a sudden laugh, short and surprising, turning heads all the way from Business Class. 'Keeping in focus, he wants! When what he needs is keeping in line!'

Ben's face said that he wasn't so sure. But he put an arm out to stop a stewardess as she passed. 'Do you serve Champagne back here to the poor bloody infantry?' he asked.

'Of course, sir.'

'Then bring us a bottle each,' he ordered. 'Please. We've got a lot to celebrate!'

**Look out for more books starring**

# Ben Maddox

### coming soon!

# MORE ORCHARD BLACK APPLES

| | | |
|---|---|---|
| **Ten Days to Zero** | **Bernard Ashley** | **1 84362 649 7** |
| **Little Soldier** | **Bernard Ashley** | **1 84121 306 3** |
| **Tiger without Teeth** | **Bernard Ashley** | **1 84362 204 1** |
| **Revenge House** | **Bernard Ashley** | **1 84121 814 6** |
| **Freedom Flight** | **Bernard Ashley** | **1 84121 306 3** |
| **Jacob's Ladder** | **Brian Keaney** | **1 84362 721 3** |
| **A Crack in the Line** | **Michael Lawrence** | **1 84362 416 8** |
| **Small Eternities** | **Michael Lawrence** | **1 84362 870 8** |
| **Hazel, Not a Nut** | **Gill Lobel** | **1 84362 448 6** |
| **Milkweed** | **Jerry Spinelli** | **1 84362 485 0** |
| **Stargirl** | **Jerry Spinelli** | **1 84121 926 6** |

All priced at £4.99 or £5.99

Orchard Black Apples are available from all good bookshops,
or can be ordered direct from the publisher:
Orchard Books, PO BOX 29, Douglas IM99 1BQ
Credit card orders please telephone 01624 836000
or fax 01624 837033 or visit our Internet site: www.wattspub.co.uk
or e-mail: bookshop@enterprise.net for details.

To order please quote title, author and ISBN
and your full name and address.
Cheques and postal orders should be made payable to 'Bookpost plc.'
Postage and packing is FREE within the UK
(overseas customers should add £1.00 per book).

Prices and availability are subject to change.